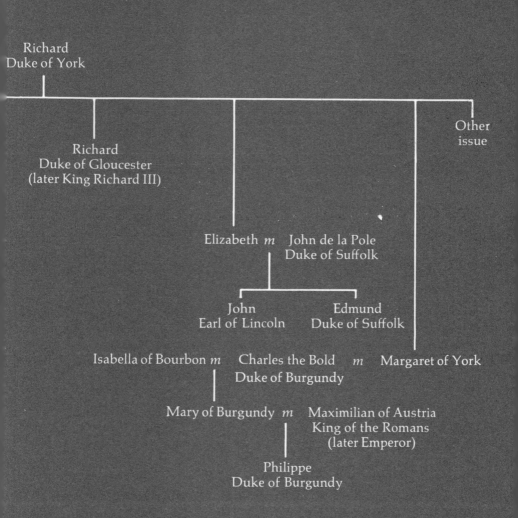

Richard
Duke of York

Richard
Duke of Gloucester
(later King Richard III)

Other
issue

Elizabeth *m* John de la Pole
Duke of Suffolk

John
Earl of Lincoln

Edmund
Duke of Suffolk

Isabella of Bourbon *m* Charles the Bold *m* Margaret of York
Duke of Burgundy

Mary of Burgundy *m* Maximilian of Austria
King of the Romans
(later Emperor)

Philippe
Duke of Burgundy

THE WRONG PLANTAGENET

Marian Palmer

THE WRONG
PLANTAGENET

Doubleday & Company, Inc.
Garden City, New York

And now it is all gone—like an unsubstantial pageant faded; and between us and the old English there lies a gulf of mystery which prose will never adequately bridge. They cannot come to us, and our imagination can but feebly penetrate to them. Only among the aisles of the cathedral, only as we gaze upon their silent figures sleeping on their tombs, some faint conceptions float before us of what these men were when they were alive; and perhaps in the sound of church bells, that peculiar creation of medieval age, which falls upon the ear like the echo of a vanished world.

. . . Froude's *History of England*

Author's Note

The territories of fifteenth-century Burgundy comprised roughly the modern states of Belgium, Luxembourg, and the Netherlands, and portions of northeastern France; they were ruled by a succession of powerful dukes whose prestige and wealth were frequently greater than those of neighboring kings. The fourth of these dukes, Charles the Bold, was killed in battle in 1477 at Nancy, being survived by his wife, the English princess Margaret of York, and his only child, daughter of a previous marriage, the heiress Mary of Burgundy: a girl not twenty years old. The immediate incursions of France persuaded Mary to a marriage alliance with the Austrian prince Maximilian, heir to her neighbor of the other hand, the Holy Roman Empire.* A few years later she died, leaving a son to succeed her, Philippe, the future Duke. During the boy's minority Maximilian with difficulty prevailed upon the Estates of Burgundy to accept him as regent, but his attention was always divided perforce between

* At that time, very approximately present-day Germany and Austria.

affairs of Burgundy and those of his native country, and he was never popular, at one time even being held prisoner for three months in Bruges after a spontaneous rising of the citizens against his government. The majority of Burgundians, it seems clear, regarded him only as an evil to be endured until their young Duke Philippe became old enough both to reign and rule. Maximilian himself succeeded eventually to the Imperial crown as Emperor Maximilian I, while his son Philippe of Burgundy, having married a daughter of the King of Aragon and Queen of Castile, in course of time fathered the future Emperor Charles V, upon whose possessions, inherited by stages from his father Philippe, his mother the Spanish princess, and his grandfather the Emperor Maximilian, the sun indeed never set.

The title King of the Romans, by which Maximilian was known for many years, was the style of the Imperial heir, and had no territorial significance.

I should like here to express my deep appreciation to the City Library of Exeter, England, and in particular to the staff of their Archives Department, who not only made available to me the manuscript of Hooker's Commonplace Book with its account of Perkin Warbeck's siege of Exeter, but spent a large part of one morning patiently assisting me through the intricacies of its sixteenth-century script.

PART 1: The Lord of Clairmont
Spring 1488

I

The Belfry of Bruges was the tallest building in Flanders. From its height one saw northward the estuary and foreport of Damme, and gray wastes of sea; to south, east, and west, the green Low Country plain. Anxious lookouts gazed from the tower across a floor of red-tiled, steep-pitched roofs and the broad bustling Grand'Place, as aloofly perched upon their watch as the birds which nested among the pinnacles; it was spring weather, with tall clouds like caravels moving in a sky of deep dazzling blue, and the morning sun flickering between warmed the Belfry's yellow brick to tawny, glanced from the spire of more distant Saint Sauveur, and returned as if with fugitive, uneasy eye to dwell on the building opposite the Halle where Maximilian of Austria, King of the Romans and heir-elect to his father, the Holy Roman Emperor of the German Nation, lay a prisoner of the merchants and artisans of Bruges in a grocer's spice shop.

They had taken away the rack and the headsman's block from beneath his window, and weeks ago the blood had dried; those sympathizers of Maximilian who had escaped the mob, learning wisdom from what had happened to their fellows, stayed hidden now indoors. Ordinary citizens who crossed and recrossed the Place on their affairs no longer halted to stare at the grocer's house with its cluster of guards before the door, having in three months become accustomed to the sight. Sooner or later, they said among themselves, he must give in. The swift-moving clouds patched the square with flying shadows, and children laughed and ran, brought out like bees by the sun; in all the morning hardly anyone, not even Maximilian's warders lounging bored at their posts, had so much as turned a head at the arrival and dismounting of one man after another —discreetly cloaked, inconspicuously attended—before a house on the other side of the square. They wore head coverings pulled low; their servants displayed no badges; but the horses their grooms led away were blood stock, and behind the well-secured frontage of the *salle* into which they retired, sunlight peering through the shutters flashed on silk and damask and fur, jewels of worth, and, where occasionally a cloak had been thrown back, a knight's gold collar of firestones and double steels, with depending from it the drooping ram of the Golden Fleece. Shrill in the quiet, the iron door-hinges complained again; and the person who had just entered having been saluted with nods or bows, a lisping voice at the other end of the room asked, "Are we all here?"

"Not yet: the lord of Clairmont is expected." It was a man sitting alone in the window embrasure who answered; he had a broad-brimmed velvet hat drawn down to half conceal his face, but his solitude appeared

4

more the consequence of respect, a privacy conceded, than of indifference to his presence. At his reply the first voice directed itself, as if recognizing authority, to him. "Clairmont? I could have spared his company. What has an Englishman to do with the affairs of Burgundy?"

"An Englishman not welcome in England since Bosworth fight," someone else remarked. "Henry Tudor would like to lay hands on him. The late King Richard's friends are too active still for his peace."

"The lord of Clairmont has lived in quiet on his estates from the time he came here after Bosworth," a younger man interjected. He wore a curl-plumed beaver with turned-up brim, which sat awkwardly in its forward position upon his brows; beneath it, his eyes were angry. "He is esteemed for his own sake and respected for the lands he holds in right of his wife's dower, and of his regency for her child his stepson. It is proper he should have been invited."

From the dimness of the wainscot the lisping voice came again: "His stepson. Oh yes, my dear Bouton, we know about his stepson." An uncertain laugh accompanied the remark, as if the individual making it had heard part of a joke once, which he would have been glad to enjoy, if someone would tell him the rest. Bouton turned to gaze at him, all the expression smoothed from his face, and the man in the window seat spoke decisively across the wrangle. "I sent for him myself, in case the burghers had not thought to do it. I might have saved my pains: he had had word from them."

Nobody had noticed the squeak of the door. From

the outer threshold, the attendant who kept it said, "The lord of Clairmont," and having stood aside for someone to enter, withdrew again, closing softly after him.

It was just possible for the dispute to have been unheard; but the abrupt silence could have been read by a man less perceptive than Philip of Clairmont. He came partway into the room, his glance sweeping the attentive faces: a man of middle height, with hazel eyes which looked brown in the shadows, clearly defined cheekbones, and a mixed humor and resolution about the mouth. His smile at Claude Bouton was a private greeting; to the room at large he said, "Messieurs. My regrets if I have kept you waiting." His French was good, and only a little foreign still about the vowels. Alone in the gathering, it was observed with annoyance or amusement, he neither wore a hat nor carried one; Bouton, as if making up his mind, doffed his feathered beaver in company, a gesture that did not escape his remaining associates. There was a slight stirring which the immobility of the velvet-brimmed profile at the window served to emphasize; then, rising, the person that owned it came forward, saying, "You have not kept us, my lord. Shall we sit?"

The light of the window falling across his cheek showed the strong hawk brows and masterful jaw; after a moment, like Bouton, he deliberately bared his head, and the newcomer bowed in acknowledgment, responding courteously, "My lord of Ravenstein."

The head of the table was yielded without question. From its advantage Philip of Cleves, lord of Ravenstein, sat facing Philip Lovell, lord of Clairmont; and the others arranged themselves like actors waiting upon

6

their turns. Equally was it left to Ravenstein to begin, his square soldier's hands linked before him on the polished wood, his eyes on the undisturbed hazel ones opposite.

"The Duke of Burgundy is ten years old; until his fifteenth birthday his government is in the hands of a regent, the King of the Romans his father. This government has lately caused discontent among the provinces, and the cities of Bruges and Ghent require pledges of reform before allowing the King to resume his office and rejoin his troops: pledges which the King has refused to give. We are here by invitation of the citizens to persuade his acceptance of their proposals, and this having been accomplished, to ensure his honorable release."

Everyone waited; the direction of his stare made plain from whom he expected reply. After a minute it came.

"I have seen the proposals: they will make an interesting errand of it for the men that take them to the King. Essentially, he is expelled from Flanders and denied his son; meanwhile the French are pressing the western frontiers, and the King having got word of his predicament to Germany, an Imperial army to rescue him has crossed the Rhine. My lords, these are matters for the Estates of Burgundy, meeting in session, not us few here."

Ravenstein said sharply, "The King of the Romans is a foreign prince, using the territories of Burgundy to advance his German wars."

"He knows his advantage, as the cities do theirs. Until lately the war was to gain them something too. That is not to say the King's taxation has not been extortionate, the indiscipline of his troops unpardonable; he was unwise, in face of this, to enter Bruges and leave his guard outside. Nevertheless, he is right in doubting the French. They will eat these provinces if they are allowed, and for all his mistakes the King knows that too."

"As the English tried to eat France?" A voice spoke blandly from the left side of the table. Bouton stiffened and swerved round in his seat, and a hand descended on his arm, silently forbidding retort. Momentarily the air was tense with challenge; then, his fingers still gripping Bouton's sleeve, the man to whom the remark had been addressed replied with equal gentleness, "One prays not, my lord, for all Burgundy's sake."

Impatient, Ravenstein struck in: "This is idle. My lord of Clairmont, that chain you wear about your neck is of our Order of the Golden Fleece, conferred upon you by the King of the Romans in the Duke of Burgundy's name; but it has not made a Burgoner of you, and you will find, if you hold his acquaintance long, that the King is readier at dispensing our honors than in respecting our customs and laws. For the present it is sufficient to say that, being English, you do not see with our eyes: nor have you hidden your sympathy with the King's position, which is not dissimilar to your own. Like him, you have a trust to keep, standing as father against his coming of age to the Brezy heir."

"Stepfather, my lord." The amendment was coolly made. "I grant you, I have been long enough a stranger here to apprehend the King's difficulties."

"One admits there have been difficulties. So it seems to me the King would more readily hear the cities' arguments from you, his natural partisan, than from any other of us here. Should the nomination for spokesman fall on you, would you accept it?"

Silence followed, while two wrought and gilded links jingled softly with the shifting of a chain on someone's shoulders, and the listeners who enclosed the table sat back as if a puzzle had been explained. Of them all, the person most affected appeared least moved; when after a pensive interval he spoke, it was to observe only, "Belling the cat." The phrase did not translate well; raising his eyes, he said, "Why me, my lord? You have given reasons, I know, but there are some here who have longer known the King, whose names have been great in Burgundy these hundred years. You cannot believe he will welcome the friendliest emissary who sees him in this plight: by now I should imagine him ready to dine off the whole chapter of the Golden Fleece. Are you sure no one could influence him more successfully than I?"

"Quite sure." Ravenstein was amiably final. "But if there is any disagreement—"

The chorus of disclaimer, hurriedly uttered, was unanimous. Nobody had been anxious to face Maximilian of Austria with his jailers' terms; hardly a man present was not quietly congratulating himself on Ravenstein's acumen in shuffling off the job where it would least redound to their collective hurt. Ravenstein, pursuing advantage, went on, "We have a schedule of the cities' demands: immunity from reprisal; surrender by his Majesty of his guardianship of the Duke of Burgundy, his son; removal of his Majesty's soldiers and an indemnity for troops to drive out the Germans if they refuse to honor their master's treaty . . ." He had a sheet in

9

front of him, which his eye barely consulted as he enunciated the articles. A few of the company, who had not heard them all before, were raising eyebrows before he was done. Rolling up the paper, Ravenstein concluded unemotionally, "When the King has agreed to these stipulations, I will escort him to more fit lodgings pending his ratification by public oath. It is right also for you to know that I have offered myself to the cities to be a hostage for his faith on the day he leaves Bruges."

A reflective quiet fell. Breaking it, the Englishman said evenly, "I take it there can be no negotiation in these particulars. His circumstances being what they are, the King may see no alternative than to yield: has it occurred to you he may not keep his word?" No one spoke; after a moment the level voice added, "Yes, and it would be well then if he knows as little as possible of who came forward to stand the cities' friends. For he will so regard it, and remember those that associated themselves with his enemies."

Ravenstein began politely, "If you are declining your services, my lord—"

"I am not declining them." The hazel eyes swept the assembly; with a shrug the conclave was ended. "I must send to the King to learn if he will receive me. My lord of Ravenstein, you will have word from me."

He had risen as he spoke; Claude Bouton, nearly tripping in his haste to follow, attained the door in time to have it shut in his face. He wrenched it open, and discovered after all he need not have hurried; the man he was after had gone no farther than the outer step. He stood thumbs in belt, his long firm mouth with its crisply indented upper lip unaccustomedly set, his eyes, in whose clear brown the sunlight showed flecks of green and smoky gray, inscrutable on the paving of the square. A little breeze curvetted and danced across the Place, stirring the topmost threads of his still thick, fair-brown hair. There was no chance he had not heard the door, but he gave no sign, and Bouton said quietly, "Philip, I am ashamed."

He thought at first he had earned a snub; then turning, Philip Lovell smiled at him and said, "What, for those in there? . . . Not of yourself, I hope." At that Bouton came nearer, and putting a hand on his shoulder said, "I am going with you to the King."

"Oh no, my dear Claude, you are not. I thank you and I understand you too, but you are a young man, properly ambitious for advancement: you have far too much to lose. My position is different. There is nothing I want in the world, not office nor title nor command, that is in the King of the Romans' gift, even if in three years I've been unable to make Ravenstein and his friends believe it."

Judicious, Bouton observed, "They're jealous, of course. They live by favor, which they dislike to share, and don't love strangers besides. You came here an exile; the King received you in the Duke of Burgundy's name, showed himself friendly to you, allowed your marriage to a lady whose husband had left her rich, and had been courted by our matrimony-minded lords for themselves, or for their sons. . . ." He added with a gleam, "Not to mention that she is pretty too." They both smiled.

It was past noon; the shadow of the Belfry tower stretched a lengthening finger, and the lookouts' heads bobbed like apples as they kept their watch. After a silence Bouton spoke again.

"Be careful, Philip. Ravenstein runs no risk by what he is doing; the King may keep his pledges or break them, but he can do little against Cleves-Ravenstein. For you, it might be another matter."

"Are you telling me I should beware his grudge? Very possibly, for what harm when he is back again in Germany it still may do. He has done wrong, and has had it done to him; there's not a man in Burgundy could bring him these proposals, and convince him he was not his enemy today."

On the other side of the square there was a stir about the grocer's door, as new guards arrived to relieve the old; it was the moment to find someone in that bewildered, disorganized confederacy who could take a message to the prisoner, and produce authority to let its sender in. For Claude Bouton, his peaked brows like anxious triangles above his eyes, the stage had long passed in their acquaintance when he might have asked, needing to understand: "Then why do it?" He thought of the room behind them, the ancient, honorable names and sleek empty faces, all waiting for someone else to agree to do what hourly was more urgent to be done; and he already knew.

Not many days later it was made known that Maximilian would consent to the cities' terms, and all Bruges burst out of doors to see the sight. The scaffold upon which his friends had been racked and died was decked with tapestries and green boughs, and an altar had been set up; before this, the young King swore on his knees to honor the pact with his good subjects of Bruges and

Ghent, to yield his son to the Estates and his regency to a council, and to forbear all malice toward those who had constrained him to his oath. He looked pale, it was observed, his dark eyes sunk deeper beneath their heavy lids, his once fresh color bleached to ivory against his flaxen hair; for three months he had lived in fear of death, or of being handed to his mortal enemy and friend of Ghent, the King of France. There was a story his jester had offered once to change clothes with him, so in the fool's motley his master might slip past the guards; Maximilian had refused, fearing, it was said, the punishment that would befall the servant for his sake.

Soon after he took his leave. The gates that had held so long against his bodyguard swung open; Ravenstein, pacing deferential at the King's stirrup, kissed his hand in farewell. Momentarily the young man's eyes dwelt on the impassive face of his hostage; then flicked past it to another he had also come to know, that of Philip of Clairmont, through whose mouth he had learned the price of his liberty; traveled beyond, gazing, searching, as if there were others he expected to recognize too. But in all the jostling crowd no noble countenance was seen, no plumes and silks adorning yet more persons that Maximilian of Austria would remember too. The knights of the Golden Fleece had scattered to their castles and manors through the provinces of Burgundy, and the dust of their passing had long settled to the unidentifiable haze of the Flanders plain.

In Bruges the bonfires of rejoicing burned until dawn. Ravenstein showed himself, to cheers; people danced in the Grand'Place against the beat of pipes and tabors, and some celebrants ascended the Belfry to share the musicians' platform, where they leaned across the thick sills, shouting encouragement and tipping their tankards until the last beer was gone. Off the square, where the light of torches threw dappling shadows among the trees, a horseman dressed for travel watched in the dusk alone; someone riding up quietly behind him said, "But will he keep his word?" Without turning, the other answered, "I have known only one prince who might have tried, and he is dead."

Like ghosts of shepherds' piping the music whispered, threading the laughter and shuffle of feet and hallooing from the Belfry tower. Bouton waited a minute before he asked, in a lighter voice, "Do you go home now to Hainault?"

"Not immediately: I've business in Zeeland first. My men have gone ahead; I only stayed to look awhile, and wonder . . . Well. We've not seen you lately at Clairmont, Claude: my wife asks if you are offended."

"I'll come soon, and eat your larder bare to prove friendship." They had begun slowly riding toward the Damme gate; Bouton went on, "Someone else would like to claim your hospitality, Philip. My neighbor Grandmont is looking for a place for his brother, and I said I would ask if you had room among your lads. The boy's a trouble at home, and as much at odds with Grandmont as with their father before him; I'm told the old man once yoked him the day through for discipline with the ass of his mill, young Hélie being then about seven years old. I promised Grandmont I'd speak to you; he's a well-meaning man, and as I judge it nearly out of his wits."

"One might well believe so. You're a kindly fellow

yourself, Claude: or at least I thought so once." They chuckled, and talked a little more, and Bouton said, "Then I'll tell Grandmont he may send Hélie to you. There's time yet to correct the faults, Philip: the boy's only somewhat younger than your stepson. Perhaps they'll take to each other."

They said good-by under the Porte, one to follow his meinie, the other returning to his lodgings in the town. Evening was apple-colored still in the west, and against its clear green and yellow the great sails of windmills turned slowly, like winged shadows. The sergeants of the bar, careless with beer and good humor, bade their visitors jovial good night, and went back to dicing in the gatehouse.

Night drew on; the sky was violet, then gray, and a half-moon rose above the city walls. About midnight one of the drummers in the Belfry noticed a red glow in the sky over Maele wood; peasants arriving soon after cried that men of Maximilian's guard had fired their huts to observe, they had said, the occasion of their master's release. All night the village burned; when morning came only ashes remained, and the echo faded to memory of the King's troopers, hurrying to join the Imperial army at Liége.

II

The house at Clairmont had been newly built on the old castle site in the last Duke of Burgundy's time: the largest and most comfortable of the several manors which Margaret de Brezy had brought as dower to her second husband. Low-walled and moated by a ribbon of water, the chateau offered its fairy steeples and roofs of colored tile from a little eminence above the demesne; hunting woods stretched beyond, oak and alder and beech, and a gleam of silver marked the course of the river where herons nested. The princely house of Chimay was near neighbor to Clairmont; eastward, hidden by distance, lay the great forest of Ardenne in which Charlemagne's horns had sounded, and Hubert, patron of hunters, met the stag with the cross upon its brow that called the Saint to holiness.

Immobile with his horse, Philip sat looking across the valley at the chateau and its girdling lands. Clairmont was not immense, compared with the Brezy fiefs he had held nearly three years in trust for Simon, his wife's young son; but one could have set Willowford, or any other of his lost English holdings, in a corner of it and had space left to fight a war. A stone's cast away some poplars leaned in the breeze, a little knot of them whose feet in England now would have been dressed with bluebells. There had been a spot at Willowford, each May, that astonished the eye and made the sky seem dim. Sometimes he wondered if Meg too remembered; but she had been taken from her father's country while still at nurse: long ago, Hainault had become her home.

The Clairmont village church was set a short distance before the manor gates, a small old building of weathered Ardenne stone, and here after his custom Philip dismounted and went inside. The parish priest entering by another door recognized his back, and hesitated; there was the question, long burning in his mind, of elevating the church tower from its present insignificance to more worthy height—an ambitious project which could be paid for only out of my lord of Clairmont's purse. But it was no great while since Monseigneur had given the new roof for God's house at the same time as his workmen repaired and rebuilt the parishioners' walls; there had been, too, the silver monstrance, masterpiece of an Antwerp craftsman, now gleaming on the high altar before which, as usual, Monseigneur had not himself chosen to pray. It was his habit to make his devotions at one of the little side altars which would not have ill-suited the least prosperous of his tenants; the unfitness of this, the priest had ceased to point out. The church smelt of beeswax candles, silently burning, and of incense and chill stone; the painted figures of walls and piers gazed with se-

17

vere fixed eyes upon emptiness and their fellows of opposing column or wall. Coming once more into the sunshine, Philip stood alone under the arch of the tympanum, carved by some artificer three centuries dead of Moissac or Lombardy, which said, "Oh man, if thou wouldst wash thy sins away, cross then this threshold."

The lodge keeper at the chateau gate offered cheerful salutations in his Walloon French; the cobbles of the outer courtyard threw up echoes and the soaked warmth of the day. Climbing the stair to his wife's rooms, Philip heard voices beyond the door curtain, and found her seated in front of a tall carved screen while the artist engaged from Bruges worked at his easel. He was a young man, a Hollander who had come to Flanders to paint in Memling's studio, and was becoming talked of in his own right. Unwilling to disturb him, Philip kissed his wife as she smiled in welcome, and went to stand a distance behind Heer David, gazing alternately at the half-finished portrait glowing on its stand—foreground of soft velvet folds, deep red and deeper blue, inviting the fingers; a square of window through whose mullions the light fell luminous on the cheek—and the woman from whom the copy was being made. He had seen her turned to the doorway even as he swung back the tapestry—David with an air of patience had halted to pretend to do something to his brush—looking toward the footstep on the stair; always, whether or not he sent word of his coming, she seemed to know.

The light was altering as the sun swung westward; soon the sitting ended, and Gerard David with stiff, respectful bows, the women of the chamber smiling and fluttering, departed all upon their ways. It had appeared to Philip, toward the last, as if they never meant to go. His eye caught Margaret's as the youngest demoiselle fumbled, bobbed, and fled, and descried in it a little gleam; before the door was closed, he had her in his arms.

It was better than a month, this time, that he had been away. In a few minutes, still without words, he led her to the window and drew her down beside him in the seat. He had hardly realized, until cherished by her tenderness, that he had ridden that day forty punishing miles; sighing, he leaned his face down upon her breast, and Margaret said, "You're tired, love. Will you have wine, or food?" He replied with a claiming arm about her waist, "In a little. Stay with me here awhile."

The slanting light defined an indentation between her brows, which would be in a few years a deeper line; her skin was fair, startling against the darkness of eyes and hair, and the brown-red nipple swiftly rising to his palm upon her breast. Noises drifted from far off, the sound of all the household at its tasks; someone would be certain, soon, to come; he would get up in a moment, he thought, and secure the doors. All the while her grave still eyes were on his face. Speaking presently against his shoulder, she asked, "What passed in Bruges?"

"A deal that might have been expected, not much besides. Ravenstein fancies himself the national hero, and had a notion for someone else to turn the spit for the ox of his hearth: in this he supposed I might do. Since it was high time that agreement was reached, I obliged him . . . You had my letter? The King has gone to join the Imperial army at Liége, having first promised to take no action against his late captors. One would be happy to believe him."

"Is he angry with you?" She was fingering the neckband of his shirt.

"I was informed so, very roundly, across the grocer's parlor, and could only tell him I was sorry for it. Large gestures, little spites: leaving out his rhetoric, adversity has not instructed him . . . Maybe it's the years between our youth and the remembering of it that paint the folk we knew then in larger size."

"That's an old man's thought."

"God forbid." He smiled, and was silent for a space, his hand absent in her hair. "I was at Sluys after I left Bruges. I'd a message from Harry Russell: he was there to see me, off a ship from Germany."

"Harry Russell?" The name was strange to her; only because it was English a chill touched her heart. Philip said, "He was with my cousin at Stoke."

She was motionless in his arms. It was a year and more since Francis Lovell had sailed from Flanders, bound for England to raise the North against King Henry Tudor. All that spring and summer Philip had waited; but when news came it was to tell only of the crushing defeat of Lord Lovell's forces near the midland town of Stoke. Of Francis himself, neither then nor after had there been sign or word.

Margaret said quietly, "Dear heart, there is nothing you can do: all that was possible you tried when you begged him not to go. He was a man grown, able to choose his way, and that was what he chose. He knew well it might be his death."

"I would have thanked God, these many months, only to have been sure of that. I kept imagining him a prisoner in Tudor's hands . . . Then when Harry wrote I thought he might have news, but they parted south of Stoke, getting what was left of the German mercenaries away. There was a rendezvous in Oxfordshire; he waited, Harry said, more than a fortnight, but Francis never came."

Beneath the high window the land lay like an arras picture, park and river and pleasure gardens embroidering the valley floor. The late sun came long and low, warm on their faces; shivering, Margaret turned her head away. Philip said, "Since I spoke with Harry I have known—I have allowed myself to realize he is dead. He had a wife and children, all homeless now—a boy the elder, and a little maid, much younger, that Francis especially loved. They live now in the protection of a kinsman of the wife, a decent man, but often I wonder if I should go myself and see . . . I was young Will's godfather at the font. If he has the least part of Francis in him, he would be grateful to speak to one who could tell him something of his father besides ogres' tales."

Her hands were cold. "England is death for you too. When Lord Lovell sailed from Flanders, swearing to pull down the man who had killed King Richard and got his throne, you would not go with him. 'There is that in Hainault,' you said to him—I heard you say it—'which must keep me now.' Have you grown tired of it so soon?"

He answered in a smothered voice, his face to her hair. She had been three years his wife, and become as necessary to him as light or food; the time had passed when he could have conceived of losing her, without whom indeed he could no longer have imagined his life. All this she was assured of, in silence, through the passionate language of his body's love; no ghosts whispered, no memory of England's pale sunlight and misty rain, of Richard Plantagenet, who had been no less Francis' friend than Philip Lovell's too, dead on Bosworth field in his haunted crown. Solitude was about them now, inviolate as a spell; Margaret only sensed without comprehending it the change in her husband's embrace, until she heard him say, "You might have knocked, Simon."

The boy stood just within the door: a handsome youth, well made and graceful, on whom Margaret's black hair had not yet been tamed to orderliness. Scarlet-faced, he was looking, or not looking, at the floor in front of the window seat; in a square of sunshine his mother's hood lay fallen on the polished tiles. Philip rose slowly, his hands on the loosened cords of his doublet; expressionless, he said at length, "Well?"

He had spoken in English, their household's other tongue, but it was in French that the boy replied, his gaze immovable at his stepfather's feet. "Monseigneur —I only wondered, I wanted to ask what news—"

"No more than what is courtyard talk by now. I would like to speak with you, but later will be more convenient. Is there nothing else?"

As if performing a feat for a wager, Simon raised his eyes. They were Margaret's too, but not so dark; it would have been easier for Philip, any time in the past twelve months, if the lad had been only a little less her son. "No, nothing. Except . . . there's a boy come

22

below, Grandmont is his name. The chamberlain will send to tell you."

"When he considers the time suitable, no doubt he will. Meanwhile, it is his office to deal with such matters." Philip waited. The silence prickled with unease; when no more came he walked to the door and held it open. "I will be free after supper, Simon."

After he had gone, Margaret stirred. She had drawn the thin chemise high about her throat; her hair, unbound, fell like midnight around her shoulders. "Philip, he may not have thought."

Sighing, Philip shot the bolt and came back to the seat. "Sweetheart, he is in his twelfth year, and not dull. Believe me, he thought very well." She shook her head in protest, and he sat beside her, smoothing her hair. "From the time he could speak, while his remembered father lay ill and shut in his rooms, Simon was all your life. Then I came. Can you wonder he feels it? He would have accepted a husband Maximilian had chosen for you far more easily than any you took for yourself."

"Some day he must learn, he must be told how it was. Only in the beginning he was too young, and now—"

"Certainly not now. If for no other reason, let it be until he is old enough to hold his tongue." After a pause Philip added, "There's more justice in it than he knows. Beloved, don't think of Simon now."

Her wide bed was beyond the fireplace, deep with pillows, its hangings worked with flowers shutting out the sun. Lying together there, they knew not time nor memory nor lengthening shadow, cool on the lids; only the scent of cassia and santal from the tumbled linens, of crushed sweet herbs that strewed the floor and gilly-flower water warm about her breasts, mingled like an enchanted cup to drink of, and be at peace.

Supper was late, past five o'clock, and served in the great parlor where the inner household dined. When the tables had been cleared, Philip beckoned Simon to follow him and went upstairs to his private apartments. He had the rolls from Saint Aubin, which he had visited coming back from Bruges, ready for the boy to see; always when he had been to any of Simon's manors he took pains afterward to explain everything that had been done. When the bailiff's accounts had been shown, there were cases of tenures: Jehan of the river field was to be forgiven this term's plowing, because of illness; for adultery with Alys, the hayward's wife, Enguerrand son of Olivier had been put to penance and fined. Simon commented, "I remember Alys: she gave me apples when I was a child. Did she really lie with Enguerrand?" Philip said quietly, "She is a kindly woman, and I think not well used by her husband. Since she and Enguerrand were both flogged in the bishop's Easter court, I have remitted the fine."

The boy's eyes under their level brows swung briefly to consider his, as if drawn by an inflection, then fell again to the correct clerk's script of the opened rolls. His face had recently lost much of its young roundness, so the bones more austerely showed; the set of mouth and jaw alone owed nothing to Margaret, although they were no less familiar to Philip for that. The silence wore on; then pushing back his seat Simon said, "With your permission, Monseigneur—" Their business was done, and it was long since Simon de Brezy had made a practice of lingering in his mother's husband's rooms. With a slight gesture Philip gave the desired leave, and sat listening to the footsteps going away through the outer chamber.

It was still early in the evening; in a while he remembered young Hélie de Grandmont, and was about to send a message to Bertrand the chamberlain that he would see the lad now, when Bertrand himself appeared. It was about the boy, he began, Monsieur de Grandmont's brother, whom he was given to understand Monseigneur had agreed to receive into the household. By his tone conveying his opinion, he unfolded the tale. Hélie had arrived in custody of a servant of Claude Bouton, and sat down to supper with the other boys after their betters in the hall had dined. A difference had arisen with Geffroi the seneschal's son of Saint Aubin, an older boy; Geffroi as a result of this had felt called upon to box the newcomer's ear, whereupon Hélie passed the blow to his neighbor of the other hand, ingeniously challenging him to continue the gesture around the board until the compliment returned to Geffroi. The seneschal's son was not popular; the riot which followed, Philip apprehended, was beyond the power of Bertrand's tongue to describe. All the boys had been beaten, with special attention to the chief malefactor, but, said Bertrand distantly, since the youth was not yet formally of the household, in his view Monseigneur should behold him before deciding to accept such a one at Clairmont.

Sighing, Philip leaned back in his chair, feeling at his shoulders the disapproving judgment of a dozen generations of Clairmont lords, while Bertrand withdrew, and shortly returned thrusting before him a big boy with blond curls unkempt about his brows, and a mixed rage and suspicion in his eyes. By Claude Bouton's telling Hélie was now about eight years old, but he was almost as tall as Simon, and only a little lighter, as Philip reckoned it, than the redoubtable Geffroi. Silently appraising, Philip noted the good forehead and sullen, intelligent mouth; saw also the stiff gait, eloquent of late discipline, and tearstains proudly scrubbed, and a reprehensible sympathy stirred. But he waited for Bertrand to recite the catalogue of offenses, which included it seemed an entire lack of compunction for Geffroi, who had ended on the floor under three of his associates. When the chamberlain had finished, Philip said, "What was the cause of the quarrel?"

Hélie lifted his eyes: from their expression it might have been the first time anyone had thought to ask. After an instant he replied in a muffled voice, "He said since I was the newest, I should serve him at table and eat of his plate when he was done. He—he said his father's office at Saint Aubin made him Monsieur Simon's man."

It was, Geffroi being considered, an entirely likely story, delivered in a tone which anticipated disbelief. Philip said mildly, "He was overbearing, and mistaken besides. There are no servants here or at Saint Aubin save mine, Monsieur Simon being some years yet from a man's age." But he expected to hear from Simon just the same, should Geffroi have the cunning to take his grievance to him. Depression bore like lead on his spirits; he was sorry for Hélie, whom he was beginning to regard as Fortune's stepchild, but sorrier yet he should have come at this time of trouble with Simon to stir the flames. Bertrand's suggestion returned temptingly to mind: it was not too late to refuse to accept the boy. Philip opened his mouth, and heard himself say, "For the time your bed will be in this chamber, and I shall require you to serve me. Since you are here to learn conduct, you must expect to apply yourself. There is wine on that cupboard: fill two cups, and bring them to Monsieur Bertrand and me."

He watched from the corner of his eye while seeming to continue in talk with Bertrand; the task was unhandily performed, but, he thought, without unwillingness. Later, when Bertrand had gone and the tented bath was brought out, he observed again that the lad appeared ready to serve, although clumsy and lamentably schooled. A malevolent genius attended upon his every gesture: sheets and towels, soaps and spiced herbs, sponges great and small at different times cascaded from his grasp, to angrily conscious blushes which were their own reproofs. What he should know, he was well aware of, and that, Philip reflected, was a beginning.

Having dressed in clean shirt and hose, he bade the boy good night and left the inner chamber. A bloom of light within the turret stair came from Margaret's rooms above, but he went first to the nursery; it was growing late, and he had not yet seen Margriet, his daughter, who within the hour would be in her bed.

Indeed, he found her at her prayers. Her brown eyes peeped across her hands, obediently folded; she had been expecting him, and heels and knees betrayed impatience within the embroidered Holland smock. Her nurse, a Yorkshirewoman who had been Margaret's too, was reciting to the blurred baby echo:

"Matthew, Mark, Luke and John,
Watch the bed I lie upon:
Four corners to my bed,
Four angels there to spread,
One at head and one at feet,
Two to guard me to Heaven's gate:
One to sing and two to pray,
And one to fetch my soul away."

In his hand were a half dozen of the dried sweet figs she loved, from a basket of them which he had bought in Sluys off a late-season ship of Spain. He waited smiling in the door, watching the candlelight leap and tremble on her hair.

III

—And Seven Years After

There had been a wedding at Chimay, to which the
household at Clairmont out of neighborship was invited.
The chateau was crowded with guests; the bridegroom
a Croy kinsman, made advertisement of his intentions
as he retired, and was sent off with jests to make good
the boast. Ten minutes later he burst from the wedding
chamber, furiously claiming redress for his dignity; the
guests, willingly following him, discovered the underside
of the bed had been wired with bells whose echo still
affronted the walls, while the bride hid among the pillows. It took four pairs of hands to dismantle the carillon,
which had been disposed with an inventive patience
worthy of greater things, and as supper ended Philip
learned the culprit had been his squire, Hélie de Grandmont. "I see signs of grace," he remarked to Claude
Bouton, who had brought the story. "Once it would
have been a charge of powder."

Bouton, grinning, was looking after a distant figure
being marched off in custody of the lord of Clairmont's

chamberlain. "You've done well with the lad, Philip. I was talking with Grandmont the other day; he would hardly know his brother, so he told me, from your letters reporting of him."

"It's a question of temperament," Philip observed. "From Grandmont's furlongs of earnest prose, I can understand why he and Hélie did not agree. For myself I like the boy, though I would be first to admit he has his own weapons."

"Is that why Simon doesn't care for him?" Bouton's little eyes were bright with curiosity. "I heard him addressing Hélie just now on this latest prank: they do not appear precisely friends." The silence was discouraging; accepting disappointment, he added, "Well, young men must have their likings, and Simon is coming on too. He made a good showing when he was with me in Vienna a year ago: Maximilian took notice of him. Between petting and courting of the new English pretender, that is to say. Is it true that when the prince was received at Malines, Simon was bidden to be presented and you refused to let him go?"

"If you mean the youth calling himself Prince Richard of York, he has been, I believe, successively recognized as the young Earl of Warwick and a bastard of King Richard—who had none unaccounted for that I knew of when he died—before assuming this most recent title, and Henry Tudor says he is the son of a burgher of Tournai. The suggestion that my stepson should go to Malines was not a command, and I was glad of it. I see no reason why Simon de Brezy should dance attendance upon this very doubtful incarnation of the late King Edward's son."

"Well, the boy has been flaunted about the courts of Europe ever since he was discovered, only to be a sting at King Tudor's tail, but there's a difference now. Maximilian is backing him to be King of England, and has promised men and money to make him so—and that, Monsieur Englishman, I should think would interest you very much indeed."

Across the hall, the door to the nuptial apartments had opened again; the new husband emerged, swaggering and holding up three fingers to his friends. There were cheers and shouts for wine, and one of the young Lannoys hailed Claude Bouton to come and join in saluting the hero. His expression thoughtful, Philip watched the braided scarlet bonnet vanish in a cloud of ambergris and peacock plumes. He was wondering if, after all, it would have been politic for him to have gone to Malines. Simon indeed had taken very ill the refusal on his personal behalf, being as inquisitive as most to look at the youth who appeared likely before he was much older to set a good part of Europe by the ears. But that winter Richard of York had gone again on his travels, this time to Vienna at Maximilian's behest; it was the year that Simon too was there, with Claude Bouton, and, Philip reflected wryly, in Vienna Simon had undoubtedly enjoyed opportunity in abundance to satisfy his curiosity, and under Maximilian's benevolent sponsorship to make the pretender's acquaintance. That the young man was an imposter Philip was quite sure; the question in his mind was whether Richard of York was being used by, or using, the King of the Romans, and upon that all the adventurer's fortunes could depend.

The chance to judge for himself came sooner than

expected when, returning from Chimay, he found awaiting him a second summons from the dowager Duchess of Burgundy, Margaret of York—self-acknowledged aunt, outspoken partisan, and, since his return to the Low Countries, hostess to her proclaimed nephew Richard of York—requiring the lord of Clairmont to attend her in her dower town of Malines. This time the framing of the message left no room for polite maneuver: if he wanted to keep friends with Margaret of York, Philip knew he had better go.

Her palace at Malines had been the English princess' favored place of residence since her husband Charles of Burgundy's death. It was a gentle countryside of moist green fields, trimly ditched and tilled: a pretty ride by good roads from Clairmont, but Philip was tired when he entered the city gates. The palace was in a narrow street close by the walls; he sent his servants to find rooms in the nearest inn, and was passed by porter, usher, and gentleman-in-waiting into Margaret of York's privy chamber.

She sat beneath a canopy of state, on a dais whose three steps were spread with arras. She wore deep purple, complimentary to the ruddy fairness of her cheeks; her hood was velvet with pearls embroidered on it, and a linen chin cloth bore up the softening flesh of her heavy jaw. He saw too that she was angry.

There were some women about her, and a young man, tall and auburn-haired, stood at her right hand. Philip stooped over the fingers she briefly gave him, noting as he did it how they had thickened so the rings lay embedded beyond the puffed and swollen knuckles. But there was neither illness nor failing strength in her voice when she addressed him, the words rapping down like hammer strokes before he had wholly raised his head.

"Monsieur de Clairmont, this is the second time you have been expected. More than a year ago there were letters sent making plain we should be glad to receive you here, with your wife's son Monsieur Simon de Brezy; to these messages you returned slight answers, and nothing more."

Philip replied gently, "Madame la Grande, you were mistaken if you understood me so. The time was inopportune, and I did not take it that I was commanded to Malines. As for Simon—" He hesitated, his eyes swinging to the bright-haired youth. "Let me speak plainly. I believed if you wanted Simon and me here, it was to present us to the man called Richard, Duke of York, that by my stepson's apparent attendance upon him his name and rank would give standing to the Duke. This prince, the younger of the late King Edward your brother's sons, was known to me in his childhood; therefore my presence also would appear a kind of sanction of his identity. It seemed to me—unwise—that I should permit my stepson to be so used, without having been first allowed to satisfy myself that this person was who he has claimed he is."

Her hand had gone to the man beside her, checking without seeming to have noticed it his instinctive movement forward. Tight-lipped, Margaret of York said at length, "I had guessed as much. You do yourself too great honor, my lord: his attendance upon the Duke of York would have earned credit for your stepson, not the Duke. Nevertheless, for your satisfaction now, here is the

33

prince: look upon him, and acknowledge him King Edward's son."

For the first time, the gesture of her head directed Philip's eyes to her companion. He, speaking in English, said with an open friendly look, "Indeed, my lord, I trust you will not disown remembrance, for I do know you. It is seventeen years since we first met, when I was married to the Duke of Norfolk's daughter who after died, and you came from the north with my uncle Richard of Gloucester to be present at the wedding. I remember my uncle throwing coins from golden basins when the people shouted for largesse; the cheering frightened me so I wept, whereat my uncle told me a prince must learn to bear such things, and smile for them; but you said, 'It is a sign of their love.'"

There were sighs and smiles among the women—Duke Richard was already, it appeared, a favorite with them —and the Duchess sat watchful as at a match of chess. An old memory drifted through Philip's mind: once, it was whispered, Margaret of York had taken a lover to supply her husband's neglect, the man being the Bishop of Cambrai. Gossip said she had even borne the bishop a son, who was sent secretly away to be reared out of her husband's knowledge and the Burgundian court. But that had been long ago; it was twenty years since in England Philip had first heard the story.

The princess spoke into an expectant silence: "Will your Highness give us leave?" Richard bent gracefully to kiss her hand; the women were already going. Philip, detained by a motion of her fingers, stood waiting while the hush of skirts ended with the closing door; the Duke, walking before, turned for a last smile at Philip as he crossed the threshold.

"And now, Sir Philip." She had spoken in English; he could not help a feeling of strangeness at the old title, so long it was since he had borne it. She saw his face, and smiled too. "Yes, it is a time since you were that: ten years, isn't it, almost, since you became lord of Clairmont? And your stepson must be eighteen now: how the years pass." She leaned back, measuring him with her eyes. "You have been plain, sir: I will be no less. It is true I sent for you because your name has value in this affair of my nephew. He is King of England by clear right, but right alone will not get him crowned at Westminster. Setting aside the help he must have only to reach his kingdom, he must be known to his people. Some gentlemen lately come from England have acknowledged him, but they go by my word and his. You, on the other hand, it is well known were once acquainted with the Duke, and would be not easily deceived. Your oath avouching him, duly advertised among the princes of Europe, will go far to advance the Duke on his road." She was silent for a space. "Sir Philip, we have been friends. I ask no more than your true opinion, and leave to make it known."

"My true opinion?" Philip said slowly. "Forgive me, madam: I should doubt it is that which you want of me."

She sat unstirring in the big chair, her hands on the carved griffins of its arms. Inscrutable, she said, "Let us try another way. You have been from youth the servant of my house; in his lifetime you were besides my brother Richard of Gloucester's friend. When King Edward died, that same Richard put aside his nephews

35

King Edward's sons, and the great men of England freely consenting, himself claimed the throne. His nephews he lodged with fit estate in the Tower, and the elder of them, the boy Edward, I am reliably informed died there. The younger one has stood before you today. You must know that since Tudor seized the crown it has been put about that while King Richard reigned—afflicted one must suppose no less in his soul than in his wit—he had his nephews murdered, and this slander has been much quoted among his enemies: surely you, his friend, would wish the lie disproved? You can do it, only by admitting that the young man you have seen in Malines is the prince Richard, Duke of York, who entered the Tower with his brother and, as I now believe, two years after escaped to Portugal. The manner of escape is most secret, for there are persons in England still whom Tudor would not thank for having helped the prince; but I do assure you, this is the very boy."

Philip answered levelly, his eyes on hers, "Since you have said so, I must not dispute it. Touching myself, some years ago my cousin Francis Lovell tried with your help to bring Henry Tudor down, and in that attempt he died. I still mourn him; and those hundreds of other deaths which he caused by that endeavor are enough for me to lay to the account of my name. I will add no more." He hesitated, still holding her gaze. "Madam, I understand your desire to be revenged upon King Henry, who has done you and your house great hurt, but I beg you will reflect on what you do. You have said that crowns are not won by right alone: they are not gotten either by the questionable support of foreign princes who want to muddy their neighbors' waters only to keep the stick out of their own. I entreat you to consider, if not the poor folk who must suffer in this quarrel, then the young man himself, and what could happen to him if he fails."

"In plain terms, you refuse. Yet it seems you know this enterprise is not mine only, that the King of the Romans and the Duke of Burgundy his son have promised their approval and aid. Is there need to call to your memory that you have offended the King once already? Yes, and when his soldiers laid siege to the rebel cities after his release from Bruges, you associated yourself with French intercession—*French!*—on the rebels' behalf. You grow great, sir: one might almost forget that when you came to Burgundy ten years ago, it was with not two pairs of shoes to your feet." There was an instant while Philip heard her furious breathing. Then, laying down the words like treasures from a long guarded store, she said, "You have spoken of considerations: I will remind you of another one. You also have a youth in your protection, your wife's son. You forget, I believe, that I have had knowledge these eighteen years that could injure him." Her eyes were on his face. "I see you understand me."

He was as white as his shirt. "I must be forgiven my simplicity. I had not supposed an old good will to have been leased out for gain, nor that I had given myself in pawn for it."

A quiet followed. Her color high, Margaret of York spoke without inflection: "You have leave, Sir Philip." She did not offer her hand. As he was withdrawing, she

37

raised her voice to say, "Nevertheless, reflect on it. I shall expect you in Malines again by Pentecost."

His servants displayed astonishment when, next morning, Philip turned back toward Clairmont; the intention yesterday had been to travel on to a hunting lodge of Simon's beyond Malines, where Meg and the inner household were next week to join them. But now it seemed that a courier had been dispatched instead an hour after the audience with the Duchess of Burgundy, warning the establishment at Clairmont to wait on my lord's return, and Philip paid no attention to the consequent curiosity. His men indeed found him remote to the point of curtness, compressing by brutal stages three days' normal riding into two, and speaking of no more than the journey's needs except once, when, pausing for refreshment outside a village inn, he drank two tankards of beer and complained of the heat. It was May, and no worse than warm; his English groom Gregory looked under his brows, clamped rheumatic knees more firmly to his horse's sides, and mentally reckoned up the miles before they should be at Clairmont with my lady again.

Toward the end of the second day they rode under the gate arch and dismounted before the stables of the outer court. It was evening, and in the shadowed corners of the lawn the daisies were folded up for sleep. Leaving his men to dispose themselves as they would, Philip walked stiffly across the privy garden; he was hot and aching in every limb, and a dull pain in his back had made of the last miles as many leagues; but for two days his body's signals had been to him no more than annoyances, to be first ignored, and then pitilessly overcome. The door by which he entered the house was chosen for its nearness to Simon's rooms; he took the stairs with a haste which brought dampness to his forehead, and discovered on going in that the owner was not there. A little page, scrambling from sleepy ease in the tower window seat, said Monsieur Simon had been in his place at supper; he did not know where he might be now.

The best thing, Philip knew, would be to ask Meg; but he went instead to his own apartments, telling himself he would send Hélie to inquire about the house. In the event he was spared his pains; entering the bedchamber he found there Hélie and Simon, facing each other across the room. The sound of the opening door fell on a stillness that seemed to breathe; it was that, not the trestle stools kicked on their ends, the wine flagon slowly rocking and spilling its lees along the floor, which halted Philip before he spoke. His eyes went from Hélie, standing with an oddly alert expression against the farther wall, and returning to Simon fell on the unsheathed dagger in his fist.

Shutting the door after him, Philip advanced two paces into the room. To Simon, he said in a voice the boy had never heard before: "Explain this." Simultaneously he extended a palm. Fiery scarlet, Simon came near enough to give him the poniard; it was fine work with a haft of gold and ivory which he had used at table since his fifteenth birthday. Philip dropped it to the chest beside him; he had already seen that Hélie, careless as usual about his belongings, was unarmed. As Simon continued obstinately silent, the younger boy began, "Monseigneur, it was a private dispute—"

"With bare hands to a blade? I've not asked you to tell me about it, Hélie. Simon?"

Rigid, Simon said, "He made me angry. I am sorry."

"I see. You may leave us, Hélie."

The squire went out. Simon, who had gone from red to very white, stood like a stone; after an instant Philip said curtly, "Stay here." He found what he wanted in Bertrand's room, and was glad the chamberlain himself was not there to question him. Returning, he closed both outer and inner doors, and laid what he was carrying on the chest: a long birch rod that Bertrand used for disciplining the squires. Simon, understanding what he intended, recoiled with dilating eyes, and Philip said evenly, "If you have anything to tell me of how this thing happened, I am ready to listen, but I warn you I can fancy few circumstances that would excuse it. When you are only a little older your position will give you power to govern many men; since it seems you have not yet learned to be master of yourself, this must help you remember. Undo your clothes."

Simon whispered, "You would not dare—you have no right—"

"We will discuss that presently. Meanwhile, if you do not obey me by the time that bell ceases, we will have in Bertrand and Gregory to help. Would you prefer that?"

Outside the gates, in the belfry of the village church the hour was sounding. It was eight o'clock; on the sixth slow stroke, with trembling fingers Simon began to unlace his doublet.

Such a thing, Philip knew, had not happened to him since his nursery days. Grimly he got on with what he had promised, feeling each cut as if it had been his own flesh which was imprinted by it; for the boy's pride's sake closing his ears to the sharply catching breaths. Twelve stripes, he had told himself, surely that would be enough; but his midriff clammed with weakness, and he had to pause only slightly better than halfway through; having waited, he could not bring himself then to resume, as if the interval had been intended only for the cruelty of anticipation. He laid down the rod and said, "That is all. You may dress."

He moved away, to allow privacy for it. Simon bent to retrieve shirt and doublet from the floor; he put them on neatly, and used especial care in tying up his hose. Almost it appeared as if nothing had happened, except for his eyes. When he had finished he looked across the room at the older man, asking without expression, "Have I leave to go?"

"Not yet. There is something else—I'm sorry, it cannot wait." Philip discovered he was leaning his palms on the table; his head seemed strange and light. He was beginning to realize he was sick with something, but pushed it aside as unimportant. "I have long wanted you to know this, but the time was never right, and I don't expect you to pardon me for choosing to let you hear it now. Tell me, since you have seldom spoken of him to me: do you remember your mother's last husband, Monsieur de Brezy, well?"

The graven face showed an involuntary surprise. "Well enough. He was ill from the time, almost, that I was born; I best remember him the day he died, when he sent for me to bid him good-by. I was nine then."

"Yes. Listen to me. In the summer before you were

born, your mother was—younger than you are now. She had been married while still a child, Monsieur de Brezy being then about fifty years of age. You must understand that it was not—a happy marriage. I may say this because Monseigneur was my friend; he was not unkind, but he did not much trouble himself about her. Perhaps this was a consequence of their ages." Turning to the fireplace, Philip rested both hands on the mantel which overhung the hearth. He felt, behind him, the boy's gaze. "In the summer I speak of, a man came to Burgundy. He had known your mother when she was a little maid, and it so happened to them that they fell in love. I say nothing for him, but keep this in your mind: that she was seventeen years old."

He searched for words. His face unreadable, Simon said, "Well? Did my father know of this?"

"In due course Monseigneur learned of it. By that time, although no one then suspected it, your mother had conceived by her lover. The child was yourself."

He sensed movement behind him, and turned to see the swung-back hand. They stared at each other, and Simon said in a thin, deadly voice, "That is a lie, and I will strike the man that says it."

Without stirring, Philip answered, "Though you do so, that will not change it." The silence was like a winter night; then, his color draining, Simon lowered his arm. Half choking, he muttered, "It isn't true. It could not be— Monseigneur knew, and called me his son? He would never have done such a thing—"

"He had, I think, his reasons. In the end he came to understand a little that it had happened to them almost —against their will. Also, he had no son or child to wrong in owning you, and he had once had a—a kindness for the man."

Blindly turning, Simon took three steps. A silver mirror hung on the wall; to his reflected face he said, "Who was the man?"

This time the pause was different. Philip said, "You do not much show your fathering, although Meg says at times she sees it. Only in the color of your eyes, and the mouth a little, maybe; and your hands." He looked down, and slowly spread his own. "It is a family likeness: my father had it too. The width between the thumb and first finger —you will find it difficult in fitting armor, as I have done; no gauntlet will serve that is not made to the pattern."

He ceased, expecting he knew not what, but no sound came from Simon except a long, harsh sigh. Beside the boy's unmoving shoulder the mirror's polished face threw back the room: the shelf of books and bare, low bed; Gerard David's portrait of Margaret smiling in the shadow; the open door into the little oratory with its plain altar and wooden crucifix above it on the wall. Philip spoke into the quiet feeling as if he were dropping stones from a cliff, too high to hear them fall. "It was for another reason that I came back to Burgundy after Monsieur de Brezy died. Bosworth had made me a pauper; although I had lately learned of Monseigneur's death, I had no intent to seek your mother as a beggar, until the Duchess of Burgundy sent you to me. She had stood your mother's friend; she knew the truth, and had taken care that in those years in England I never heard it."

"Madame la Grande—the Duchess of Burgundy knows?" For the first time, in the frozen reflection something showed. "And how many others, that will love to tell me of it one day?"

Philip said after a moment, "Simon." His breath was like an obstruction in the lungs; he waited, his shoulders to the buttress of the fireplace, until his son faced him. "No one else knows. There may have been gossip when we married, some may have remembered I was in Burgundy that summer long before; but no one else now living for a certainty knows."

There was a medallion with the Brezy crest, massive and old, on a chain around the boy's neck; he reached up, dragging at the links, and when they broke apart dropped the medal to the floor. "But I know. This is not bastard's gear; someone should throw it in the fire."

It was, Philip recognized, the reply he would have made himself. In a great solitude of pain and growing dark he groped outward, and the mist clearing momently they stood eye to eye; then like a spring uncoiling the shaking body repulsed him. "Take your hand from me. Do you think I will forgive you this as long as I live?"

Philip tried to check him as he turned, but the movement brought his back from the support of the chimney, and of a sudden the room swam with horrors. The sleeve he touched felt stiff and rough, like bark on a dead tree; in the glittering circle of the mirror his wife's picture winked and grimaced, and the wooden cross burst with flame. Through a singing in his ears he heard the sound of feet running; his legs carried him after them, in a dream of hot buffeting winds and rivers that foamed and roared breast-high, and shrill ironic laughter. Then all at once the smooth frame of the antechamber door braced his palms; an arm came out of the blackness to bear him up, and someone exclaimed: "Monseigneur, you are ill." He fumbled to know the arm, for everything was dim and far and voices no longer told their owners, but it was not Simon. Then he knew, and remembered thinking, "How big he is, he has grown again only since Epiphany. He is taller now than I." All the strength was going from his knees; Hélie's shoulder thrust in his armpit, and he fell into endless night.

Someone was talking in low, decisive tones: "No more bleeding, it is inadvisable after the fourth day. The fever may be expected to abate in a little, and syrup of poppy will reduce restlessness." Thinly, from an impossible distance a woman was screaming, "Blessed saints, the pox, we shall all die of it. Blessed saints, I came here to wash sheets, let me go while I am still whole . . ." The pox? Philip thought confusedly. Great God, and I lie here; I must get up and deal with this. Then he heard sobbing, and Margaret's voice as it must be at the door, "I will come in, do you think I can endure not to be with him? Hélie, you have no right to bar the way." Hélie replied softly, "Madame, he would be first to forbid you. What of the Demoiselle if you should take it too? Truly, you can do no more for him than Maître Jehan and I, and I will send each morning to tell you how he fares."

Jehan of Tournai, Philip said to himself. But that is two days and a night from Clairmont; we have not had him here since Margriet's fever. The sound of Meg's crying distressed him; he said aloud, "Hélie, what is the matter?" and the squire's shadow stooped above him. "Monseigneur, you are ill of the smallpox. Will you have your lady come to you? Remember, she has never had it."

There was a prickling over all his face and limbs, something that was an irritation even through the terrible burning and aching of his body, the tortured rawness of his throat. Philip moved his hands across his chest, and felt the first hard lifting of the papules under the skin; when he touched his face they were there too. He turned his head on the pillow, whispering, "Tell her no. Tell her to kiss Margriet for me."

Consciousness was going; he heard Maître Jehan's heavy padding step at the bedside, but was no longer able to distinguish the physician's moonlike countenance. There was a smell of myrtle burning in pannikins, and cloths soaked in something cool and astringent were laid on his eyes. Then darkness shut down once more.

Time passed, bewildering and unreckonable, broken only by the feel of Hélie's arm supporting his shoulders, the taste of broth or barley water acidulated with pomegranate juice grateful on his tongue. When not uneasily sleeping he was a restless patient, asking repeatedly what date it was, and how long since last he waked. After a while—it was the week following Pentecost—Hélie stopped counting it out, and gave only gently answers to soothe him back to sleep. But it seemed to the boy it was about then that his patient grew quieter, and asked no more.

Once, rousing as Hélie lifted him into fresh sheets, Philip came enough to himself to notice the scarlet hangings drawn about the bed; even the linens had been dyed with madder, and the curtain at the window, so he lay as if in a world of blood. It was to prevent scarring, Philip knew; a court lord in waiting only last year had been five weeks on a couch draped to the ceiling in red, but arose from it nonetheless with his face, as it appeared, half eaten away. Suddenly his mind was very clear; he was afraid, and asked, "Hélie, have you had this sickness?" The boy looked round, smiling to hear him speak, and came to the head of the bed when he saw him struggling to sit. Holding his shoulders, he rejoined cheerfully, "Oh yes, when I was a child. See, here is a mark."

Presently Maître Jehan recommended oil for the ripening pustules, and showed the squire how to rub the itching scabs so they would not be torn or chafed away too soon. Sometimes, waking at night, Philip would see the physician dozing in his chair by the fire, his several smooth chins disposed on his breast; when Hélie slept, he hardly knew.

The days went by; the sun was warmer, and beyond the window falling apple bloom drifted like snow. One morning Jehan entered beaming with a mirror in his hand; this he gave to Philip, saying with a smile, "Now Monseigneur may see," but Philip was looking past him at the door. For the first time, Jehan had left it open; in the outer chamber he heard Margaret's voice, and Hélie's answering as he brought her in.

She had Margriet with her, the little girl carrying a book which she had covered in velvet and embroidered with her own hands; his daughter's expression told Philip quite plainly what, despite Jehan's satisfaction, he would look like for some weeks to come. His wife's tear-wet face lay momentarily against his own; Hélie, tossing Margriet high on his shoulder, informed her with a flattering astonishment that she had become a young lady while Monseigneur was in his bed.

They went away soon because Jehan was watching,

and the patient weak yet; in the afternoon Gregory was allowed briefly past the inner threshold, and Bertrand the chamberlain with felicitations from the household. The day was no more than half gone; Philip leaned against the pillows, his fingers between the leaves of Margriet's gift, his eyes on the door. Hélie busied himself about the chamber; to a suggestion that he let somebody else take his place now in the sick room he had shown a mutinous lip, and promised to sleep in a little while. Suddenly gazing, Philip asked, "Hélie, how did you come by that scar?" He meant a white mark on the boy's temple, nearly hidden by his hair; unthinking, Hélie put up a hand. "This? Oh, it's a bite I had from one of my father's dogs when I was young—" His voice died. Philip said, "Yes, in this light it does not have much appearance of the pox."

There was an interval while Hélie fumbled with his hands. Discovering eventually a knot in his girdle, he devoted some attention to unraveling it. "I got that mark when I was four years old; one of the dogs flew at me when I went into the run while they were feeding. My father beat me himself because, he said, I might have excited the hounds at their food and set them fighting: he valued them, you see." He lifted his eyes. "How could I have said differently to you? Until I came here, I never knew what a father might be."

Philip said softly, "For God's sake—" He had turned his head aside. Abruptly scarlet, Hélie stared at the floor as if committing to memory the pattern of the colored tiles. In a moment the older man spoke quietly: "Is my wife coming again today?" Margaret answered from the door, "I am here, beloved."

This time she was alone. Hélie had fled away, not waiting to be bidden; at length loosening his arms, Philip whispered, "Simon—" and she replied, "He has told me."

He sensed something from her voice: words not spoken, the soreness of long shed tears. "What did he say to you?"

"Very little, and of that, nothing unkind. It was as if he were teaching himself to believe it yet."

Anguished, Philip moved among the covers. "I must see him, it's past Pentecost and there's a danger he can't know. Madame la Grande—has there been word from her? She's been waiting to hear from me better than a month, God knows what she may have said or done by now—"

Margaret's hands, warm and strong, closed upon his. "A gentleman came, the grand almoner of her household, with a message for your private ear: I told him you were sick and could see no one. He said Madame would be very sorry to hear it, and that he was sure she would receive you with friendship when you were well enough to wait on her again."

Philip said steadily, "What, then?" He saw from her face there was more.

"Simon went to Malines three weeks ago. The Duke of Burgundy wrote to him, commanding him upon his duty to attend the prince Richard of York, who was shortly to go upon his enterprise of England—" Her eyes, deep-ringed from long sleepless watching, were on his. "The Duke's letter came from his hunting lodge in Luxembourg. He was several days there last month with his father, the King of the Romans, for sport."

Lying back on the pillows, Philip stared at the canopy above his head. Philippe of Burgundy—since he became fifteen years old he had been Duke in fact as well as name; but not for nothing was that sleepy-eyed, plump-lipped youth nicknamed Follow Advice. Here at last was Philip Lovell's gift from Maximilian: the paying of a seven years' spite. Suddenly rage burst in him like fire; he sprang out of bed, and throwing open the press began to search in it for clothes. "It's time my young lord of Burgundy learned a little of the provinces he rules. Simon is not of age, and cannot be commanded to any duty without my leave; and the council my little Duke was careful not to take with him to Luxembourg will have something to say about a vassal of Burgundy being used to decorate the King of the Romans' favorite imposters—"

He was wrenching hose and doublet from their cases; her arms, flung out to check him, turned and held him to her breast. "It's too late, you cannot stop it now. The ships have sailed."

PART 2: Simon de Brezy
July 1495–October 1499

IV

The gentry and countryfolk of Kent were surprised by the Duke of York's Flemish ships, but nevertheless beat back his landing at Deal with a loss to the Duke of more than two hundred men. This was a disappointment; he had been led to expect a better welcome from Henry Tudor's subjects, and supposed them to have been made hostile by the sight of his foreign men. Sailing on to Ireland, he found there warmer haven; the Earl of Desmond received him in Munster, and supported him in an attempt upon Waterford. The city, however, refused admission to the besieging lords; the failure of Francis Lovell and his Irish hosts, who eight years before had tried the same leap from Ireland to Tudor's England, was still fresh in mind, and Irishmen were done with dying for the house of York.

It was time to remember the King of Scots, whose money had first helped launch the expedition from Flanders. James Stewart was young, generous, and not in love with his English neighbor; he had besides already recognized by letter the Duke of York's title, and might be worked upon to do more. "And I should have tried Scotland in the beginning," the Duke said to Simon, as they leaned together against the poop rail, watching two sailors haul up the anchor stone. "What good are these sacks and killings to me? I want the people's hearts." He glanced at his companion, whose eyes were on the green hills lying in smooth reflection across the harbor. "How is your arm? I thought you were favoring it this morning."

Simon looked down at his forearm, bulky in linen paddings. "Almost well now: the surgeon says the splints come off next week." Richard of York shook his head at him, laughing. "May it be a lesson to you. Next time I want someone to have a look between cannon shots into an unfriendly town, leave climbing the rigging to a sailor that understands it—or to anyone else in the company, for that. There's not a man of them that hasn't better need than you to make a name for himself." He reached to touch the straps. "That bandage is loose: let me fix it for you."

Without moving, Simon said, "Geffroi can attend to it." He had stiffened in spite of himself. Slipping two fingers under the linen, Richard tightened the slackened knots. "There now. Would Geffroi have been half so clever about it?" He smiled into the younger man's eyes.

If he had meant anything by it, he would not have chosen a ship's poop deck for the gesture, and having discovered how keenly he felt rebuff, Simon could not bring himself to show what he thought. A wandering life, half royal, half adventurer's, had made of Richard of York a mixture of knowledge and innocence; in this, his rank had fenced him from what other boys learned as pages before they were ten years old. Yet when it came to knowing cloths and wines and spices, or sailor's skills, no one could have been better; he had done a good deal in his life, he used to say gaily, to put food in his mouth.

The ship stood away, and Simon looked along the deck to where Geffroi Marot leaned brawny arms on the rail, watching the sunpath on the sea. From his expression, he was wishing himself at home again in Hainault, once more safely the seneschal's son at Saint Aubin. Briefly, Simon thought about it himself. He had paid a courier of the Duchess of Burgundy, overtaking them at Cork, to carry a letter back to his mother, telling her about the Irish visit and that they were sailing now to try their luck with the King of Scots. It had been difficult writing; now, months after their parting, his mind's eye saw only a girl seventeen, giving herself to a wandering Englishman one long-past summer in forbidden love.

King James received them at Stirling, throned on a dais of state with his nobles around him and all the royal plate, hurried from Edinburgh for the occasion, shining on the board. Before James and his Council Richard of York spoke with simple dignity, rehearsed his lineage, and begged the Scottish King for shelter and aid. It was the kind of occasion which showed the Duke to his best advantage; he had dressed for it with instinctive correctness, elegantly but without too great richness, and his auburn hair, brushed to gleaming, lay on the dark blue shoulders of his tunic like fiery gold. His voice was light but pleasant, admirably complemented by the restrained and graceful movements of his hands; at some time between rovings with knightly or merchant protectors, someone had taken trouble to teach him how to stand and speak. James was impressed; by Saint Ninian, he swore, in Scotland my lord of York should find the welcome he deserved, and, having embraced him warmly, he took a jewel from his finger and placed it on the hand of the Prince of England his guest.

His Council, meeting some days later, was less susceptible, being divided in its attitude to the nation's historic bane and pastime, another war with England. The upright and prudent Chancellor Elphinstone, always for peace, was known to be strongly opposed; so was James' brother and heir, the Duke of Ross. The great nobles— Hepburn of Bothwell, Gordon of Huntly, Buchan and Angus and Argyll—kept their opinions for the present to themselves, but some of the younger ones were all for James' proposal to restore the Duke of York by force of arms to his father's throne, and the arguments, as James later cheerfully admitted, flew like shillings on fair day. From the enigmatic amusement in his eyes, it did not appear as if he had made up his mind yet what he meant to do; Richard, accurately reading his host's gently smiling look, returned it in kind across the gaming table, and drew another card. James was fond of gambling; that night in a temper Richard won four pounds from him, and wondered after to Simon if he had been wise.

A Scottish court, Simon was learning, differed markedly from that of Burgundy; being so far separated from much of Europe made Scots dress and manners seem rude and old-fashioned, copied from the styles of a few years earlier in France, and the clansmen were as stiff-necked and thorny as a pride of kings: of one chieftain it was told that an ancestor had refused Noah's hospitality in

the Ark, having, so went the story, a boat of his own. But Simon liked King James, who whatever his future intentions for his visitors, so far had proved himself as good as his word; he made the Duke of York an annual allowance of thirteen hundred pounds, and had accepted without cavil his train of better than a thousand followers.

One evening he beckoned the Duke after supper, at the same time drawing forward a lady. She was Katherine Gordon, the Earl of Huntly's daughter, famous for her beauty. It had come to his mind, James said, that his kinswoman Lady Katherine having but recently returned to court, she was yet unacquainted with his Grace the Prince of York. Bending deeply over her hand, Richard saw a girl slightly younger than himself and almost as tall: slender as willow, with cloud-gray eyes set wide apart that spoke, or appeared to speak, of mysteries and enchantment: of fairy chases where unicorns sank their wild heads to a maiden, of sirens singing far off on their rock, wrapped in their sea-wet hair. James having moved smiling away, they stood alone, as solitary together among the lights and dancing as in a winter wood; but she was Huntly's daughter, and when Richard had passed from fluent compliment, to stammering, to hot-cheeked, devouring silence, she answered all his admiration by saying in a light, collected voice, "You speak English very Frenchly for a Duke of York, sir, if indeed you are that prince you say." He replied with a flickering look, "Then you must teach me that tongue again in your sweet Scots, sweet Kathi, and I will use no other for my life henceforward—" Her hand in his trembled but did not withdraw itself; her skin, which was very

pale, showed its first color as he gazed. His heart beat so it seemed to choke him, and he whispered, "If the brow be so white, what should be the breast? Maiden, I never wished more greatly to be king in my own land than now, with such a lady to sit beside me queen."

A month later they were married in James' lovely, lake-girt palace at Linlithgow, watched glumly by the Duke of Ross and his partisans, and with corresponding delight by the war faction of the court. Huntly bestowed his daughter at the altar, and James held a tournament to honor the Prince of York and his bride, giving as a present to his new kinsman a suit of armor with over-dress of purple damask, furred with ermine and powdered with Yorkist suns. It was Twelfth Night, in Scotland called Uphaliday; guisers in false faces scowling or fantastic or gay had come to profit from the openhanded King's Christmas largesse, and a drummer was King of the Bean. After supper there was piping and dancing, while James watched sitting with Richard and Katherine at the high table. The hall was crowded, the men looking tired in their fine array; James himself had his hand in a bandage from a thrust under the gauntlet during the afternoon's *mêlée*. The dancers had ended a turn; in a lull while some singers arranged themselves, Currie the King's buffoon and his wife Daft Ann (they had had a gift from young Ross) advanced mincing and bowing to the dais. Currie was spokesman, while blaming it grinning on his wife; she was wanting a husband for their daughter, and wondered if the King would kindly let them have his son the lord bastard Alexander—his Majesty being lately disposed to giving his relatives from friendliness, without ever a pedigree that was proven, forbye. Three

58

quarters of the table roared, with a promptness which betrayed how many had been privy to the joke; uncrossing his legs, Richard said easily to James, "A good fool, my kinsman: have I leave to reward him?" He slipped the heavy purse from his girdle, and without looking inside flung it chinking to the jester. Expertly catching it, Currie louted low. "Much thanks, royal gentleman: you may be King, Emperor, or Pope in Rome for me, and King Jamie your fool—" He pranced off, loudly counting coins to his wife.

It seemed as if from that time a change began in James' feeling for his guest. He failed in no courtesy, but he made it plain that he expected the Duke of York to be of use to him; and his courtiers, responsive as vanes, found him less ready to frown at Ross' or Buchan's jibes. As winter passed into spring Richard met with slights from men who had been most forward in supporting him; he suffered from this immoderately, bruised both in his pride and the self-esteem which, like a citadel without defenses, could be penetrated by a single dart. In those days he turned with passion to his wife, again and again drawing her from hall and revel to lie with him in their great chamber, and this was the more strange for his not having appeared the sort of man to be obsessed by a woman: hearing him, in fact, when he first spoke at Stirling upon being welcomed to Scotland, one of the Campbells had put round a witticism about my young lady of York.

In the spring the Spanish ambassadors, sour observers since Christmas of the love feast of Stewart and York, sailed home to Madrid, bearing with them a promise from King James that he would take a Spanish princess to be his bride if a suitable lady were offered. The ambassadors' chief business in Scotland had been to persuade James into keeping truce with Henry Tudor so that English attention might remain undivided and available to the Holy League of Spain, the Emperor, and the Pope against the Most Christian King of France, and the King of Scots' willingness to marry into the Spanish royal house carried with it a guarantee—soon gleefully circulated around the court—that should he get his Spanish lady, he would in consequence entirely forsake the Duke of York. Though some doubted that an infanta would be forthcoming for James, the promise meant that until a reply was received, there would be no war with England on Richard of York's behalf.

There was an alehouse in Edinburgh, not far from Holyrood Abbey, where Simon used to go that summer. It was kept by a young woman for her brother, who had a brewery down the street from his tavern's sign; she was tilt-nosed and dimpled, and spoke in a friendly way to the foreign young man so far from his home. Her name was Christy.

The first time he kissed her was as much a surprise to Simon as, he suspected, it was to her. He had been telling her stories of Ireland—she was as curious as a magpie about other parts, and kept a bird a sailor had left once for debt: a raucous creature with a red tail, that had startled Simon when first he heard it by swearing at him in dockside Dutch. She was leaning her crossed arms on the table beside him, listening with parted lips; suddenly she turned with a question, her mouth a hand's breadth under his, and he set his own upon it.

It seemed, after the first motionless instant, that she did not find that experience unpleasing. Her arms bound him to her as they rose together from the awkward seat; by the soft movements of her body, he knew she understood as well what was happening to him as to herself. It was past noon, and the house was empty of customers; she was pulling him after her to the loft stair when a step sounded heavy in the passage. A man's voice shouted, and Christy whispered, "It's Kerr, my brother. He'll beat me sure if he finds us together." The brewer's tread faded toward the kitchen; she leaned close again, her sand-colored curls tickling his cheek. "It's no' safe here. Is there a place we could be together, up yon, if I came at night?"

"What if Kerr finds out?" Simon asked the question mechanically, sure she would have an answer. His hand slid down her back to her waist, pressing her round so they were breast to breast.

"I'll tell him they sent for nut-brown for the King's cellars, and offered me a bed after. Shall I come tonight?" He kissed her quickly, and said, "Yes."

Climbing back up the hill to the castle, Simon caught himself looking at the sun, and reckoning the hours until dark. He had not had a girl since he was in Ireland, and then it was only a harbor drab that Geffroi had met first, and then dared him to go with too. Afterward he was ashamed, and remembered also what he had heard of the danger of the French sickness in such women. He thought of Christy, the clean smell of her hair, and her merry eyes, gray-green like an autumn sea. She had been married when she was fifteen, she had told him once, but

61

the man abused her, and she had not been sorry when two years ago he died.

Sunlight flashed on the Nor' Loch, and the town roofs rose like steeple hats below the castle hill. As a city Edinburgh had been grown from its rock; and on a fair day, when the air sparkled as quick and lucent as mountain water, one saw from the citadel fifty miles to Perthshire and the first highland peaks. On the Lang Stairs two men with the appearance of servants passed him, idly talking as they strolled down into the city; they saluted Simon politely by name, calling him "my lord," but it seemed as though they exchanged looks. For a moment Simon paused outside the gate, staring after them; but then he remembered Christy again, and shrugged and went inside.

The young lord of Saint Aubin enjoyed certain privileges not shared by the majority of Richard's poorer followers, and among these was a room in the castle which he shared only with Geffroi. The business of explaining that his companion would be considerate to find a bed in the hall that night was accomplished more easily than anticipated; Geffroi only winked and said he would expect Simon to do as much for him, another time. When afternoon faded and the night guard had been set at the gate, he took a present to the captain, asking him to keep an eye on the postern, and when a girl came, to let her quietly in. The officer, a jovial soul, joked as briskly as Geffroi, and offered congratulations on a better night, as he said, than he expected for himself. His neck warming, Simon walked away; by now he felt as if half the household were observing him, amiably wishing him well.

When supper came it was nearly dusk. Simon ate what

arrived before him, and as soon as the pages had passed with ewers and bowls and napkins he sprang from his seat, meaning to go out to the postern and wait. Richard overtook him at the door; it was becoming an evening custom for him to ride down to Holyrood to visit with the canons, and often sleep there after, since it was common talk that the Duchess of York lay more easily these nights alone. Everyone knew the reason: James himself, with that half-scoffing lightness which nowadays was for Richard his usual tone of address, had offered to stand godfather when the hoped-for event took place.

Outside, the courtyard was mysterious with night. As they crossed the square Simon heard someone shouting, and the clatter of feet; the sounds drew nearer, and by the light of a torch which flamed against the tower wall, he recognized the captain of the gate. What he was saying seemed confused; he called to Simon by name, and said something about murder, and that they were to come quickly. Then Simon heard him say, "My lord, it's the lass you were looking for—" and, shaking off Richard's arm, he started to run.

Pounding along beside him, the captain gasped out what he knew. He had been watching for her, or he wouldn't have seen it; she had driven her cart up, and as she was alighting two men that appeared to have followed her rushed out, and before the captain or his men could shout or stir, put their dirks in her back. He thought, when he left, that she was still alive—

Beyond the gate, white moonlight struggled with the yellow flare of torches. The darkness was alive with faces, floating like masks before the blacker shadow of the tower; Simon pushed through them, and dropped on his knees. "Christy, *how—*"

She was lying on the cobbles because no one had dared move her, like a doll thrown when children have finished their play; one of the guards had rolled up his coat to stuff under her head. A spreading wetness trickled from beneath her back. Crouched above her, Simon whispered, "Is there a doctor coming?" Someone said yes. He heard footsteps behind as Richard came to stand at his shoulder, but did not turn, for he had felt Christy's hand move in his. Her eyes fixed on him, hazy with the surprise of pain; she said catchingly, "It hurts," and he set his teeth in his lip. After a moment he asked, "Who, Christy? Who would do it?"

She said huskily, "They came in to drink, they saw I'd heard them talking, and I suppose they were afraid I'd tell— They must have watched outside after, and when I came up here they thought I was going to warn your Duke—"

"The Duke of York?" Richard spoke sharply, leaning down to peer into her face. "What warning for the Duke?" She replied vaguely, not recognizing who he was, but responding to the jewels on his hands, the plumed cap and lace at throat and wrists: "There'll be men waiting when he rides down to Holyrood tonight. They're to take him and have him over the border to England before tomorrow night: there's money paid for it—" And she said once more, "They thought that was why I was coming, to tell him. . . . As if I cared for dukes." Her mouth twisted in an urchin grin to fancy it, and straightened sharply again with pain. The captain, who had been grimly listening, looked across her as two of his

64

men came tramping back up the hill; to the silent question, one of them said, "Just the two. They fought, so there was no taking them for to question: half dronken, and gey scared besides for what they'd let slip while in the beer—" He jerked his thumb. "Down there, both of them."

The circle of watchers parted, to let in the physician fetched from the castle: a little, round-bellied man in a camlet gown, openly annoyed at being troubled. He stooped, flicking back a slashed and ragged sleeve, and one of the guards brought a torch nearer. It had seemed to Simon that she was quieter; even the hand he held was unclenched now, as if she slept. He was about to say so when the doctor shook back his cuffs and rose from one knee, remarking curtly, "I am a physician for the sick. This woman is dead." There was mud on his hose; he scrubbed at it, and turning, walked away.

The torches bloomed her cheeks with color still, and her skin was warm as life. The captain was an older man; he said quietly to Simon, "I'll have her taken inside, my lord. My wife will do what's needful, you can be sure of that—" He hesitated, and added delicately, "Would there be—had she a husband?"

Simon looked up. Suddenly his white face burned; he answered slowly, "Just a brother. I'll go down—I'll see that he's told." The cart stood a little way off, the empty hogsheads of her subterfuge arranged in rows behind the backless seat. He remembered the talking bird, and wondered who would take care of it now.

Some of the crowd lingered, staring and muttering behind the smoking flares. Abruptly lifting his head, Richard signed them away. As they drew off, with backward glances, Geffroi appeared from the shadows; he had got to think lately that such dismissal must be intended for anyone but him. Speaking just as if he had been invited, he said, "The King should know of this. Someone has been plotting against the Duke of York while he is the guest of Scotland: the King must hear of it."

He stood gazing from Simon to Richard, his thumbs in his girdle. Angered by such obtuseness and the very abrasion of his presence, Simon returned shortly, "Not if we have our wits. It may be Ross, or Buchan, or any of a dozen lords that are against the English war. Do you expect King James to quarrel with them for the Duke of York's sake? He'll profit how he can from us while he gets it cheap, that's the worth of his friendship nowadays." He went over to Christy's cart and stooped for the reins. Shocked, Geffroi said, "You aren't going to drive that down yourself, are you?"

"If it worries you, go away so you needn't see." His fingers shaking, Simon put a foot on the step up to the seat, and Richard, who seemed hardly to have listened, wheeled round to address Geffroi: "You have had permission to withdraw."

When he had gone, the Duke came over to the cart. Softly stroking the little donkey, he spoke across her back: "My wife's with child, poor lady. If it should be a boy and live, he will be my heir and England's." The donkey nuzzled his palm, expecting salt; he looked at Simon, his eyes wide with hopelessness and fear. "What shall I do?"

Had Simon answered as he thought, he would have said, "Very ill, if you must ask me at all." At the back of his mind, memory returned of the day when he had

66

first been sent for to Malines: his own voice, wrathful and arguing, "But he is the rightful king," and Philip Lovell's replying, "God pity the boy, if he has no more to help him to a crown than that." He felt cruel with his own hurt, and would have been glad to make someone else suffer too. But he said presently, "Do? Why, talk of long-nosed Spanish virtue, and how cold it is in bed: there's no one like King James to take that to his heart. Nobody believes in the Spanish marriage but him, and if it fails, he'll march you to England in front of ten thousand men."

The last torch flickered by the gate, and the moon stared down. Clicking his tongue to the donkey, Simon uncertainly shook the reins. It was true he had never done such a thing in his life before: there had been reason for Geffroi's astonishment. As the cart lumbered down the hill, he realized he had not even excused himself, nor begged the Duke of York's leave.

V

The Spanish infantas, a much proffered commodity, proved to have been disposed of elsewhere; one of them, in fact, was going to Henry Tudor's eldest son. This information, diplomatically conveyed by a new ambassador from Spain, wafted fresh courteous breezes in the direction of the Duke of York, whose fortunes seemed once more on the flood. Shortly afterward a gentleman from France arrived, the Seigneur de Concressault, with whom Richard had been very friendlily acquainted some years ago while a guest of the King of France. Concressault, indeed, was a face out of a happier and less doubtful past; he saluted the Duke with affection, spoke at length of their former days, and laid balm to the young man's sores by seeking him out at every opportunity, his readiest and most deferential courtier. Being both fond of cards, they formed the habit of playing together of an evening while others looked on; one night, passing on the way to his inner chamber, James paused to watch as Richard, laughing with delight, capped the

Frenchman's hand with the grimacing painted Fool. Everyone applauded; Concressault, smiling defeat, pushed across his last coins, and James said, "My lord of York, I would like to speak privately with you."

His face told nothing, but a score of eyebrows rose. Private conversation with the Duke of York was a pleasure of which James had not lately availed himself; someone behind Simon muttered, "He's made up his mind. Faith, he's been the bonny while about it." Tossing his winnings to the yeoman who was clearing the game away, Richard accepted the King's companionable arm around his shoulders for the length of three intervening rooms and a principal gallery, while bets trailed the progress like a comet's tail. Neither of the individuals concerned displayed any consciousness of the interest attending them; when they entered the King's bedchamber Richard was chatting easily about the Seigneur de Concressault, and his happiness at seeing him once more. "While I was in France, he commanded the guard of honor assigned to me by goodness of the Most Christian King. The duties were not heavy, but we saw much of each other, and it was a real grief to part."

"Indeed?" James said dryly. He was pouring wine from a flagon. "Perhaps you should know the Seigneur's present errand in Scotland for the Most Christian King is to offer me a hundred thousand crowns, for your person delivered to France." As pleasantly as at table, he offered the cup to his guest.

It slipped from Richard's hands. Wine splashed the blue and mulberry of his doublet with darker red; he stood with the color dying from his face, while James hitched a leg over the bedside chest and sardonically regarded him. His mouth working, the young man whispered, "This was his errand? I thought he was my friend."

"He's one you can spare then, and his master too. The King of France is beset by the Holy League; if he can buy English neutrality by offering to clap you where you can do Tudor no hurt, he'll jump at the chance," James said coolly. He waited, long-nosed, hard-mouthed, with fine brows gently curved like a girl's above the politic eyes. His Stewart-bright hair, straight as wheat, hung loose to his shoulders to catch the light and be changed by it to fire. As if unable to consider or comprehend beyond the fact of betrayal, Richard covered his face; and the Scotsman said softly, "Man, who sent you about this business? You're like a wee pebble thrown in the loch, that will put out ripples long after it's gone to the bottom."

It was like talking to a figure of stone, or clay. Springing from his seat, James took a turn about the room, the stalks of bent grass rustling about his shoes. At length halting, he stood looking with narrowed eyes, in the manner of one that has wagered on a questionable horse, but will stick to it rather than cancel the bets. "I'll take you to England. I'll call up my men, and give you arms for yours, and supply artillery. In return, I want your promise sealed for the castle and town of Berwick, and one hundred thousand marks."

Something—the stab of contempt, the understanding of escape—restored the other to composure. He dropped his hands, and stared at James with the chill unreadability that had earned him his name for pride. "Berwick? I remember, my uncle of Gloucester took it away from your father, near fifteen years ago."

Amused, James put up his brows. "So you've teeth. I wondered." Once more seating himself, he swung his foot.

Richard paced to the window. He said, "Fifty thousand." The Scots King smiled. "Done."

Once resolved upon it, James pushed forward the English war with all speed. Letters of summons went out to nobles and clansmen from Caithness to the Tweed, and at Edinburgh and Stirling the light of forges burned through the night. James himself included with his restless autumn peregrinations a visit to the highlands; at Darnaway he looked into the progress of his northern musterings, and beguiled the time between with a boar hunt during which two alaunts were killed, and Simon, too near the covert for prudence, was gored in the thigh. The accident sent him protesting to bed for a fortnight; he had to go back to Edinburgh in a litter, with Richard sometimes dropping back in the procession to ride alongside, alternately scolding and diverting with jests his disappointment. They both knew the mischance had cost him his part in the English campaign.

They were hardly back in Edinburgh before a ship of Flanders put in at Saint Andrews, carrying letters and more troops from Margaret of Burgundy to reinforce the invasion. A palace page, with the scrubbed Scots sand-and-freckles complexion that still brought Christy back, came to Simon's room with a packet off the Duchess' vessel for him. There were letters from his mother: two, written a week apart, and another which he stared at a moment before taking it in his hand. Presently rising, he limped to the turret window and, throwing open the shutter, broke the seal.

It had been written, it seemed, when news of James' English purpose had reached Flanders. Following quickly upon the opening lines, there was a reference to this—"In my young days it was the kind of expedition I spent my service in preventing, but as the saying is, Other masters, other times. You will find border fighting different, I think, from your previous experience, which, as I understand from your mother, has enlarged in better than a year. Your prince has my good wishes for his fortunes." There was a little more in the same awkwardly restrained style—one saw the writer imagining an unauthorized eye perusing it—and a last sentence, which must have taken as long to devise as all the rest: "Your mother thinks of you always, with that special affection of a parent for the beloved absent son; by that, and the substance of our own last speaking together, you may judge also of mine." The signature had followed after so long a hesitation that the quill was thick from repeated dippings in the horn: it was only his name, Philip Lovell.

Simon was still sitting in the window, turning the sheet in his fingers, when the sandy-curled page squeaked from the threshold, "His Grace of York," and ducked away. Richard came in, looking tense and ill at ease; he had had letters himself from the Duchess of Burgundy, written in what, from his expression, Simon presumed to have been her customary north-wind style. This time, it seemed, she had included an emissary to reinforce encouragement: a reverend gentleman at present abed in Saint Andrews while recovering from the rigors of passage and a rheum. Restlessly wandering the room, Richard said, "He'll never be here before we march. You must see him for me, Simon: make my excuses, tell him we are practically in London, that England is ours, anything you like that will give him a good report for Madame until I can send escort for him. Maybe he hunts: you can find out."

"He came to see you, he'll hardly be pleased to have me for substitute," Simon objected; his mind was divided between the letter in his hand and the familiar jumping of his heart that, with every emanation from Margaret of Burgundy's court, reminded him of the glass he stood on. From the corner of his eye he studied the high-bred profile, at once haughty and delicate, which had so often turned to him as, among all the Duke's adherents, the nearest equal and friend; tormenting as vermin in a hermit's shirt, fancy inquired of him what Richard of York would say if he knew.

Richard was still moving about the room; he was always unquiet within doors, hating walls about him, and a small room's the most. "Well, I've little acquaintance with the gentleman myself, and I'm not grateful to Madame for hanging him around my neck now. Just do what you can to keep him out of my way until the campaign is over; you'll have met him, probably"—he stood at the shot window, his eyes on the arm of the Forth like pewter flashing in the sun—"he's the Bishop of Cambrai."

Before the high altar of Holyrood Abbey, King James and the Duke of York knelt together in faith and brotherhood, and to chanted prayers the English war began. Ox-drawn wagons were already trundling south bearing picks and powder, spades and siege engines, and Mons

Meg, pride of Scotland's cannon, had been dragged
with piping from her watch at Edinburgh Castle to join
the train. A few days later James and the Duke followed,
riding before the mounted knights and infantry of the
polyglot army—Flemings, Irishmen, English Yorkists, and
Scots—with which they meant to uncrown King Henry
Tudor. It was fine autumn weather; the reaped fields
showed neatly cropped stubble, and sunlight was thin
and clear on the Lammermuirs. As they rode, James remarked lightly to Richard that King Henry, taking fright,
had offered him his eldest daughter, Margaret, to make
peace between them; if accepted, the marriage would
put the King of Scots next after the princess' brothers to
the English throne. Impassive—he had gotten used by
now to James' humor—Richard asked, "And will you
have her?"

Grinning, James glanced behind them at the plumed
and glittering files. "Not this year."

They crossed the Tweed into England by Coldstream
ford, and turned east toward the Till valley. A few settle-
ments lay on the way, empty of life, the inhabitants fled;
these the invaders put to the torch, and destroyed as
they found them the crammed pele-towers of refuge.
They were poorly defended, often with no more than
some old country knight and a handful of village boys;
at Cornhill one such lad flailed on with his cudgel long
after the rounding up of cattle had begun, until a Scot,
tiring of the sport, finished him on a ten-foot spear.

At Twizel a stone bridge spanned the Till into the
valley farmlands beyond. It too was undefended, but
there was a castle on the river bank to guard passage
over; before this, while the huddle of huts around it

went up in flames, the gunners disposed their pieces. Richard, who was sitting among his followers a little distance apart, broke off a conversation with an aide as the Scots King approached, turning to James a pale, troubled face; they had sent out heralds, days before, to proclaim that every Englishman who came to King Richard's allegiance would be safe and unharmed, but the shouts of his messengers through the Northumberland villages, he now learned, had met with silent stares. Apprehending the reason for his disquiet, James reminded him with irony that upon entering England they had put a price on Tudor's head, for who cared to claim it: did his Majesty feel, perhaps, that they should increase the offered prize? Grimy-browed, the snout of his helmet pushed back to let in the air, he sat gazing at the glum faces of the Duke's English councilors; miles behind, the smoke of their passage hung like mist. Ignoring the sarcasm, Richard kneed his horse forward to gaze at the devastation and its sullen pall. "This is no place of note: what need is there to spoil it and take their few poor beasts? We came to fight an army for my kingdom, not rob its folk."

His color rising, James wheeled his horse to point an arm north. "Do you travel back a few miles," he said evenly, "you'll find muckle places to grieve for in Scotland that are like heaps of stone. We've been at this business here for two hundred years, with the best of it going to the English; and forbye, you show a great concern for persons that want no part of you, seemingly."

"Am I made of iron?" Richard exclaimed passionately. "They are my people: can I see them suffer and not be moved?" He leaned down, and with his gauntleted fist

75

struck the match from the gunner's hand. "I'll have no more of such work here: bring the guns away."

James did not stir. "You're in the aim of my piece," he said, spacing the words with precision. "Gin you do not move yourself, you'll make a grand entry on a cannon ball into that castle."

Their eyes locked. Flamboyant in the wind, the great banners of England and Scotland whipped above their heads: suave-faced Plantagenet leopards staring out beside their arrogant lilies, the Scottish lion clawing his golden field. The gunner's pan of coals hissed on its trivet; then Richard said bitingly, "Not in my name. Get on with your sacking and sheep-stealing, since it's what you came for; you'll do it without me or my men to countenance you."

He signed curtly to the marshals, disregarding the gape-jawed dismay of his English advisers. One of them—it was the London merchant Heron, whom Tudor had mocked by spreading it about he had run away from England for debt—edged up to James, mouth arranged in placation; the Duke of York, his expression implied, was fast running out of kingdoms to shelter in. Paying no attention, James dismounted and stood hands on hips watching as the gunner touched his glowing tool to the breech; there was a flash and a roar, and the stench of sulphur rose; and the ancient masonry of Twizel Castle began its slow, ordained bowing to the assault.

In Edinburgh, Simon was engaged in his designated task of entertaining the Bishop of Cambrai. Sumptuously welcomed by the canons of Holyrood, the bishop had disconcerted his hosts by quitting the abbey for the castle almost the instant after his foot had touched the cloister lawn; Simon, hastily readying himself to wait upon the visitor at Holyrood, was astonished to learn he was at that moment alighting at the castle gate, and barely gained the Duke of York's chambers in time to receive him. They were not wholly strangers, the bishop having been a frequent figure at the dowager Duchess of Burgundy's court while Simon served there as a page. The son of an ancient and noble family, Henri de Berghes was a man now nearing fifty, as respected for his erudition as his charity, with grave fine brows and a beautiful small mouth which it struck Simon he had seen somewhere before. It seemed to him also that beneath the bishop's princely dignity and composure was discernible the strained, tentative manner of one who sits on powder.

If he was disappointed at the Duke of York's absence, however, he concealed it well, remarking on the expedition with which King James was meeting his commitments. He asked about the strength of the force which had marched, and his brows went up. "Only two thousand? A small army to take a kingdom with: I should have thought the King of Scots would have judged a greater troop required." Simon explained that it was expected large numbers of the Duke's countrymen would join him as soon as he showed his banner in England; the bishop nodded, and smiled. "A difficult decision for their Graces to have made. Englishmen look notoriously ill upon a prince who arrives before a foreign army, and yet they have shown themselves slow also to join one who does not come to them strong with followers. A curious people." He recollected himself, and added graciously, "But I must beg pardon for forgetting your own share of Englishness, my son."

There was a fractional silence. Simon felt his head come up as of itself; a fist seemed to have been driven into his belly so he ceased to breathe. The bishop, non-plussed by the very blankness of the expression turned upon him, said after a moment, "I refer, of course, to Madame de Clairmont, your mother. A lady of great loveliness, whom I remember from the time of her first coming from England to marry Monsieur de Brezy: she was only a child then, but already with a promise of beauty."

A pause followed, while Simon struggled in vain to make sense of his part in the conversation. He knew he was failing miserably, but the reaction of relief had been so shocking it made him feel sick. To hide it, he rubbed his thigh where the bandages made a bulk still beneath his hose; if the bishop laid his abstraction to discomfort, it would serve for excuse. Henri de Berghes, however, had fallen into no such error; whatever its reason, he knew an unhappy spirit when he found one. Being kindly by disposition, and because also he remembered the serious, proud child of a dozen years ago in page's silks, he put aside briefly his own deep cares to talk gently on. "I had the pleasure of speaking with Madame de Clairmont shortly before sailing from Flanders; she begged me especially to seek you with her blessing and love. She grieves for your absence, which has been long, and it would lighten her heart to know when you will return to Burgundy."

Immobile in a spar of sunlight, the compactly muscled boy's body rested in the window seat which the guest out of consideration had indicated. His hazel eyes, colored of mixed earth and slate beneath their black level brows, met the bishop's like a guarding sword. "I have promised to serve the Duke of York until he comes to his right. When he is crowned in England, it may be there will be nothing to keep me more in these kingdoms—" A quietness fell, while dust motes danced in the suntrack. "Say to Madame, I have need to earn my name. She will understand."

When the bishop had gone Simon went back to his own rooms, which seemed emptier for lack of Geffroi's large presence. He had ridden with Richard's company, not caring to linger in Edinburgh through dull days of waiting for news, and Simon did not blame him for it. Presently he rubbed his leg again, and began to wonder what prevented him from following the army himself; he could still ride a horse, and, he told himself, if need be fight from it too.

He had wisdom enough to keep his purpose from anyone else in the household, making surreptitious arrangements with a stable boy when the ostler was busy at the other end of the stalls; but as he was leading the gelding toward the outer gate he met Sir Nicholas Ashley, Richard's chaplain and secretary, back from the loch with a fishing rod over his shoulder. He was a young man with bright twinkling eyes, on whom the circle of his tonsure sat with the inconsequence of a titmouse's cap; taking in the scene at a glance, he said, "You'll be in trouble with your surgeon, and have half the Duchess' ladies around you in a wailing wall"; and then, "If I come with you, I can't tell."

They followed the route of the army's march to Haddington, where they spent the night and found a guide to take them as far, next day, as the mustering ground at Ellem. The forsaken camp was a litter of old tent poles, broken-down carts and campfires black-out; beyond that point, any plowboy or farmwife could point them the way.

They made Coldstream late in the afternoon, where Ashley, casting an eye around the horizon, pointed east to the haze of smoke and said briefly, "That way." Simon rode beside him, thoughtful; he was having his first glimpse of England, and at every turn met in his mind the ghost of a young Philip Lovell, riding behind Richard of Gloucester's banner to keep the northern peace. When they reached the first village, which was smoldering yet, he began to remember what his letter had said about the differences in border war. "Englishmen hate all Scots, who return the kindness," Ashley observed once. "In fact, it's something marvelous in England to meet anyone that can hear the country's name spoken and keep his temper; a man may be brought to law in York, for miscalling his neighbor a Scot."

Presently they started to meet the first stragglers: looters who, having early burdened themselves with plunder, were disinclined to follow their King further into England and risk losing it. Simon lifted his brows as they passed; with many more of such, James' army would soon shrink past any hope of solid conquest for the Duke of York. Everywhere was emptiness and ruin; he was wondering where, in all the desolation, they would find a place that night to lay their heads, when before them they heard the clash of weapons.

He was pricking a heel to his horse's flank when Ashley seized his arm, saying softly, "Wait." They rode quietly up a gentle hill; beyond and below a spinney which turned the way toward Twizel, a knot of sheep and men heaved together athwart the road, swords and spears uncertainly flickering in the swiftly falling dusk. The spearmen were on foot, and hampered by having half their minds on the sheep they had been driving determinedly home toward Scotland; the few horsemen appeared travelers encountered by chance, and set upon in hope of further gain. Back of the fight, two or three sumpters stood huddled. Simon hesitated, glancing at Ashley; then, above the clang and scuffle and bleating of the sheep, a woman's voice cried out.

She had been with the sumpters, and one of the Scots had crept up to try to drag her from her palfrey. The rider who seemed in command of the party, looking round, tried to back and hack his way through the press to her side, and Simon said abruptly, "You look after the woman: I'm going down to help him."

It was, they both knew, a hare-brained scheme; Simon had only his sword, his armor being stowed on the carrier horse left grazing on the crest, and it was questionable how great heed would be paid by the marauders to the exhortings of an interfering priest. Pelting down toward the affray, Simon reflected cynically that the girl was most likely a bawd that would be happy enough to change her man if a long purse went with the bargain. From the corner of his eye he saw her rein her horse about to face the man behind; her arm went up, and something—it looked like a leather ale bottle—came down on the Scotsman's head. The stopper flew out on impact with drenching effect; Ashley shouted an encouragement laced with blessings, and the fringes of the scrimmage enveloped them like a glutinous and indecisive tide.

Very soon it began to retire on itself, separating into the individual persons of men and horses. The assault from behind had been the deciding factor for the raiders, no more than half a dozen in number, who were already tired and in two days had grown used to easier pillage. They broke and ran, leaving their plunder behind them, and, returning from a last sally to encourage them on their way, Simon found the Englishmen dismounted and clustered about their captain, who was nursing an arm. He looked up as Simon approached: a young man with dark hair and eyes, a little pale now with discomfort and the residual traces of anger. Swinging from his horse, Simon walked toward him, remarking with a glance at the milling ewes, "You've acquired some livestock, unless you might know who owned them once. Have you any notion how to recognize a sheep?"

"None in the world," the other rejoined briefly. He chafed his arm again, which had been bruised parrying a spear, and looked Simon up and down, taking in the foreign-style hat and hose, and cloak lined in Scottish patterned cloth. "Well sir, I am indebted to you, for whatever your reasons, but if you're thinking of ransoms I warn you my sister and I together will fetch a fair's-end price." He stared up the hill, as if wondering how many more alien horsemen might be awaiting signal to descend, and Simon said smiling, "No, you've more men about you than I." He realized with a shade of humor that the admission could make a hostage of himself, and went on quickly, "I hope you've no injury from this business: I doubt the Duke of York would be pleased with it. This is not the way he means to win his kingdom."

His lip curling, the dark-eyed man said, "Then he should have found out something of border wars first. Any crofter hereabouts could have told him. I was taking my sister to Warkworth for safety—we've kin in the North, and were visiting near Branxton when we heard King Jamie was on the march." As if prompted, he added then, "My name is William Lovell. Here is my sister, who will thank you too." Ashley was conducting the palfrey and its rider toward them, but Simon, his back to their approach, had his gaze on the other man's face. Ten years ago, as a child in Hainault he had seen that profile: the finely modeled structure of brow and cheek, and strong, mobile mouth. Every line and feature of his face, Will Lovell had drawn from his father; and he wore them like princes' leavings, ill-becoming and accepted from need. When he thought about it, Simon could understand that he would have little cause, in Tudor England, to be grateful he was Francis Lovell's son. Awkward, he said, "But then, Viscount Lovell was your father. I met him when I was young, in Hainault while he was refuging there after Bosworth fight; his cousin Sir Philip Lovell married my mother that same year."

"The late attainted Viscount Lovell," the young man corrected curtly; the amendment was automatic, as from long habit. His eyes swung to Simon, a faint interest kindling in his expression. "So you are Philip Lovell's Burgoner stepson? I remember, we heard in England that exile had mightily prospered him. Well"—he found somewhere a smile, and put it on like company dress—"I suppose in some sort we are kinsmen."

"In some sort," Simon agreed gravely. He did not know why it should amuse him, except to think of that solemn face should Will Lovell find out how closely related, in fact, they were. Flanders and the Duchess of Burgundy had never seemed so far; his spirits lifted reasonlessly, and he turned to the girl on the palfrey with his best court bow. "Simon de Brezy, mademoiselle: a liege of the Duke of Burgundy, and your good servant."

She looked at him by the light of a torch which had been brought to dispel the dusk; even in the shadows, he discovered her to be younger than he had believed. She was so muffled now in cloak and hood that only her eyes showed, dark and widely spaced like her brother's; from that, Simon judged her to be pretty, but she had drawn the lappets of her hood across her cheeks so he could not see. He thought it gentle and maidenly in so young a girl; then he remembered the ale skin spouting over the Scotsman's head, and wanted to laugh. Beneath his breath, Will Lovell having turned to an attendant's whispered word, he said, "A swingeing blow, my kinswoman: the fellow will have a headache all the way back to Tweed." She answered in a clear voice, only slightly muffled by the cloak, "Did you truly know my father in Burgundy? I have always thought I remember the last time I saw him, when the nurse held me at the window to watch him ride away to Bosworth. He was all in armor with scarlet plumes; ever after, Saint Michael never seemed so fine to me." Her brother looked round from speaking with the servant, saying sharply, "Maud." She drew back, as if put in remembrance; an instant before, Simon was sure she had smiled.

At length returning from his conversation, Will Lovell

spoke past his sister to Ashley, bright-eyed and silent at the palfrey's bridle: "Sir, a man is injured here that may die of it. Will you do your office for him?" He did not offer to accompany the priest, but stood waiting as Ashley hitched up the skirt of his robe and, riding whip clutched in his other hand, followed the pointing finger. Across the road, some men crouched over one stretched on the ground; there was a torch at his head, reddening the gaunt watching faces and stand of piebald birches beyond. Simon, his constraint returning, spoke some words of regret to the master for his servant's hurt, and Lovell said shortly, "He is my mother's kinsman the lord Talbot's groom. I have neither lands nor folk; this is an escort lent to get us to Warkworth." It was true, Simon had forgotten the father's proscription would have stripped his son; suddenly he remembered again the young man's voice, saying of Philip Lovell, "We heard exile had prospered him."

It was the girl Maud, silent once more on her palfrey, who first heard the pat of hooves. She said softly, "Listen," and leaned forward, touching her brother's shoulder. A minute later the sounds came again, mixed with the night breeze but nearer now, east from the direction of Twizel. Instinctively Simon and William Lovell looked at each other; whether Scots raiders or English patrols, horsemen on this road portended ill for one of them. To Maud, Simon said quietly, "Come down from your horse: you are too much seen a woman there." Holding her around the waist, he brought her swiftly to the ground; a servant, urgently signaled, stifled the torches. They stood listening, peering in the gloom, until points of light glimmered through the trees; someone stumbled, to French curses, and silk of scarlet, gold and blue rippled beyond the leaves. Many flambeaux illumined the roadway like noon, and Richard's voice said in amazement, "Simon?"

The light revealed his face haggard and drained of color beneath the blazing banner; the hand he gave Simon to kiss was slack with tiredness. Ashley he greeted with similar surprise, and glanced curiously at the others, clustered by the roadside with the surging sheep. Hastily —for he could see some of the Duke's men already eyeing the trove—Simon explained, "These are English folk, that renegades from the King of Scots' army would have robbed. They are peaceful, and there is a woman with them."

His mouth tight with bitterness, Richard said, "The King of Scots has made the example: his men do as he shows them." Speaking more loudly, he addressed William Lovell, who after an instant came forward at his sign. "I am indeed sorry for this trouble, sir, which I would not have had befall you for half my kingdom. If you have suffered loss, it shall be made good: Sir Nicholas, take note of this young man's name, and call it to my remembrance again." But when he heard it he turned to Simon as if in question; reluctantly, for he suspected what would follow, Simon said, "The gentleman is a kinsman of my stepfather, the lord of Clairmont."

"William Lovell?" Richard repeated. "Oh, but your name has been especially commended to me: your father was the good servant of all my house." He leaned from the saddle eagerly to give his hand; an arm's length from his reach, Lovell answered unmoving, "And suffered for it. With your"—he paused long enough to make omission of the title plain—"with your leave, I would like to continue my journey; the ways being so full of brigands, I am in fear for my sister's safety."

Richard drew back. Behind him the Irishmen muttered in anger, but after a little silence he replied calmly, "I understand you. Well, you have reason." The drooping lid over his left eye, always more pronounced in weariness or discomfiture, alone betrayed his chagrin. He sat still, mechanically fingering the reins, while the Englishmen slowly collected numbers and set off, a single torch going before, toward Warkworth. Soon the noise of horses faded; the light flickered and blinked for the last time among the trees. It had seemed to Simon that one or two at least might have pulled caps from crowns, or looked back once at their dead King Edward's son, but no head turned, and all the voices that were raised belonged to the worried sheep, circling forgotten and uneasy around the Flemish lanzknechts in the middle of the road.

Night was coming on; the darkness would shortly be too thick for strangers to travel further in. To Richard, absorbed and sad with his eyes on the emptiness where his countrymen had been, Simon said presently, "My lord, where is the King of Scots? We must make camp, unless he has found a castle whole enough to shelter in till day."

The blue eyes turned to him, recalled from far off. "The King of Scots? At his pastime behind us somewhere, I should suppose. I am going back to Scotland, and all my men with me: I told the King, I will have no part in what he is doing to my people of England."

Like a dewlapped moon beyond the prince's shoulder, Simon saw John Heron's face; he could have laughed, another time, so sour was the merchant's look. He thought of Geffroi riding off all hot to conquer England: he had seen himself made lord of many manors in reward.

As if the reflection had been reminder spoken aloud, Richard laid an arm on the younger man's shoulders. "Simon, there is ill news, and I must ask your pardon that until now I forgot. Geffroi Marot your friend is dead." He snapped his fingers in command, and one of the Flemings led from the rear a knights' destrier, caparisoned for war. An instant later Simon realized it was not after all without its rider: a man's body was thrown across and covered with a mantle. He went close and lifted it, and saw the face.

He was surprised at the heaviness of his heart. For months now they had been an irritation to each other, chafing like sand; many days Simon had demanded of himself why of all the young men at Saint Aubin he had asked this swaggering, thick-hided youth to come with him beyond seas. Yet seeing him now, he could only think with pain that but for him, Geffroi Marot would not have sailed away from Burgundy to die in a foreign land. It had not happened in battle, Richard said, for they had encountered none. There was a house sacked which they came on, riding back from Twizel; the stones were loose where they still stood, but there was talk of plunder left, and Geffroi going too near, he was under the wall when a piece of it fell on him.

The breeze buffeted their faces, blowing keen down the valley from the upper Tweed; there was always wind in these parts, raw and uncomfortable to one bred in the fruit lands of Hainault. The fringed mantle whipped in Simon's fingers, tugging against its gay embroidered binding of Arras work. He remembered Christy lying outside

Edinburgh castle gate; and he said, "This is the second person that has died because of me."

Richard's eyes opened wide. He stared round the darkness, which every second breath of the shifting wind tainted still with the reek of old fires, and he exclaimed, "Only two?" His voice broke in laughter, or it might have been tears. Digging spurs in his horse, he jerked an arm at his men to follow, and galloped off down the road toward Coldstream ford.

VI

The Bishop of Cambrai sailed back to Burgundy, with what impressions many would have been glad to share. He had had an embarrassing errand in Scotland, being at once councilor to young Duke Philippe of Burgundy, who had lately reversed his diplomacy to make treaty with England, and long acquaintance of Margaret of York, in all Europe now the Duke of York's only friend. Richard was withdrawn with the bishop, who in turn displayed restraint in seeking out one whose affairs must have formed the principal purpose of his journey; they met as strangers of whom fate has made conspirators, and what they talked of when necessity brought them privately together, no one knew. In October the young man rode with Henri de Berghes to Saint Andrews, where the last ship waited before winter storms closed the wild northern seas; at the harbor side he kissed the bishop's ring, and stood watching with blowing hair as the sails grew small, and dropped from sight.

King James' war with England went on, but the pre-

tense had long been abandoned that it was on Richard
of York's behalf; it was in fact widely speculated that
when truce was made, as finally it must be, one of the
chief articles of the peace would be surrender of the
Duke of York's person to the English King. Why he
lingered in face of such danger was beyond understanding, except perhaps there was nowhere left for him to
go. His wife, who had been lately delivered of a child,
looked sullen; the babe that should have been a prince
to be his father's heir had proved a girl, so sickly and
small she was daily expected to die.

James had packed off home to Ireland and Burgundy
the bulk of Richard's hungry locust followers, with the
comment that they had eaten long enough from his
bounty, and that while it was commendable in a Christian
to seek the promised land, Scotland was no such place.
Simon, being regularly supplied from Burgundy, was glad
to be one of the few remaining who had no need of the
Scots King's gifts, although James had given no indication he would prefer the young lord of Saint Aubin
to leave his court. He even went from his way to speak
friendlily with him, and once said that if it should be
that the Duke of York departed again upon his travels,
there would be no need for Monsieur de Brezy to feel
himself dismissed from Scotland at the same time. They
were in the great chamber at Linlithgow; across the
room a storyteller was recounting to listening women
the tale of Lady Cressid of Troy town, and on the settle
near them Richard leaned his shoulders to its velvet
back, his pale, fair profile a little turned from the rest.
Simon looked at James, whose gaze had paused thought-

ful on the Duke's face, and he said, "You don't like him, do you?"

Crookedly smiling, James responded, "My dogs don't like him. That's enough for me." Restless, he leaned down to scratch the ears of a wolfhound bitch, lying with her head on the square of carpet at his feet. "Devil on the fellow, there's that about him that would curd cream, for me. Have you never felt it yourself?" His eyes rested curiously on the boy's face, which the lamplight carved with a strong and resolute beauty. The darkness of his hair and brows was an exact and vivid opposite to Richard's lucent fairness: Hylas to his prince's Hercules, Master Dunbar the poet used to say derisively, after the new fashion for Greek things: although not when Simon could hear him. Now, when he sat silent with his arms clasping his knees, James added in an altered voice, "Had it been left to him, you'd have made kites' fare at the Darnaway hunt. He was nearest to help, but moved not a foot to do it."

Abruptly formal, Simon said flushing, "I do not forget it was your Grace's spear that saved me from worse injury that day. For the Duke of York, it would be a kindness to remember there has been little in his rearing, being dispossessed and a wanderer most of his days, to teach him how to kill a boar. He has been busy getting his bread."

"I doubt all the instructing in England would have profited him," James rejoined cynically. "Lad, you've something to learn yet of yon milk-faced Duke." He stretched, stood, and walked away. Beyond the window a full autumn moon hung warm and golden; the candles were no more than half consumed on their prickets, and

Margaret Drummond, his new mistress, had turned from the ended tale to smile at him across the firelight.

Richard of York loitered in Scotland until the next year's summer. The war went on all winter through into spring; King Henry, maddened at last by the gadfly incursions of his adversary, was mustering an army to send against James that had, for its instructions, the King's warrant to burn and ravage wherever it found itself on Scottish soil. This, unlike previous reprisals, was serious; envoys began to go back and forth between the two kingdoms, and in their letters the name of Richard of York—Henry called him Monsieur Warbeck, asserting him to be in truth the son of a burgher of Tournai—grew large. All this Richard knew; but his wife was pregnant again, and wept to be sent traveling with her husband so near her time.

Spring came, and one afternoon in May Simon leaned with folded arms against the ramparts of Edinburgh Castle, looking without seeing toward the lion hill of Arthur's Seat, and the silver sleeve of the Forth. The day was sunny and what passed for warm in Scotland; in the estuary a Flemish trader that had loaded at Kircaldy was standing slowly out to sea, riding down in the water like a fat gorged bird. One of Margaret Drummond's ladies halted as she passed to catch his arm, saying mischievously, "You are far off, Monsieur de Brezy. Stay with us yet a while." He laughed and answered lightly; but it was true he had been thinking of Hainault, where for nearly two years he had not set his foot.

The King of Scots, long fending off the demands of

Tudor's ambassadors, offered Richard of York a ship to take him out of Scotland, big enough to carry himself and his wife and children, and the thirty or so followers who continued still in his service. It was a Breton merchantman called *The Cuckoo,* and the great captains Andrew and Robert Barton would escort the Duke in their own vessels, to ensure he came to no harm. The day of English peace was drawing nearer; Richard waited now only for his wife to be delivered, and enough recovered to accompany him. All in a night, she bore her second child: it was another girl, as weakly as the first.

A fortnight later they embarked at Ayr. Letters had come to the Duke from Cornwall, where rebellion had been recently suppressed, entreating him to show himself there as King Edward's son; but he sailed first to Ireland, remembering the past friendship of Desmond and Kildare. John Atwater, the sometime mayor of Cork, stoutly proclaimed his support, but Kildare was lord deputy of Ireland now, his peace with Tudor made, and Desmond, once so great a friend, was looking for Richard Plantagenet now only to deliver him into King Henry's hands. With Atwater's help Richard slipped down the coast to Kinsale, where the resourceful Irishman had got news of two more ships: a Spanish trader returning from Flanders, and the kraeck *Jacqueline of Antwerp,* under charter to help the Spaniard transport his goods to Santander. For a consideration, and with Spanish gallantry toward the misfortunes of so charming a prince, the Castilian master agreed to carry the Duke of York over to Cornwall, and accompanied by the mayor himself, his son Jackie, and a few score Irishmen looking for adventure, they set sail for England. It was raining hard, with a prankish wind varying the solid, rhythmic drumming on the decks; a day out from Kinsale, through a rift in the curtaining rain they saw ships coming out of the north: four merchantmen, high-castled and well armed, overtaking them fast. When the first cannonball splashed at *The Cuckoo*'s stern, it was clear they were no friends.

Having no guns, they could only run for it. *Cuckoo* and the Spaniard, a long-bowed Biscayan built for wilder weather than this, drew gradually away, but the short-masted, high-prowed kraeck with every rag of canvas on the yards could not outrun her enemies. When the fastest of them had edged far enough ahead to turn across her bow, she hove to and waited, pitching listlessly, while the boarders scrambled over her side.

They were Munster men, that from loyalty to King Henry had put out to catch the Duke of York and bring him back to Waterford. While the *Jacqueline*'s master protested bitterly that he had never heard of the Duke, being himself a peaceable Brabanter plying between Antwerp and the Irish ports, the captain of the boarding party sent his men to search the kraeck. He himself oversaw the work from amidships, standing with legs braced wide against the lift and fall of the deck, his eyes traveling from the long rake of the bowsprit, trellised with tackle, to the oak-railed poop. At the foot of the mainmast some barrels emptied of stores sat, lids askew; on one of them a tousle-haired seaman with the look of a Walloon was perched, eating an onion. Presently strolling toward him, the captain said in loud English, "Your master has told me he does not carry the pretended Duke of York: is this true?" An uncomprehending stare answered him, followed, as the Irishman tapped

95

his foot, by a thick, *"Comment?"* Two of the searchers had come out of the poop cabin and, shaking their heads, disappeared into the hold; irritated, the captain repeated his question, at the same time seizing the sailor's arm so he descended abruptly from his barrel top to the swimming deck. "Stand to your betters, fellow. Have you seen the Duke of York?"

Confusedly propitiating, the man pulled a woolen stocking cap from his head, uncovering thereby the reminder of a thatch of sooty curls; these he thoroughly scratched, and having taken a last bite at the onion said again, *"Comment?"*

Exclaiming in disgust, the captain turned on his heel, started to walk off, and then, changing his mind, took up a position beside the unmoving Walloon. The wind had slackened, and the rain beat steadily down, coursing in rivers around the lips of the half-covered casks, or resounding on the lids. The minutes passed; in a quarter of an hour the last man had returned to report failure. Red with anger, the Irish captain strode to the rail and, shading his eyes, peered after the vanishing masts of *Cuckoo* and the Biscayan. He believed not at all in the Low Country master's description of his errand, but lacking irrefutable evidence could hardly compel back to Waterford a subject of the Duke of Burgundy, with whom King Henry was currently enjoying the warmest relations. He jerked his thumb toward the tall shadow of his ship, riding easily to starboard, and with a final resentful stare around prepared to follow his men off the kraeck. As he started down the rope ladder to the merchantman's boat, rocking like a cockleshell at the *Jacqueline's* side, he saw from the tail of his eye that the Walloon had discovered in his blouse another onion.

It was several minutes after the Irish ship had begun to draw away, and, her sails filling, headed with the wind back to her sister vessels, before anyone on the kraeck stirred. They stood gazing as the white sails and tall spines of the masts edged away north, and the seamen's moving heads diminished to seem no more than beads, slipping back and forth above the shield-hung rails. Then, his rain-wet hair whipping his brows, Simon dropped the onion and, leaping for the barrel on which he had been seated, wrenched off the lid. Richard's head appeared in the aperture; he was laughing like a schoolboy. While a dozen hands stretched to help him from his hiding place, Simon leaned trembling against the mast. For better than ten minutes he had been standing beside the Irish captain, listening to the dull, unmistakable sound of raindrops hitting the lid of a barrel, supposedly empty, by its echo crammed to the brim, and it would be bedtime, he considered, before his nerves had recovered from it. Richard, turning gleefully to embrace him, chaffed him unmercifully about his pallor, and promised he should have onions for his supper.

Of them all, he showed himself least unnerved by the closeness of escape. Indeed, the reaction of relief seemed to have brought back the young gaiety of his first adventurer's days; it was as if some fetter of constraint had snapped, leaving him at ease and free to become some new, barely realized other self. Presently, as the *Jacqueline* hauled up and set off in pursuit of her companions, he leaned still flushed on the poop rail, staring toward the gray sea line over which the ship that bore his wife and children had disappeared. There was hardly a man but believed he could guess his heart: it was long since he had had triumph to lay down, like a lover's gift, at Katherine Gordon's feet.

By evening the rain had stopped and they had a fair wind at their backs, carrying them swiftly toward England. Richard, restless yet, wandered the little cabin; it had been hung with canvas cloth to make two apartments, and in the outer room the squires' pallets were already laid. His legs curled from trampling by Richard's pacing feet, Simon was making what sense he could of letters and lists from the Duke's Cornish friends; since the executions after the late rising, the malcontents had been without leaders, and told twenty different tales. "Here's a gentleman of Polperro that is yours to the death," he remarked, holding up a sheet. "But you are on no account, he says, to trust in his neighbor of Looe, who will tell you the same thing but is really in Tudor's pay. The Looe villain writes the same of Polperro, except to add that Polperro has dealings with pirates too. *Déa*, what a folk."

Shrugging, Richard glanced at the two letters. "Both magistrates," he commented. "Well, I believe it about the pirates. This is Cornwall, Simon." He drained his wine cup, refilled it, and played with a corner of the paper. "Why bother yourself over this? It's Ashley's work, or Ned Skelton's; I'm sure you were never bred for it."

Without lifting his head, Simon said, "May I not learn?" There was an edge to his voice in spite of himself; he had suffered in council from Sir Edward Skelton, the Duke's captain and strategist, who was ironic about green youths being included with my lord of York's advisers, but from the beginning Richard had insisted upon it. Smiling now, he squeezed his favorite's shoulder. "Does Skelton worry you? Never care for him, my dear: he's only—jealous."

He hesitated over the last word. Simon stood up and carried the papers to an open coffer pushed against the bulkhead. "Skelton knows his job, or says he does. He's no need to be."

Indulgent, Richard responded, "Skelton is a tailor's son; if you've forgotten it, he has not. Anyway"—he came across the cabin, the cup in his hand—"never mind Skelton." Simon was kneeling to lay the papers in the chest; standing by him, Richard lifted a strand of his black hair. "How the light shines on it. When I was young, I used to wish my hair was dark."

For an instant, while the lamp swung gently in its chains, and the lattice shadow of the lantern cage slid back and forth with the roll of the ship, Simon thought he must be drunk. Then, as the tentative, exploring finger stole down his cheek, comprehension broke like a shock of water. He sprang to his feet, his arm swinging back; in the moment that Richard saw his eyes, the *Jacqueline* yawed and half heeled with a shifting wind, and the heaving floor, violently listing, flung both men together to the bulkhead. While Richard lay as if stunned, his face gone bone-white against the slow dilating of his pupils, Simon got from his knees to his feet, and heard a voice he hardly knew for his own say, "There are papers in that chest that have been this day waiting for you to look at. Do you not soon get to the cares that brought you here, you'll be put to it to keep a head that has any kind of hair on."

99

He went out past the canvas curtain, ignoring in the outer apartment the sleepy rousing of the boys, who had heard, they said, something fall. He answered shortly, and outside climbed the ladder to the poop deck; there in the darkness he leaned over the rail and was sick into the sea. Many things, now, came back to mind, incidents at the Scottish court he had hardly noticed when they happened: a girl when he had kissed her behind a curtain last Uphaliday, giggling and protesting he did it so well as her friends would never believe; William Dunbar, sharp as his quills, with his sly Greek jokes. If he had been younger by only a few years he would have understood; one did not go a squire into even Margaret of Burgundy's household without learning very soon about which boys caught the interest of certain of the unmarried men, and why. He thought of Skelton, and his hands closed on the sea-scoured rail. There had been good reason for his hatred: a soldier of experience, and a man, being pushed aside for the Duke's fancy boy.

Lamplight shone from the windows below, thrusting like spears into the dark. Only to remember the loathed being so near him still in the cabin beneath his feet made their soles prick, and him to wish he was with the ship's boy, high on his mast; nor could he bring himself to go down to bed with Ashley and the squires, divided only by a wall of canvas from that inner room. It was coming on to rain again, a thin mist like feathers tickling the cheek; he found a sheltered spot in the huge bellying shadow of the mizzen, and lay down, although not to sleep, until day.

In the morning the Flemish master looked at the

sky, and after consulting his compass, a needle rubbed on lodestone and floated in water on a straw, said that if the wind held they should raise Land's End in three days. "Bad luck to it then for an ill-wishing name," remarked Jackie Atwater with a grin; Richard only laughed and shook his head at him, and having nodded civilly to Simon, invited Sir Edward Skelton down to his cabin to help estimate, from the Cornish letters, what forces and of what kind they might find awaiting them. There was a mark on his forehead, where the cup had cut him as he fell.

The wind held fair. On the third day, early in the afternoon, the lookout shouted, and, thronging to the side, they saw far ahead ruffles of foam, and the low granite headland of the point of Cornwall called Land's End. *Cuckoo* and the Biscayan carrack were lying to north of the reefs, in Whitesand Bay.

They had been waiting since yesterday evening, plenty of time for the news to have spread; when Richard and his officers were rowed ashore, they found the cove as busy as an anthill, and almost as populous. One old gentleman in sober country-cut clothes burst from the crowd as the Duke walked up the beach, and, falling to his knees, gazed steadfastly into the young man's face. "God be with your Highness," he said through his tears. "I was at Westminster in your late father the good King Edward's time: I know you now as I did then, his true son and our undoubted prince."

The *Cuckoo's* boat was nearing shore, carrying Katherine Gordon and her children, she herself clasping the elder girl's hand, and a nurse holding the baby, warmly wrapped against the blowing spray. When the boat grounded, Richard went down to its side, and having long embraced his wife, lifted her over the water to land. The Cornishmen had brought horses for the Duke and his gentlemen, and a gentle palfrey trapped in blue velvet for the Duchess of York. They set off westward, drawing after them men from every hamlet until Skelton began to look serious and wonder about their provisioning. But the gentlemen of the county were as friendly as the common folk, and sent foodstuffs and fodder wherever they could not themselves receive the Duke in their halls. Tudor's exactions in Cornwall had been as rigorous as in other places; it has cost him one rebellion there already, and King Edward's memory lingered yet among West Countrymen. Others, who had been servants of Edward's brother Richard of Gloucester, were as ready as any to salute the heir of York, although at first slow in coming forward; it was, after all, Richard of Gloucester who had set aside King Edward's sons as being born of a marriage not lawful, and afterward put them in ward while he took the crown himself. But the Duke of York, apprehending their embarrassment, was at pains to seek out his dead uncle's friends, took them heartily by the hand, and repeated in proclamation what last year he had published abroad in the North: that although desire of rule had bound King Richard, in his other actions he was noble, and loved the contentment of his people. That brought them swarming out with cheers. When he spread his banners a great shout went up: they were two, a child escaping from a wolf's mouth, and rising out of a tomb.

They took the eyrie fortress of Saint Michael's Mount, crossing over when the mainland causeway lay open at low tide: this was a base about which even Skelton could be pleased, that might be supplied by land or sea, and whose monastery would be a safe refuge for Katherine of York and her children, while her husband marched on toward London. Richard was two days there, sending out letters, reviewing troops and supplies, and receiving friends; in the evening he kept hall for old adherents and new, sitting by his wife under a canopy blazoned with the royal arms of England. Everyone said how kingly he bore himself, and how just it was that he should wear the crown: his very father's son, they said, reminding each other of King Edward's gracious dignity that put every man at his ease.

Of that time, after, Simon was obliged to take anyone's word, since he got drunk the first evening, and stayed that way until they left the Mount. What he was doing there at all, he could not endure to think; he would gladly have run away, if there had been a spot on earth where he could show himself with the reputation his own carelessness and the Duke of York had given him. He knew how fast such stories traveled too; once he dreamed himself with Richard again in the ship's cabin, which in an instant changed to the master's room at Clairmont, with Philip Lovell looking at him from the door.

By the time he entered Bodmin, the Duke of York, who had left Scotland with thirty followers, had an army of four thousand men. It seemed likely he would roll up England before him as his father had done more than five and twenty years ago, when he returned out of exile unwelcomed and near friendless, except for England's people. They could risk Exeter now, the first great objective; and that, John Atwater prophesied jubilantly, would fall like a ripe apple. He had dropped back from the vanguard looking for his son, and found him riding knee to knee with a dark-haired companion about Jackie's own age, of whom Atwater had been hearing something. With a shade of uneasiness the mayor repeated his cheer, his gaze on the young man whom, in view of stories going round, he would have preferred to see farther from his boy. It was an expression that Simon had recently begun to identify; but when the mayor went away again, and the younger Atwater—blue-eyed, black-banged, his Irish color like poppies in his cheeks —broke a prolonged silence to ask what he was thinking, he roused to say lightly, "Nothing much. Do you know where Skelton did his fighting before he came to the Duke of York?"

The Irishman was surprised. "In Italy somewhere, I think; it's a grand place to be getting experience. Doesn't everyone know?"

"Perhaps they do. I was just wondering how he meant to take Exeter without guns."

Atwater reflected on that, his eyes on Sir Edward's broad, armor-clad back a dozen yards up the column. "Does he mean to fight for it, now? I thought we were to show ourselves at the gates only, and the good folk of the town would come flocking to invite us in."

Simon said dryly, "With only sixty horse and no engines, we had better hope they do." Having spent two winters in association with James Stewart, he knew something by now of what was needed for a successful siege. But perhaps, Jackie offered with an urchin grin—he was not fond of Sir Edward either—in Italy they campaigned by different rules. A village girl stood barefoot and ankle-deep in dust, watching them pass; he threw a kiss that made her dimple, and spurred off down the road, singing:

"Western wind, when wilt thou blow,
The small rain down can rain—
Christ, if my love were in my arms,
And I in my bed again!"

They made the march from Bodmin to Launceston by way of the Bodmin Moor: a lowering solitude of harsh bare hills, and one silent sheet of water haunted, so said the Cornish, by a giant condemned to bend forever over it, emptying away the water with a sieve of limpet's shell. Against the humped skyline the trudging files of men and horses looked small, their pennons washed of color by the brooding gray above them; even the destriers stepped flinchingly, as if on mistrusted ground.

Next morning they crossed the Tamar into Devon, and two days later the Duke of York lay with an army of six thousand on the hillside overlooking Exeter. The city gates were shut, but the walls displayed a frieze of bobbing heads, and Richard sent a herald to call upon the town to surrender. While they waited for reply, Skelton paced back and forth beside the Duke, squinting into the sun as he pointed out the lie of the land and discoursed of the advantage of trying first the north gate, from which, once penetrated, they might attack the castle on its inward side, as opposed to that of the west with its greater natural defense. Simon looked at the glowering red battlements which the Normans had called Rougemont, rearing like cliffs above the city walls, and thought they must be surely troubled in their wits to talk of breaking their breasts against that colossus; but he held his tongue. In a short time the herald returned, and speaking on his knees said, "They will not admit your Grace. The Earl of Devon and his son are in the city, and a great multitude of gentlemen."

There was a little pause, and then Richard said quietly, "They leave us no choice. We will force the gates, and the blame is on their heads."

He nodded to the trumpeter, a freckled Waterford lad, who blew out his cheeks until they glowed like fruit with the fury of the blast. Slowly the long column descended to deploy before the walls, the Duke leading with as undisturbed and cheerful countenance as if he had considered no other course but to break into Exeter by the power of his arms. He wore the silvered armor, polished to blazing, which the King of Scots had given him on his wedding day, and rode a stately war-horse the Cornishmen had brought to meet him at Land's End. It was a bright September morning, with a breeze that smelled of the sea; the mounted lances dipped pennons, and raised a cheer for King Richard, fourth of his name.

Hours later, tired, hot, and baffled, they were in their same places before the city's north gate; the same taunting banners waved above the ramparts; and, far from conceding to the Duke after a decent show of resistance, the citizens had sent messengers for help, letting them down on ropes over the walls. So much Richard knew, from having captured one of them; but he must presume more to have escaped, and a relieving force under King Henry's general, Lord Daubeney, was on the way. Standing hands on hips with his beaver lifted, snoutlike, above his brows, Skelton gazed at the obdurate stone as if insulted, and cursed beneath his breath. "They have not five hundred men in arms: they cannot fight us and win. Something has happened, maybe, that we cannot know of, to change their hearts."

"They have eyes to see," Simon observed coolly. "For what damage we may do them with these tools, they can bear us here to Judgment Day. It takes a mighty bowman to shoot through stone." He was as exasperated as any, and felt as great a fool; most galling of all was the reflection that it was an impasse they could have foretold. Richard was staring at the gates, his lips closed tight on a disappointment that might be guessed. He had counted on the men of Exeter opening to him, after such token opposition as was indicated by prudence and the mayor: so, perhaps, had Skelton. Simon glanced sideways at Sir Edward's heavy, barrel-bodied figure in dust-streaked mail, and flushed, irritated countenance— like the great god Mars with a bellyache, an unregenerate inner voice remarked—and addressed the owner's pre-occupation in what he tried to make a friendlier tone. "I've been looking at the east gate, Sir Edward; there's little natural defense, and it's not strongly manned. If a good force kept up the attack here in the north, it might be possible while the townspeople are engaged by it to breach the other gate."

The impatient eye came round, as unregarding as if a child had plucked the plated sleeve. Skelton said shortly, "We have no implements to break down the gate, and no one to command such a diversion, myself being the Duke's only officer. It is a second captain's work to lead such an assault: by misfortune, his Grace has none but me." His gaze stayed long enough to take note of, and offensively discount, the significance of the younger man's armor: Leave fighting to men, it advised, that know something about it. Simon perceived his meaning, and losing his temper retorted, "There's a hillside of trees to make rams, and most of your Cornish are better used to axes to fell and trim them with than they will be this twelvemonth to their poor spears. As for the question of a captain, if you can assign no other to lead them, I'll do it myself."

Later, working with a team of Cornishmen and Jackie Atwater as they sweatingly cut, trimmed, and loaded onto makeshift sledges the thick trunks of three Devon beeches, he could not think what had possessed him. He cared no more now for Richard of York than the Old Man of the Mountain, three hundred years dead in Paynimrie; it was the old sting to exceed that had goaded him, and the stupidity of six thousand men camped before Exeter, waiting for Daubeney to come.

They got the strongest ram in place before the gate, and formed a column of six men to carry it, two abreast. Half a dozen more flanked them close, carrying bundles of brushwood over their heads to make a shield from arrows. Not many of these came down, since most of the citizens were manning the north wall; the Earl of Devon and his men were nowhere to be seen. The gate was old; with the first blow it protested and shook, and when soon the next team of men bore forward to relieve their fellows, the splintered wood burst apart so suddenly that ram and carriers together were thrown halfway through the aperture. While axemen widened the breach,

Simon shouted to the trumpeters and with the Cornish-men pressing behind plunged through the shattered gate. A street of tall houses stretched before them, whose topmost floors leaned above the lower so two men might have joined hands across the way. By pressing close to the buildings they avoided what descended from above; a chamber pot crashed to the cobbles at Simon's feet, and the yard-long shaft from a longbow sprang quiver-ing from the timbered porch where Jackie Atwater had paused a moment earlier. Away to the right, the slope began to the citadel which the Conqueror had built because who held that, held Exeter, and all Devon and Cornwall too.

They had gained the turn into the little twisting street which led up the castle hill, forcing back the raw citi-zens' levies hand to hand, when Devon arrived. He and his son had rushed up their men to catch the waist of the invaders' column where it pushed and struggled out of the high street, and the inexperienced Cornish began to find out the difference between opposing their bodies, however willing, to others as slightly equipped, and men in mail of proof. They gave, and gave again; and from the rear Atwater sent word that if Simon did not pull the vanguard back, they would soon be cut off and trapped between Devon and the castle walls. It was a time for reinforcements to hearten discourage-ment and overwhelm with numbers the better-furnished enemy, but although a message had gone to Skelton when they first broke in the gate, no help came.

Daylight was fading; in the west sunlight glowed fiery, and a great shadow lay long before Rougemont hill. Simon knew he must get his men out of Exeter before darkness fell: night fighting is for the man that knows his ground. He went among them, cheerful and unhurrying, trying to stave off the panic which, once yielded to, would break soldiers back into the plowboys that a month ago they had been, and send them flying into the narrow alleys to be hunted down like felons, or dogs, after the gates were closed: trying to be all places at once, from the rear of the column, fending the brunt of the assault, to the flanks where every courtyard's mouth threatened a flight of arrows and more troops forcing a path across the retreat to cut it in two, to the staggering, exhausted head. His bones throbbed with weariness, but had anyone told him he was doing three captains' tasks he would have stared, or wept. Nothing he could persuade his body to seemed of significance beside the staunchness of these rough, raw men with their simple weapons, standing like brothers before Devon's steel; and he was still young enough to be shaken that such gallantry could be without reward.

It was the stench of fire, before its noise, that was their first warning. Before ever they reached the gate black plumes hung above the rooftops, and when the vanguard came near enough to see through the haze, they understood why Skelton could have sent no men to help them even if he would. A great fire had been kindled in the breach, green wood and old sending up smoke and sparks together, with broken bits of furniture and torn-off shutters from nearby houses helping the blaze. Wedged against it one saw here an irreverent prentice's hand —was the overturned carriage of some rich citizen, silk curtains shriveled to fluttering scraps on the roof hoops, paint and gilding melted to sleekness in the flames. Out-

110

side, some of Atwater's countrymen had tried to approach near enough to scatter the pyre; these had been driven back by archers newly posted in the gate tower, all the watch the city could spare, or that the gaping entry required now. One could say so much for the citizens: they knew how to make circumstance work for them so it appeared their choice.

They cleared the gatehouse first, smoking the birds from their nest after a good example, as Atwater said with a soot-smeared grin. Wood piled within the tower doors, first fired and then half smothered, sent the occupants coughing to the roof, where they enjoyed an option of lying flat beneath the parapet, or lifting heads for the Cornish bowmen below to shoot at. Afterward, while the better-armed of the Cornishmen held off Devon and his men, others dispersed the fire, using billhooks to snatch away the burning brands; the carriage itself—more effective than its contributor could have guessed—Simon had himself eventually to shoulder aside, swathed to the elbows in someone's leather jerkin that had been cut up and soaked in sewage from the town ditch, with two spearmen similarly protected hauling on the poles. The blazing skeleton heeled over with a crash and a flight of sparks like fireflies gauding the half-fallen dusk; the rest was done with bills and boots, dragging and kicking until the cobbled street lay clear, and, keeping fair order yet, the Cornishmen withdrew through the blackened stone gateway, leaving behind them, as Devon was shortly with anger and disappointment to learn, not twice twenty hurt and slain.

Of that escape from Exeter, Simon knew nothing and only hours later heard. Memory had ended a bare instant after the fiery hulk left the pressure of his shoulder, and the terrifying rush of heat through the steel plates of pauldron and beaver brought his hands up, blindly fumbling, to tear off the helm. He remembered the September evening cool on his face, and like a picture forever fixed, the head on the gate tower rising cautiously above the parapet: the glint of an arrowhead as it left the string, the gray goosefeathering of the shaft vanished to invisibility against a grayer sky; then a shock like a thunderbolt blasted consciousness away. It was Jackie Atwater and an archer from Marazion who together dragged him through the gate.

He woke in discomfort, to the jolting of a litter swung between two horses, and bright afternoon sunlight warm on his shoulder. All around him were unfamiliar green hills and files of trudging men; he saw near him young Tom of Waterford, the Duke's Irish trumpeter, and Heron the merchant's brigandined back. One can tell a great deal from the set of men's necks: these spoke defeat. Simon felt his head, which ached as if ready any moment to burst apart; there was a blood-soaked clout around his forehead, staunching the graze of the gateman's arrow, and a mess of unidentifiable composition daubed over his cheek and neck which did nothing to help him forget where the unlined steel of his helmet had burned them. He owed it to the quilted arming doublet, he supposed, that he had not been boiled like an oyster in his cuirass. He lay motionlessly staring at the puffs of cloud passing overhead until Jackie Atwater arrived, leaning down with his sallet riding between his shoulder blades; he looked disgruntled and dead tired, his round baby cheeks stubbled black with yesterday's beard, and when Simon asked, "Where are we going?" answered with a shrug.

"On the way to Taunton—so you're better? I'll send a wee boy with a drum up and down to tell the news, and save myself pains." Over the edge of the litter, Simon became aware of an unobtrusive jostling as the nearer men pressed forward to look at him; one or two, catching his eye, grinned awkwardly, or gestured in diffident salute. Without bothering to lower his voice, Atwater said, "They know who got them out of Exeter, those that went into it, and they know who was to blame that they had to come out again too. That grand hero Skelton was near pelted last night when we found him still on his fat hams under the north wall, telling the Duke what a foolishness it was to try to take a town without guns."

The litter swayed gently as it jounced along. After a moment Simon said, "Well, he's probably right about that. It's no use blaming him for not getting men to us, no one could have through that fire. How many did we lose in Exeter?"

"Not many, thanks to yourself. No, he couldn't put men over the fire, but there's some would like fine to know what he was doing while it was getting built." With a mouth of vinegar, the Irishman added, "We raised the siege this morning. They got the guns down from the castle last night, and there was no standing to that once they were above the gates. So the Duke sent a message to the city, courteously praying them to allow us peacefully to depart, which the mayor was in no case to refuse. Faix, I could wish me in Cork again."

He rode off in a chinking of bridle rings, and Simon rested with shut eyes in the litter's cradling lift and fall, listening to the dull sound of the horses' hooves stirring the dust, and the soft blowing of their breath. He was thinking that, by so much, Atwater was better off than himself: he knew of no place in the world he could wish to be now.

By the time they reached Taunton the first deserters had begun to slip away, and those remaining had the look of men with ropes for necklaces. The Bishop of Winchester's bailiff came out to excuse the town from receiving Richard of York within its gates, the place being ill suited to accommodate so large an army; since they had no food but what the country people chose of fear or friendship to give them, the common men could only sit on the grass among the watch fires, and think of their empty cooking pots. Richard himself had the host's one tent: a simple thing sent anonymously by a gentleman of Taunton, not rich, but that could not bear, his message said, that King Edward's son should lie out in the fields like a beast. By now rumor had it that Daubeney's vanguard was less than twenty miles off, grown greater by the addition of many West Country gentlemen and their retainers, and King Henry was marching from Oxfordshire with a second army no smaller than the first: reason enough for anyone to be shy now of admitting a friendliness for the Duke of York. As twilight deepened it began to rain, although the sun had set cloudlessly in an apricot sky; leaving those of his councilors that desired it to huddle in the tent, Richard walked among the weary men, hatless, his coak rumpled and wet with rain, stopping by every smoldering fire and pausing frequently between, to speak with kindliness or cheer to as many as he saw sitting apart from their fellows, or nursing unskillfully tended wounds. They gazed after him with love, knowing him as hungry and tired, nearly, as they; not one doubted that, when he asked where such a man's village was in Cornwall, or if another had had proper doctoring for his hurt, he had a true wish to know.

Council had been set for late that evening; as the town bell struck ten o'clock, and Skelton's thick person appeared in the lamplit entry of the tent, his head thrust forward into the dark, the Duke came across the grass with his quick, light tread and halted beside some men casting dice by a half-out touch. One lay as if watching, with bandaged head turned sideways on his arms, and Richard said quietly, "Come, Simon." He had spoken in French, using the soft, intimate *viens* of their earliest times; so greatly had his following altered that there was no other now with whom he could converse in the tongue which was most familiar to him.

Over the black-out fire, Simon met his eyes. He had not set foot in the Duke's councils since that night in the *Jacqueline of Antwerp*'s cabin: his private choice, which in the beginning had Richard queried it he would have defended with explicitness. Now, although for an instant his mouth went straight, and the day's journey he had unwisely finished on horseback reverberated in his fever-tight limbs like an unsilenced bell, he rose and followed the other man up the slope to the tent.

The voices of several persons talking all at once stilled as the Duke entered, but an atmosphere of dispute lingered; Skelton, almost breaking in over Richard's greeting, began the discussion abruptly by saying, "The chief thing is to secure his Highness' safety, and decide upon a route for his escape beyond seas." His bulging eye stared round their faces, from the mute rebellion of the elder Atwater, to Nicholas Ashley, inscrutably studying his fingers, to Heron, his pendulous jowls and soft merchant's hands together tremulous before a kind of deficit that could not be written off. Richard himself stood like a schoolboy while his teachers are busy, waiting to be remembered; it was as if the walk round the camp had taken his last resolution, leaving him able now only to hear what others would decide for his good. Skelton had spread a rough map drawn large at their feet; he was looking down at it, tracing an imagined course from Taunton to the south coast with the tip of his sword, when Simon said, "The Duke of York came to England to get a kingdom. Did he expect to achieve it without a battle?" The moving sword paused, its point dragging a hole in the paper between Yeovil and the Purbeck hills, but Atwater, having discovered an ally, grunted emphatic agreement, and Ashley remarked blandly into the silence, "The lord of Saint Aubin's opinion might be worth hearing, since he is distinguished by being the only person here to have had experience, this campaign, of fighting hand to hand."

Richard interposed warmly, "Indeed, we know what we have owed my lord of Saint Aubin. But Simon, if the odds are so unequal as reported—"

Once more Skelton's heavy voice overrode his master's. "They are so unequal. There is Daubeney here"—he thrust at the place on the map—"and King Henry behind him, and a fleet off Exeter, I am told, to guard the western ports. I see no help but for his Grace to forsake this camp tonight, as his royal father did without shame or blame at Doncaster, when he fled out of England and in a better season came again."

Ending a baffled quiet, Richard said gently, "You see, sirs, there is no other way." He looked grave, but not inconsolable; it occurred to Simon that, from the hour they had reached Taunton, this was probably what he had meant to do. Disgust was like a taste in his mouth; he swallowed so every man heard it, and walking to the door of the tent plucked back the curtain to point into the dark. "And what of those out there? What way does your Highness see for them, that risked all they possess for your sake?"

Ponderously ironic, Skelton struck in, "The lord of Saint Aubin believes himself at home in Flanders, where he had men whose lives, possibly, were his concern," but Simon flung words past him at Richard's scarlet face. "I have fought with them! Will you run off like a thief and leave them to face Daubeney alone?"

What he had said was borne on them slowly, as an avalanche slides from its crest. His color gone from red to white, Richard whispered, "That is enough! You forget yourself, and have done it more than once too: get from this place, and learn respect before you beg speech of me again." He swung round, his shoulders stiff with angry hurt, and addressed Skelton. "Sir Edward, those that are mounted must leave this camp as soon as they can be mustered; we will make for Southampton and hire a ship there. In the matter of the Cornishmen, I charge you: they are to be wakened so in the night they may scatter and escape Daubeney, and make their ways home again." Skelton and Heron burst out together in protest, the merchant being especially eloquent: someone, he said, was sure to slip off to Daubeney with news of the Duke's flight, only for the reward it must bring, and where would be their advantage of the hours until morning then? Richard allowed him no more than commencement of this argument before cutting him off. "It is not in my honor to buy twelve hours with five thousand men. Now go: and remember what I have commanded." With a gesture as imperial as any of the flame-haired despot he had claimed for father, he dismissed them all.

Outside the rain had stopped, and weak moonlight silvered a ripped bank of cloud. Simon, unexpectedly discovering himself braced on John Atwater's arm, muttered, "He should speak to them himself, only he'd never face them with it. Monsieur le maire, thank you but I'm very well—if you'll excuse me, I'm going round the camp myself now, to wake the men."

"Why do that?" the Irishman asked comfortably, without relinquishing his grip. "You heard the Duke: the Cornish will be warned and Daubeney get some burned-out fires and the Duke's bed furnishings for his trouble. Lad, you're sick yet: you spoke well, but your legs will never stand under you while you shake up five thousand snoring heroes, and there's a grand long ride in front of you to Southampton besides. Come and rest an hour, now."

His pink plump face in its half-circle of closely cropped hair was Jackie's over again, with an expression indicative of adjusting views. Unconscious of it, Simon let the mayor guide him down the slope; a dozen paces on, Atwater pushed him to a spread cloak which was thick and dry, and having groped within the folds brought out a leather bottle of something which, when introduced between the younger man's chattering teeth, ran a stream of pure fire from palate to belly and nestled there, warmly radiating, in a way, Simon estimated dizzily, fit to dry the earth under him a handbreadth deep. "*Uisge beatha,* the very water of life," Atwater remarked informatively, while he coughed and gasped and shook his head to another draught. "Man, it'll lie on your stomach like milk." And as his patient turned a cheek to the rough Irish cloth and shut his eyes, he stowed the bottle away.

When Simon woke he found himself already sitting, one arm dragged over Jackie's shoulder and the round Irish voice calm at his ear. "Up with you, so. The horses are ready, and we must be the same if we're to beat Daubeney out of Somerset. Come now." The moon had slipped behind a cloud, and the camp was a waste of motionless black humps in the faint light of stars. As they reached the horse lines, Simon looked back at the unmoving silence and said, "Why are they all asleep? There's been time to get them up by now, and they should be in as great hurry as we are."

"Not quite so great: they are common fellows, and Daubeney will be less eager to catch them than us." Skelton's voice came smoothly out of the dark. "We think it best the Duke should be gone before the men are wakened; they might try to keep him with them, otherwise, in some foolish conceit of what might be gained from battle." He was waiting by the great stallion that carried him, the reins in his hand. The shadows were busy with dim figures, standing, mounting, or already in the saddle; about half sat waiting for the Duke's command. Simon felt Jackie's palm under his foot, heaving him into the saddle; as he straightened, fumbling with the reins, Jackie's father handed up the whiskey bottle with a little tongue-cluck of encouragement, and moved off before the young man could part his dry lips in thanks. It was by then midnight, and in the widening gaps between the clouds, the sky was bright with stars.

They had cause to be glad of that, and more grateful still when presently the moon appeared again to show their path. The ground sank and squelched beneath the horses' hooves, heavy with rain; about ten miles south of Taunton they came on the untended scar of the Romans' road from Exeter, and rode as hard as they could until day began to lighten over the bald chalk spine of the downs. Not daring to be seen, the party turned aside then to lie up in a fold of hills, and Nicholas Ashley, himself a Hampshire man, went off alone with cross and beads displayed to find someone that could say where they might be. He came back naming a village which he knew, and said they were not quite half their way to Southampton.

They rested for the day in the hidden valley, mostly sleeping, to make up for the night's long ride. Once the horses had been unsaddled and turned out to graze, there was nothing else to do, for they had no food, and only water from the stream nearby to drink. It was warm for September; high on the slope yellow gorse bloomed, and some grasshoppers, the last of the season, sent up a chorus in the dying grass. Simon listened to them from the makeshift bed of his cloak, which Jackie had spread for him over a pile of leaves: fussing, Simon told him, like a Kerry grandmother, and sent the Irishman grinning away. On the other side of the glade Richard sat with chin on knees, the wind ruffling his hair, his wide gaze fixed on distance like a shield that warns intruders off. It is not difficult, among sixty men, to avoid looking at one of them; through all that day, his eyes and Simon's never met.

That evening, as they pressed on east, Ashley learned from a farmstead about armed horsemen that had earlier passed that way for Poole, after King Henry's great rebel, the man called Richard of York; there would be others like them, obviously, making for the Hampshire ports. The news frightened Richard's council from waiting out a second day in hiding; as dawn broke they left the open road to push on over rough heaths until from the height of a gorse-grown hill they beheld a great floor of treetops, floating as far as they could see. As they came nearer they began to discover these woods to be not impassable with growth, but scattered stands of birch on sparse, poor grass and flowering hawkbit, yellow as butter. This, Ashley said, was a royal chase, where in time past men had lost life or limbs for hunting the King's deer; they would encounter few folk and fewer villages here.

To feel the forest close at their backs was like the sound of some great haven-fortress' gate clashing down after them. It was true what Ashley had told them, that the place was three parts of it hardly known to man; after being a third time deceived by a little hummock of grass and whin that looked exactly like the last, they started even to wish they might meet someone—an incurious wood-man, maybe—of whom they could ask the way.

Dusk came, and the moon rose white on a wilderness interwoven with shadows: a thin woodland cleft with gullys where streamlets trickled, clumps of birch and alder and willow, and bare ghosts of thorn. Sometimes the growth thickened, so they pushed on with heads pressed to the horses' necks to avoid low-hanging boughs; ducking too late, Simon was struck in the face by a lashing branch, and moments later felt an oozing wetness where the wound on his forehead had reopened from it. He wiped the blood clumsily, but it ran down again; he had thrown away the bandage when it loosened an hour ago.

They were crossing an open space among the trees, riding fast because of the easier going, when Richard's horse stumbled and fell, and scrambled up again to stand trembling. Richard himself lay groaning, and when his nearer companions sprang down to assist him, he cried out and struck their hands away. "Mary Mother," breathed a soft Irish voice as the last-following horses came to a snorting, sliding stop and Jackie Atwater passed back the word, "Mary Mother, could not her great lady-ship of Burgundy have taught him to *ride?*"

It was Ashley once more that acted, while Skelton and Heron hesitated, at a loss; presently sitting back on his heels, he said quietly, "I believe the arm is not broken, my lord. We are some hours yet from Southampton: can you go so far?" Richard had sat up, leaning his face on his knees while the hurt arm dragged beside him; his lips pinched, and he shook his head. A mutter began among those who had heard the question, and settled into appalled silence; only Heron and Skelton exchanged glances, and the merchant took a sideling step toward his horse's stirrup. Overhead, the moon had started the downward swing from its zenith; soon the first gray would break in the east, and there were villages to get through before then, that once awake would wonder about a troop of sixty men.

Not far from where they were a thread of water glistened, a little river hung over with alder and willow. Looking at it, Ashley said, "That is Beaulieu Stream, where the Cistercians have their house. I know this place now, we are no more than a mile from the abbey. You must ask sanctuary there, and they will give you food and a bed, and bind your arm. It's not a place in the way of travelers: with luck you may rest there and be gone again without anyone but the brothers knowing of it." It was only as he finished that those who listened realized he spoke as if he did not mean to go to Beaulieu himself.

There was a stir among the Cornishmen; after whispering and coughing and nudging of neighbors, one stood forward. "Then it would be best, my lord, for us to go our ways. We came so far with you for love, but we are as safe in Cornwall as in sanctuary here, and for sure we had liefer go back to our villages than beg beyond seas."

An uncomfortable silence followed; and then Jackie Atwater came stepping through the press, scraping back with one broad tough palm the tangled hair above his brows, his blue eyes like seawater under an April sun. "Why, my lord, this works for your good. The better part of us left will push on for Southampton and find us some honest captain to carry a parcel of Yorkists over seas; when we are sure of him, we will send word to Beaulieu, where meantime your Grace has rested like a babe in its nurse's arm, with the good brothers about you thick as bees, only wanting you should speak a wish. And let you not send one coin or jewel with us, for there's enough in my pocket to buy us food, and we will pay our captain when yourself has your two feet on his deck, just, and no minute before." He stood smiling and flicking the cap he had doffed against his knee, his eyes guileless as a child's on Heron's disappointed face.

His color having returned a little, Richard said, "Let it be so, then. You good men of Cornwall, I release you gladly, and am sorry to my soul that I cannot reward your faithfulness. If one day I succeed where this time I have failed, I promise you will be remembered. Nick"—he turned to the chaplain—"will you guide me to this abbey? For without you I may miss the way, and you will be safer besides with the monks than abroad in Southampton looking for a ship." He had stretched out his good hand; after an instant, taking it, the other man answered gently, "Be sure I will come with you." Heron and Skelton unexpectedly joined in, protesting they could not leave the Duke and would accompany him too, and Jackie Atwater looked on with a sweet, abstracted smile.

It was his father who drew him apart, whispering; in a moment the Irishman came back to the cluster around Richard, where one by one the Cornish were pushing forward to say their farewells. "There's someone else must go to Beaulieu too," he said, "for he'll get no farther than that without the trews of him nailed to the saddle. Sir Nicholas, would you have knowledge of how to stop bleeding from the head?" His father had gone back to Simon's stirrup, and was using both arms to get him down; under his breath Ashley said, "Holy Saint Michael," and hurried to help. Obedient in their hands, Simon slipped to the ground; his face was masked in blood, his eyes strange and fixed, as if sight were difficult and his surroundings a surprise to him. "Have we reached London?" he asked Jackie's father. "How wide the river is, it is like the Danube. I was in Vienna once, for the

Emperor's funeral, do you know it, monsieur le maire?" Since he was docile with drowsiness, it was easy to persuade him to lie quietly while Ashley tore his own shirt for a bandage; later, the Cornishmen supplied half a dozen pairs of arms to help put him up before the chaplain for the short ride to Beaulieu. Then they parted: the Cornish going as they had come, Atwater and his father and their remaining countrymen riding east with a little scratched map from Ashley's tablets to show the way—to the great slash of Southampton Water, he had said, then north and over the first crossing to the other side. Southampton was an important town of several thousand souls: they could not miss the gate.

The way to Beaulieu was through scattered birches, over soft boggy ground the horses hated, and trod unwillingly to a constant spur. The white graceful trunks rose and receded before Simon like the columns of a mighty cathedral; he wondered why they were on horseback in such a place, and how long it must be until they came to the high altar, which he could not see at all. Once, becoming sensible, he recognized Ashley's arm supporting him, and his voice, vividly profane as he addressed the jibbing stallion, and remembering something thought of long ago, he asked, "Nick, how is it that you became a priest?" With a grin that could be heard, the Englishman answered, "When I was young I liked my books better than falling off a horse at the quintain. My father considered this too clerkly to befit a gentleman, and packed me off to Holy Church before I shamed him for a lie-abed son." He gestured largely with his free arm around the silent woods, and felt the younger man's shoulders shake; the sound of laughter drifted back to

Richard, riding hunched and speechless directly behind, and Heron and Skelton together at the rear. The fat merchant's head jerked as he heard, and his hand closed about the bag of saints' relics he wore always at his neck, for safety's sake and to prosper his dealings. Since the flight from Taunton he and Skelton had kept close as brothers; even in quiet one felt their thoughts flittering one to the other, like moths made restless by light. It was enough, Jackie Atwater had said, to make you wonder what was between them, that no one else knew.

They had come to a high wall, well maintained and built solidly of stone, which stretched along the riverbank as far as they could see. Ashley said, "This is where the monks' land begins. We are not far now." But it seemed so, for the Cistercians' holding was large, and their wall enclosed it to the last acre. Farther on there were cottages with little gardens of onion and cabbage and peas, for a village had grown about the monastery gate. In one of the huts a light gleamed while a cow lowed in pain: some husbandman was up, tending his sick beast, but Heron leaped as if he expected a troop to ride out of the byre, crying halt in King Henry's name. Tumbling headlong from his horse, he ran the last distance to the outer gate on foot, and seizing hold of the bell rope dragged it up and down until the echoes beat at their ears. By the time a yawning porter put out his head, he was bellowing "Sanctuary" so loudly that every house in the village was astir and the gateman's inquiries were scarcely to be heard. When the huge doors opened, Heron and Skelton bolted through together, clamoring that their names be registered for sanctuary men; breaking in on this, the Cistercian addressed the three that waited still outside, saying, "And you also? Do you require sanctuary too?" Being sleepy and cold, he was inclined to impatience, and swung his lantern to and fro as he looked from Ashley, struggling to lift his burden to the ground, and back to Richard, who had made no move to dismount. The horse's reins trailed where he had dropped them, his right arm being crossed over his chest to hold the injured left one; his eyes were pits of darkness in the yellow light. He answered in a dull, tired tone, regarding less the pale-robed brother than the mighty towers behind him, "Sanctuary? It may be: I will speak with your abbot first, monk, before asking that my name be set down. I have a small hurt, and there is another with us that will need your best tending, I think, if he is not to die—"

He was trying to get down from his horse, one-handed; it was years since he had done it without an attentive arm, but Heron and Skelton had both disappeared. Something about his voice made the Cistercian more careful; he stopped playing with the lantern, and even walked forward to look at Simon, whose arm Ashley had got round his neck. The boy's eyes hardly flickered when he held up the light. Presently lowering it, the monk said, "Yes, your friend is sick," and then—for Richard had not turned, and was staring yet at the gate—"You told me he was your friend?" He lent a brawny shoulder, well-muscled beneath the good wool robe. Richard said only, "He was once," and, still supporting his unsound arm, went haltingly before them through the gate.

In his last rational moment as the monks laid him down, Simon thought: Here we are safe. But he rested ill, more fainting than sleeping between the slops of broth or milk they fed him, and imagined he was with the Irish whore again that Geffroi had found. She was as frowzy and dirty as the first time, and when she leaned above him, her great bare breasts sagged down to crush his face. He exclaimed in horror and tried to push her off, fighting for air and to keep from vomiting at her stink; and woke choking, with someone's hand clamped on his mouth while a young novice with intent, scared eyes whispered, "Hush!"

Trembling with weakness and the effort of catching his breath, Simon obeyed. After a minute he became aware of voices, as from far off; muttering against them, the brother told him he had slept from lauds round again and into the next afternoon; only a few hours ago, Lord Daubeney's men had come. It being unlawful to violate sanctuary, they sent representatives to the abbot, asking for speech with his chief guest; their friends meanwhile deployed before the gate to ensure neither the false Duke nor the councilors who had abetted him escaped. King Henry, they said, desired them all.

A distant bell rang for nones; having once more pointed toward the murmuring voices and put a finger to his lip, the brother hurried away, and Simon lay staring at the dusty ceiling beams. He tried to recollect what he had heard of sanctuary law in England, and on what terms King Henry currently was with the Duke of Burgundy, who was Simon de Brezy's liege lord and protector. Then he remembered the monk's whispering and look of warning, and that he had been carried into the abbey without having given his name: it might be Daubeney's men did not even know he was here. At length rising on one arm, he crawled from his pallet toward the voices; there was a peephole cut through the screen which overlooked the lower hall, hidden on the other side between two carved folds of the Virgin's robe, and he set his eye to it. The first thing he saw was Richard's face.

He was talking to somebody out of Simon's sight, one hand playing with the medal which hung from a chain about his neck. His left arm was wrapped in linen but not splinted, and lay in a sling; the monks had done something for his clothes too, which were fresh and well brushed, and his bright hair shone. He was easy and smiling, as if more truly happy shed of the responsibilities of a six years' gamble, and with only his life, now, to save. Simon heard him say, "Well, I have heard your promises, which your King has made very fair, but why should I trust myself to his word? I am safer in sanctuary, whose privilege as all the world knows is not better respected anywhere than in England."

"Respected, but within certain forms." It was a heavy, slow voice that replied, with an accent that suggested the country fellow, some farmer-knight or rich squire, but with something also of command. "The law permits forty days' asylum to a felon; having then confessed his fault and sworn to abjure England, he must come out in his shirt and go on foot to the nearest port, where if there be no ship he is obliged to walk every day into the sea to his neck, crying for passage in God's name and the King's, until a vessel is found to carry him away." This was rehearsed as if the speaker had lately looked it up; yet there was another note too, a kind of malice, that pictured the man who had proclaimed himself King of England walking the common highway with a penitent's candle in his hand. "That is the law. But if a criminal has offended too many people, it has been known for them to follow him on his way, and in violation of custom and statute so beset him that he dies. It might be that the Cornishmen you misled into treason will come to wait outside these gates, and they are in such detestation of you, having learned how they were deceived to worship a low-born foreigner for their prince, that I could not answer for your life. I am not meaning those few dozen horsemen we found here and there through the forest, but the thousands you forsook at Taunton, who until he may pardon them are now King Henry's prisoners."

"The Cornishmen I left at Taunton?" The pendant hung frozen on its golden chain. "But they broke camp the hour of my departing: those were the orders I left behind."

"You should have stayed to see them done. Your army slept the night through without ever knowing its captains gone; in the morning, discovering their desertion, some that had their wits about them made off in time, but most are in Lord Daubeney's hand, greatly wishing to thank the man that brought them to that pass, and then ran away."

Since he had sailed to Portugal as a child not twelve years old, hanging on the skirts of one exiled Yorkist or another in exchange for what the experience might bring him, Richard Plantagenet had known how to deal with insolence that forgot to whom it spoke. But he waited, his expression like one of those masks the Scots put on for Uphaliday, his blue eyes steady on the unseen other face. The voice had advanced a step, and by straining Simon could see the person that owned it: a blocklike, stiffly built man with dark hair going grizzled, and hard fleshed shoulders and thighs. He spoke without civility, looking the other man up and down from crown to heels. "You are no prince of England, and it is time this play was ended. King Edward's sons are dead: you are not one of them."

Staring him in the eyes, Richard said gently, "Are you quite sure of that?"

"I have cause to be sure—" He had a loud, hard laugh, with an edge of iron. "The game's over, lad. You led King Henry a dance for half a dozen years, let that be your satisfaction, and give yourself up trusting in his good will. I promise you, he is your best hope; there's not one of the Christian kings who set you on that cares a penny piece for you now."

"I know that well enough." Unexpectedly, the young man appeared to consider, his gaze on the scoured and strawed guesthouse floor. "What if I do, then? What terms does he offer?"

"So far he has made none: you must put yourself on his mercy. Yes, and a matter remains of your friends that came with you to Beaulieu; they have helped in this treason, and must be taken too."

There was a small cheerful fire on the hearth, of scented cherry wood. Leaning his hand on the chimney over it, Richard said, "If you mean Sir Edward Skelton and his dear familiar, Master Heron, you are welcome to them, for me. And if they should rest on their holy privilege, tell them the Cornishmen are on the way that were left at Taunton; they'll take horse for King Henry faster than rats leaving an eaten-out barn." The firelight crossed his face with scarlet shadows, flickering and leaping; peering from above, Simon saw his mouth shake, and his fingers bite the stone so mortar flaked rustling down.

"Yes, I was told two such had given their names for sanctuary," the dark-haired one rejoined, unmoved. "Also a fellow called Ashley, a lewd priest."

After a slight pause—"And Sir Nicholas Ashley."

"Good. Was there anyone else?"

Richard turned slowly, looking across at the carved screen as if he saw the eyes behind it. "No," he said. "There were no others at all."

"Then we will wait on the father abbot and tell him that from tomorrow morning you require his hospitality no more." By sheer weight of purpose compelling the other before him toward the door, he halted for an instant, having got close up, to stare openly at the young man's face. "There was too much you did not know, ever to have succeeded in it. For example, you did not know me: yet I was ten years your pretended uncle Richard of Gloucester's servant, and enough at his court for his nephew to have remembered me. My name is James Tyrell."

Vespers had been sung, and about eight o'clock, compline to end the day, with the chanting of the Cistercians rising like walls, lucent and changeless, to enclose in crystal their ancient ones of stone. For a few hours then quiet fell, while the monks slept. Some time before lauds Simon's friend the novice crept in with a rush candle, whispering, "I could not come before. Are you asleep?"

Lying chin on wrists, Simon turned his head toward the boy. "No. What has happened to the Duke of York?"

"Why, they say he is no duke at all, but a low French-man that lied to the people. He is going away with Sir James Tyrell tomorrow, to beg the King's pardon for it; the others that came with him here are going too." Kneeling beside the bed, the youngster added softly, "You must get away tonight, my lord. By tomorrow, when he is leaving, Sir James will know he has not every-one with him that he should. Sir Nicholas Ashley asked me to say to you, the Duke is not the only one that can tell Sir James you are here."

He was a lad no older than Simon, with square brow and hands and an accent that suggested more the family of some merchant than a proud lord of lands; he had, also, the conspiratorial, partisan air of the young toward others of their age. With his head on his knees, Simon gave consideration to the matter of Skelton and Heron, who would seize gladly on the chance to do him ill and themselves good with King Henry and Sir James Tyrell, all in one breath. When he thought of it, he was surprised at himself for not having remembered those two before: if he did not want to join them in captivity, he had better go.

Pressing his hands on the pallet either side, Simon got to his feet, saying to the lad's anxious eyes, "They're all about the gate, you told me: how can I get out?" The boy grinned, and stooped over something he had left beside the door. "I brought a rope."

They threw it over the wall beyond the wine press, on the other side of the vineyards and removed by half a mile from the guard-ringed gate. The blackness of the inner precinct was changing to pewter color with the faintness of dawn; in the church they saw lights with shadows moving against them, and heard the sleepy brothers—fewer than for compline—raising their voices in the first office of the day. As Simon swung outward from the mortared blocks, bracing himself with his feet to work down the other side, the boy leaned above him whispering, "Take care you stay on the paths, there are bogs about. *Benedicite.*" He grinned again, and waved; and his white-cowled shoulders dropped behind the wall.

Night was fading; low in the east some gray appeared and spread slowly up into the star-pricked dark. Simon watched it as he sat against the wall, catching his breath; he was sweating, although the air was cold, and there was a weakness in his belly and knees. He thought he should have given the young brother something for his offering box, in token of thanks, except he had been without money since leaving Saint Michael's Mount: a thing that in all his life had not happened to him before. He told himself he could have arranged a better time for the experience.

Everything was very still. When he began to walk there was a strangeness about it, after the long days on horseback; his steps seemed small, the distances of heathy levels so vast and slowly accomplished that he appeared hardly to move at all. The birds awoke, first one or two, then as the sky lightened a thousand-voiced chorus feeding among the berried trees—rowans, they were called in Scotland, so Christy had once said.

He grew thirsty, and looked for a stream, but although the hillocky ground was seamed with rivulets, the whin and scrub made them hard to find. Presently thinking he heard water, he was pushing through some willows when a shoulder of earth crumbled, and he snatched at a bough that snapped in his hand. Suddenly there was an emptiness beneath his feet; young withies scratched and lashed his face, and a mild blue sky, tender as spring above the trees, flashed kingfisher-like as he rolled over and over down into the unseen gully of the stream.

Here, after unknown time, the forest floor seemed smoother, being spongy with moss and half-molded leaves; a finger's length on was bare earth, and the noise of water purling in its shallow bed. Painfully, with hands full of dirt and body flinching from the hurt of torn muscle and abraded skin, he began to raise himself, and something clasped him by the feet which, when he wrenched against it, gave a sucking sound. His mind was tired; before he could think he had pulled again, and the coldness lapped upward to his knees. Understanding then, he lay stiffly, only lifting his head to look over his shoulder at the soft quaking wickedness in which his legs were swallowed. It was so small a thing, no broader than two men are long in its walls of rising ground, that he could not believe he might drown in it; but when, carefully gathering strength and will, he tried with repeated lunges to fling himself clear, he ended as helpless as before, choking with exhaustion and the huge, uneven boundings of his heart, and the bog was halfway up his thighs. Then he knew that if he was not to die here, someone—and in all the morning he had not seen one soul abroad—someone must find him and help.

The sun climbed higher, its brightness flaring golden through the leaves, but no warmth could reach this sunken shadowed place. His hand lay on a hump of

135

ground beyond his head, flexed in the earth to check the drag of his body into the waiting malice below; his eyes fixed on the long, dirt-engrained fingers and over-wide separation of the thumb, and he heard a voice saying again, "You will find it difficult in fitting armor, as I have done—"

He was so cold that when a worm slid under his wrist, he would not have known but for the sense of its moving. The distant sounds of the stream came more loudly, clear and individual, as if the ear might feel each cool carven shape, then faded all away.

VII

They addressed him as Monsieur de Werbecque, with an edge that, when King Henry's pleasure became known, might be turned either way. At first he refused to answer, but James Tyrell was a resourceful man: he gave orders that until the prisoner replied when addressed, he should have no food. It was a journey of some days, following the King's westward course; on the second morning, he gave in.

Skelton, Heron, and Ashley rode some distance back in the train. During a halt, the chaplain offered his former master a cup of ale that had been given first to himself, a gesture which brought a scowl from Tyrell, and which Richard accepted in silence, without meeting the other's eye. To Skelton he spoke once, breaking out in passionate reproach for the Cornishmen's abandonment, which, he said, had made him odious in all men's sight. "Do you call yourself a soldier? You have been the worst coward in the world, and made me like you." Tyrell, reining back in time to hear, burst out laughing

and said, "He a soldier? He was a tailor's prentice that ran away from his indentures; he gave his title to himself, for no one else ever knighted him. Do you know so little of fighting men that you took this for one?"

His eyes beneath their shelf-like brows lit with pleasure at the young man's mortification. Since the discovery of Simon de Brezy's escape over Beaulieu wall, there had been open hatred between Tyrell and the man whose lie had made it possible: his monsieurship might be sure, he had said, that it would be remembered against him.

Late on an afternoon they came back to Taunton, and saw the fields around still spread with men. Sunlight had shrunk up the valley to lie in tonsure on the Quantock Hills; below, where shadows were deepening, pennons bearing the dragon badge of Daubeney or portcullis of Westminster fluttered from pike and pole. The captain of the castle gate said that the King had arrived last evening and sat up late, being so pleased at how matters were falling out that he lost nine pounds at play without once failing in his smile. That made Tyrell laugh: Henry was clutch-fisted.

In a small chamber halfway up the gatehouse tower, Tyrell left his chief captive and went away. Alone, Richard paced about; though well-lit and dry, the room was hardly greater than a cell, and he had always been ill at ease in close places. It was growing dark, but no one brought a torch; he began to wonder if they would wall him in here to die, as had happened to King Richard's bastard son, so when people asked what had happened to the Duke of York, Henry could answer that he knew no more than they. He thought of Kathi, dwelling not on the bitter last days when he understood

he had disappointed her, but the long, luxurious hours of the time that had gone before, the kissings and clippings abed in their high sunlit chamber, with only the gulls wheeling above the Forth to see. He remembered Hainault where he had been a child, as peaceful to his mind's eye as a painted landscape, and Madame la Grande, who had sworn he should be King of England so he was persuaded to want it too; and he saw again the face of Simon de Brezy, whom he had loved as dearly, almost, as his wife, until the night when too much wine had taught him the reason why.

Only the tall west window now held the light. He flung himself at the embrasure, tearing at the rusted iron bars until the hurt to his half healed arm defeated him, shocking in its renewed pain; then wept, and reminded himself who he was, and shuddering dried his face, holding it up as if to bathe all of him that could reach it in the sweet, free air. This room had been a prison before; faint in the stone, someone had scratched in long-ago hand, god helpe . . . god helpe.

About an hour after nightfall, a squire of the body came with a guard of soldiers. They bound his wrists, dragging his arms so tight behind that he exclaimed in anguish; when he realized how little they cared if they hurt him, he was sorry to have let them know. A yeoman of the chamber lit the way down the stair, which wound so steeply that only the man's echoing footsteps guided them, and the light from his torch glimmering upward on the turret wall.

Outside the tower, they crossed a court and entered the keep by a big iron-studded door. Nearby was a noise of voices, men talking and laughing in the hall, but the yeoman went on without glancing toward it and halted presently before another door, this one little and low, with a bar across the inward side that grated back at the attendant's knock. An usher opened; within there were a few men standing with heads uncovered, and one seated at a table facing the threshold. He wore a dark, close-fitting hat with a jewel in it, and Richard saw that everyone who had come in was doing reverence to him. He stood rigid among the bending heads; then someone struck him behind the legs so he fell, and two soldiers held him kneeling. A man in the group beside the table said laughing, "His Majesty King Richard the Fourth."

He had bruised his head on the table, and the ache in his arm was like fire shadow, red and leaping; if only they would cut the cords on his wrists he could better think. But the voices went on around him, appraising, discussing, as if he were a beast that could not understand them, or not present in the room at all. A man in a gilt-inlaid cuirass said, "There is a little likeness, I suppose, if a person wanted to find it: there are always those that would," and another answered, "Better than a little: see the coloring, and the shape of the chin." He came round the table and took the bound man's jaw between finger and thumb, handling him without regard, like a dog he knew would not bite. "A quite remarkable resemblance to King Edward, in fact. The nose and brows"—he flicked a finger over them—"oh yes, with such tools one sees how the imposture was done. Well, there are more ways than one to have got them—with all respect to our late sovereign lord." He winked, and dropped his hand.

The dark-capped man leaned back in his chair, stroking with his forefinger a thin, smooth-shaven lip. He was narrow-faced and spade-jawed, his hair being of mixed gray and yellow with a trace of curl; his eyes were patient, temperate, and watchful, set close to a large, bold nose. "Master Osbeck, some years ago you said you could prove yourself the late Duke of York by the evidence of three marks on your body, and declared yourself ready to display this proof even to my face. There are those here that in his childhood knew the Duke: would you care to show it now?"

In the long silence, they saw the young man's teeth set. He moved his shoulder, trying to ease the pull of the cords, and a clerkly-seeming fellow in good camlet gown said drawling, "Shall we strip him to see? We may at least behold as much as the King of Scots' kins-woman in the marriage bed." He pushed back the nearest guard, thrusting his fingers in the neckband of the pris-oner's shirt, and a voice like the descent of a mallet said, "Empson!" It came from a gentle-faced man who had not before spoken; he had an embroidery on his sleeve of dragons' wings joined in a knot, and after an instant the man Empson stepped back, responding sar-donically, "My lord Daubeney."

There was a little rustle as Henry changed position in his chair; it was only the skirt of his robe falling aside as he crossed his legs, but the eyes of every man turned at the sound. He said quietly, "On the way here from Beaulieu, young sir, I am told you continued to pretend yourself the Duke of York, and required persua-sion to reply when called by your true name. Had you a special reason for this foolishness?"

Richard said huskily, as if he were choking, "It was not my name."

"You know well it is, and you would be wise to earn

mercy now with honesty, even after a half-dozen years of lies. Your history has been long known to me: I know your father's name, which is Diericq de Werbecque, and the place of your birth, the city of Tournai; as a young child you abode under the man Werbecque's roof, which was that of a respectable citizen, and were known to be his son. I know of your travels while still a youth, and of the many persons who used you until you began to use them."

Richard lifted his eyes. He had stopped straining at his bonds, and knelt between the guards as quietly as if at prayers. "You have defamed me so to the princes of Europe since I was with the King of France. But if you know so much, then you know Diericq de Werbecque is not my father. He was good to me, he and his lady who was like my mother while I was in their house; but they are no kin to me." All at once he spoke as if they were alone, with no others by. "You will not harm me, because you know I am not what you have said. Do you think me so simple as to deny my best safety?"

With a glance at his councilors, attentively listening, Henry remarked suavely, "I have said before, one day they will crown apes in Ireland. My good youth, it is your excellent fortune that you cannot prove yourself to be what you say—or indeed, to be anyone of importance at all. Because this is so, all that is required of you is a confession before these gentlemen of your true name and condition, and you will be put into an easy custody which I promise will be short. After that, you will have a place in my household proper to your station, and be as free in it as any varlet that serves me well." He added, "You are but three and twenty, well favored and in sound health. One would suppose you eager to enjoy the pleasures of life, not, as it appears, determined to persist in a deceit that must bring you great suffering, and, in the end, death."

He waited silent for an instant, gazing at the young man's haggard face. His expression, which was habitually of a grave calm, changed and grew hard; one remembered the man who had won at Bosworth, and watched King Richard die. He said, "You have been guilty of treason. Have you seen a man hanged and unboweled alive? Master Empson, you are learned in the law: explain to this fellow the penalty for one condemned of his offense."

He nodded to the lawyer, who stepped forward as at an expected command. He spoke in a low, agreeable voice, his hands clasped lightly behind him, his eyes fixed on Richard's blue ones. "It is to be drawn on a hurdle at a horse's tail to the place of punishment, and on a scaffold hanged by the neck but taken down while alive; to have the privy parts cut away and bowels taken out, these being severally burnt before his living eyes; and after, to have his head cut off and body quartered and the parts set up in some high place for a detestation to men and a prey to the birds of the air."

He signed to a soldier standing ready, who of a sudden flung a strap like a noose around the prisoner's neck; so quickly had he moved, the leather was biting into the bound man's throat before he could move or cry. His body thrashed, or made to thrash, but since he was pinioned between two men's hands there was hardly a noise. His face darkened and became blue; his eyes started; his mouth gaped like an animal's so the palate showed, and his tongue thrust out. After several moments someone kicked forward a stool and they threw him on his back across it; the man with the strap let it fall and came round before. Dragging apart the young man's outer garments, he bent and pushed the point of a knife against his members through the thin hose cloth. The small room seemed alive with crying, but what came from his mouth was like no sound a man could make, and gushes of vomit, which, since his head hung low, ran upward into his nose and eyes. Staring down into his face, Empson said gently, "Young sir, this is the commencement only: we have not yet come to the headsman. How will you fare with that, if these little troubles so work upon you?"

There was a spot of blood on the hose cloth. Released, he fell on his side to the floor and lay sobbing, his knees crooked to his belly; in a while some words came, which were French and all the same, *"Maman, maman."* The King's councilors around the table watched as if their eyes were fastened to the sight, and Henry, when he knew himself unobserved, watched them.

Empson stood like a man whose work is done. His eyes meeting the King's were answered by a barely perceptible motion of agreement; astride above the shuddering bound body, he stooped and with his dagger cut the cords.

Among the captive Cornishmen, herded next morning in the wake of the King's army as he made his way to Exeter, a whisper began, was scoffed at, and rose again in the ragged columns like smoke from an imperfectly damped fire. A few strained their eyes toward the center of the procession, but it was almost noon before a herald cantered slowly along the files, brandishing a parchment and shouting it was the true history and confession, signed with his hand, of the Frenchman Pierrequin Werbecque, who had fooled them into believing him King Edward's son. He made it, so said the herald, to save his life, which the King of mercy had granted; the young man himself had been brought to Taunton last evening, and might be seen now by anyone that wanted to look at him, riding in the King's train.

They were most of them too tired now to care. Some that were nearest briefly craned their necks, and became angry again to see the remembered princely figure borne in unfettered ease while they trudged footsore toward what fate might be intended for them; some, the closest of all, yelled curses to make the proud head turn that had bent so graciously upon them: they could have forgiven him, almost, if he had only once looked back at them in shame. But he rode on. In Exeter, some days later, a new tale went round the prisoners' tattered camp: how when that poor gentlewoman the imposter's wife was brought from Saint Michael's Mount, her husband was made to repeat on his knees before her the full account of his deceits, at conclusion of which the unhappy lady begged the English King's protection with tears. Even Henry had been moved by her beauty, describing her as fit consort for a King's general, and sending her and her children, with honorable escort, to his wife, the Queen.

In the cathedral close next morning, a solemn comedy was enacted. At a window of the Treasurer's house, before which half the trees had been felled that the show might better be seen, King Henry appeared; below, as many of the rebels as could be pushed into the close were assembled with halters around their necks, all with upstretched hands entreating the King's pardon. This, with a handful of exceptions, was granted as to life only, the royal clemency stopping just short of restitution of goods; and so, throwing away the halters and crying upon God to save King Henry for his mercy, they went home.

In time, when the hands of the King's collectors were reaching into every pocket, and all the south and west from Hampshire to Cornwall was paying, borough by borough, man by man, for having done no worse than stay with locked-up arms at home while the false Duke and his men passed by, they began to think more kindly of him. They recalled his comeliness and dignity, and how he had walked among them in the rain at Taunton when others were glad to stay dry inside, and legends grew: for sure, they said, it had been King Edward's son. As months went by they heard he had been taken to London and imprisoned in the Tower; later, that he had been released and assigned a place about Henry's court, although strictly watched. Almost a year after, so slowly did news come to Cornwall—for to cross the Tamar was described by the men who lived west of it as going into England, and few below a gentleman spoke anything but their own Cornish tongue—it was told among them he was Henry's pensioner still, a figure of wonder that the foreign ambassadors were invited to gaze upon, and view as an example of Henry's generosity and power. A gentleman of Truro lately home from court reported he had seen him, carrying wine to a visiting Scottish lord: at least, he said, he had been told it was the man.

VIII

A finger scratched his face, the sharp nail of a hard little hand that vanished before he could catch it. Moments later he felt it at his ear, this time curiously exploring; because it tickled he jerked his head aside, and the impish touch withdrew to an accompaniment of high-pitched scolding. Someone laughed.

Bolstered, upholstered, and supported to suffocation with down-stuffed bedding, Simon uncrooked his arm with difficulty from its position under his cheek, and used it to push himself away from the pillow. The monkey perched out of reach of his hand, gilt-collared and scarlet-coated, its wizened face puckered with mistrust; beyond, in a lacework of shadows thrown by the sun-filled lattice window, a woman sat smiling. She wore dark blue, a fine say of Flanders cut low, and a short hood without a coif tied well back to show hair of palest gold; there was a perfume of almond about her, and of the scented water that English wives liked to make in their stillrooms from rose petals, or the gilly-

147

flowers called sops-in-wine. As Simon stared in confusion, and, using his other hand to rub his head, discovered his wound new-wrapped in clean linen which had no feel of the Beaulieu brothers' labor, she leaned toward him, saying in a dove-like voice, "Poor gentleman, are you recovered and alive? We have watched over you the day and night since you were carried here, my servants and I. This house is White Ladies of Tickthorn, and I am Mistress Flower."

It seemed to Simon that his brain lacked its functions yet. He tried to remember, and brought back only the cold horror of the bog as he sank into a darkness from which he had been sure he would not wake; finding himself here alive was to be Lazarus stripped of his graveclothes and called to feast. He stared with new interest at Mistress Flower, whose attention had fastened modestly on the keys at her girdle, and became abruptly conscious that the only coverings to his body were his hostess' sheets. From her demure expression, he fancied she knew it too. Her bosom being half bare, the sunlight lying on the lucent baby skin warmed its tender rounds to ivory; he swallowed, and began, "*Madame, je vous remercie—*" Surely he was weak-headed still. "Mistress, I'm indebted to you, for I think you have saved my life. If there is a way I can show my thanks to you and your good husband"—he presumed there was a Master Flower, although it was work imagining him—"I will be grateful to know it."

The monkey had stolen nearer, inspecting him with button-bright eyes; she bent to gather up her pet, and as if thoughtlessly remained leaning toward Simon, her elbow on the lace-fringed pillow. She said pensively,

"My husband, Master Flower, although he is from home, is a careful man. You must understand, sir, that you spoke a little as my men drew you from the marsh, so we knew you to be French, and had no doubt you were one of those poor misled gentlemen that have been found everywhere through the forest, who followed the false Duke of York. Dear monsieur, you need not have the slightest fear that anyone will betray you, but my husband, Master Flower—he has been some weeks in London now, on his affairs: he is often from home—is so careful, I am afraid—" She sighed, and wound a fallen lock of hair about her hand. "There will be a matter of ransom, you see."

"Ransom?" Simon's mouth fell open; in this room, with the builder's dust as he would have guessed hardly swept away, it was like a rattle of mail three hundred years old. "*Déa,* madame, and have you a dungeon ready for me until I shall buy my way to your grace?" He flicked a glance sideways, and was rewarded with a blush. "You should not suppose such a thing. Your *parole d'honneur*"—this came out proudly, in the accent of convent French—"that is, your promise to stay here my guest would be sufficient for you to have all the house to walk in."

What this could mean, he was intended to see; he answered in like manner, his eyes on the fringed and figured canopy above his head. In a while, a darkness crept up his cheek; he was reflecting that, for one who had sworn to earn a name that owed nothing to any man, in two years he had done less than conspicuously well. An assortment of bodily mishaps and the debacle at Exeter were ignominious enough; to these, it now appeared, he must add the humiliation of addressing himself meekly to the household at Clairmont, asking for money from his estates to free him so he might come home. The more he thought of it, the more disinclined he became; he had been prepared to be grateful for his rescuing, but not fleeced. From the corner of his eye he considered his apparent keeper, who had put down the monkey to smooth the bedcovers; although it must be long since she had walked with hanging maiden hair behind the bride cup and rosemary branch, his two hands could have imprisoned whole her breasts, and to be unstirred by her he would have needed to be blind, or dead. Presently sinking back upon the pillows, he said sorrowfully, "Alas, madame, you shall do with me what pleases you. For I cannot remember my name."

Her eyes lifted, gently appraising; of a sudden her hands were motionless on the coverlet. With an effort he constrained his mouth to melancholy, and touched the bandage around his head. "I think there must have been a blow—have you seen the place, could you tell?"

She shook her head, her eyes still thoughtful on his face. "My man Clement, while we were tending you, said he would have supposed it not new, for when we had washed the spot, a part of it was already healed under the blood." Her cool fingers brushed his temple, lightly following the line of cheek and jaw down to his throat. "There were burns too, the blisters are hardly gone. Poor gentleman, and now to have such affliction added to all that has passed. But such cases have been cured, with time and tending: you must trust yourself all to me."

She went away then, leaving him staring between

the bed-curtains at the ceiling beams. These were severe in a way that surprised him, having seen in Cornwall the kind of flourish a rich English trader considered his due: the only carving was a shield with a lily upright upon it, which he could guess to be a merchant's mark. Everywhere one looked, one saw it: on the overmantel of the fireplace, above the door, in the six lights of the window, colored yellow and red.

At length throwing back the covers, Simon went to look out. The sun had disappeared in the usual sudden English fashion; morning was early yet, and the light lay on wood and meadowland like pearl. When he pushed open the casement there was a fresh smell of earth and leaves, and woodsmoke from the hillside where a farmer was burning waste; far off, a late cuckoo called. He remembered something he had heard Philip Lovell speak of from his youth, about rising early for hares before the dew had dried; and it came to him that, however his mind rebelled from thinking it, this was both his parents' land.

Turning from the window, he heard the soft grate of a key in the latch, and then the brush of skirts going away. When he looked toward the door, he saw in the molding of the wainscot a little shadow where the builder had not quite concealed a hole. That she had locked the door on him was no surprise—he had already discovered that none of his clothes remained in the room, and the window opened on a drop of thirty feet—but it made him flush, imagining her peeping from the other side.

Not long afterward a young man arrived carrying boiled beef and beer, an English idea of breakfast to which Simon resigned himself. As he ate, he listened to the talk of the youth that had brought it, a blond-haired, spotty-faced individual in prentice's fustian, who seated himself in the window, very much at ease. His name was Stonor, which he was given to explaining meant something in Oxfordshire; Simon gathered from his remarks that Master Flower was to be complimented Edmund Stonor had been sent to him to learn the cloth-making trade. For it appeared this was Peter Flower's business; he bought wool and had it spun and woven and finished, and sold it again in London. He had become rich from it too, being no longer obliged to have his servants carry the wool from cottage to cottage, but hiring laborers instead, who came to White Ladies to work in his spinning room and dyehouse. Simon tried to find out more about Master Flower, and got more than he expected; the lad sniggered and gestured impudently with his fingers.

"He gets gold night and morning, that's his pleasure, and my mistress may make what she likes of it. He's in London the best part of the year, the old woman his mother looks to his business here. She's half blind and three parts deaf, until it comes to hearing one wheel stop in the spinning room, or paying the weavers their hire: the last time they had reward from her for good labor, wethers did fly." He added, "My mistress told me her husband's incapable, she's had no good of him in bed these seven years past. She would get annullity of her marriage and do better, had she some kinsman to speak for her: she has often told me so."

He was a lad no more than eighteen, not ill made except for a boniness about the knees, and with a sore place on his chin where he had shaved a newly coming beard. Speaking of Charity Flower made him wet his lips, and his light gray eyes to glisten: gentle Mistress Charity, Simon reflected sardonically, your godparents named you well. He was distasted by a feel of intrigue that embedded him like the slime he had been dragged from the day before; only this was mud that would not wash away. He began to consider how he might escape, but he had no notion in what part of the country he was, and with neither money nor attire he would not get far: they had stripped him even of his rings. When next he saw Mistress Flower, he mentioned carelessly that he was well enough to be up now, if he might have his clothes; she smiled in her usual melting way, and said they had been spoiled in the marsh, but she would find something for him. The aglets to her hood swung and sparkled as she turned her head; the tips were of goldsmith's work, that when she stooped hung forward to brush her cheek.

Just before supper, she came back with a thin shirt of holland cloth and woolen doublet and hose. There would be shoes tomorrow, she said; the Tickthorn shoemaker had promised to cut them the instant he had the pattern. The outer garments, measured from the old damaged ones, had been delivered from Bartholomew Tailor not an hour since: the doublet of light broadcloth, fashionable and short, and hose particolored murrey and green and lined with holland. The shirt was very fine, embroidered in a running pattern around the neck of leaves and flowers; the stitching was so delicate that Simon asked if he had been fitted with her husband's linen, and wondered why she laughed.

At supper he was presented to the elder Mistress Flower, a mastiff-jawed old woman in a widow's hood, with eyes so faded it was impossible to say what color they once had been, and a fringe of hair on her upper lip. They ate in the parlor, Simon himself, the young woman and the old one, away from the servants and prentices in the hall; at table Simon was invited to share Mistress Charity's plate and cup, and saw Edmund Stonor, through the opened door, watching with jealous eyes. Simon had heard how apprentices in England sometimes shortened their way to wealth: if Peter Flower had the grace like many an elderly husband soon to leave his wife a widow, Master Stonor, it was plain to see, had been given reason to hope for his reward. Throughout the meal the older woman hardly raised her head; her hearing was bad, and when she spoke it was in the loud, penetrating tones of the nearly deaf; it did not appear to Simon that she noticed much beyond the food in front of her, and the contents of the pewter standing cup called Harry, which no one ever used but her. (It had been Edward more than a dozen years ago, before Henry Tudor overthrew the last Yorkist king: mother and son, as Simon was to discover, the Flowers believed in moving with the times.)

The food was good, a frumenty of venison, and brawn from a bull that had been baited, seasoned with cinnamon and ginger and pressed to a mold; Simon and Charity whispered and jested over it together, taking turns with the wine, or offering to each other from the choicer bits of meat. She called him Master Lewis, because she said all Frenchmen were named so, and appeared to take without question that he could not remember himself.

When he tried to raise the matter of what he was to do, she told him her husband must be consulted when next he came home, and meantime, he was her guest. He asked joking if that meant he might have back his rings, whereupon she replied without a blush that they had been removed while he was being bathed clean from the marsh, and she would certainly return them.

As soon as supper was over she gave him a lute to play, and later they sat at tables over a board of inlaid work. Afterward, when a rear-supper had been carried to her private solar above the parlor, and he made a show of withdrawing the other way, she said he must come and share refreshment with her since she disliked eating alone. Upstairs there was no woman waiting to attend her, which was as he had guessed; only a night candle burned, and the comfits and wine were set on a short joined table before a seat just broad enough for two. Her monkey crouched on a chest, nibbling the nuts she had thrown him: a thing Simon did not like, for the beast sat watching all the while they were in bed together, with what seemed a human stare; but when he asked if there were no other place she could put the creature, she laughed, and, drawing a finger down his breast, asked if he was unable to content a woman with only a little ape by. After that, he could hardly get up and go away.

Next morning descending into the hall from his own chamber, Simon heard a voice angrily upbraiding, and the slap of a palm. When he looked, he saw Charity with another woman whose back was slight and young: one of the girls sent as was the practice to learn housewifery away from her home. It was getting toward the middle of the morning, for he had slept long after the pastime in the solar, and Charity was coifed and aproned for some household task; he wondered what had put her out of temper so early in the day, but wanting no part in women's brawls, he was going to the outer door when he heard Charity exclaim, "And do you not come stealing upon me again in my stillroom, for I cannot endure your ugliness that would fright a man home from war."

There were other persons in the hall that could have heard; the girl turned in silence, her shoulders like a tautened bow, and being curious Simon glanced at her face. Then he forgot himself and stared, for outside of battle he had not seen such disfigurement in his life. Half her face glowed purple-red, repulsively birthmarked as if a great gout of wine had dyed her from forehead to mouth: one could believe if one had doubted it before, that such marking was God's sign, sent as a warning of malice like a dwarf's or hunchback's, that will bite and spite the world for no reason except he has been born to do it. She was already leaving by the garden door; to a maid nearby polishing brass, Simon said softly, "Who is that gentlewoman?" The wench hardly heeded the question, being clearly more interested in him; for an instant she looked down the hall at Charity, and then back at Simon, peering with a sly meaning that confirmed what he had judged of the mistress' fame. "She is Maud Lovell, that Lord Talbot sent here until a convent will have her. Good Master Lewis, is it true you have forgotten so much, you must learn all a man does again as if you had never known?"

He would have laughed, so transparently was she

imagining his instruction, if he had heard. Dumb with astonishment, he could only stand gazing while the maid presently tossed up her chin and swept off, and at the other end of the hall the girl's spoiled face turned briefly to his before she too was gone. No more than a year ago it was, since he had met Will Lovell and his sister on the road from Coldstream ford; he recalled like yesterday the proud poise of her head, and the pleasure he had taken in her voice, which was pitched low and of singular beauty. He told himself this woman could not possibly be the same; and then he saw her again sitting her horse in the twilight, the hood drawn across her cheek so he should not see.

The door through which she had passed was paneled oak, with a vaulted porch beyond at whose end one saw flower beds, and a patch of lawn. She had not run so far; he found her in the entry passage, motionless under the floriated stony bosses of leaves and roses. Most women he had known employed tears like battle swords, but she, hearing the hinges creak, dropped her hands without looking and made as if to go. Simon reached out to hold her back; though she must be younger than himself by half a dozen years, he felt as clumsy as a child that has blundered all unknowing into a grown-up world. He said, "She is a foolish woman, that one, not worth your care nor pain." And then, because she had not looked at him and he could think of nothing better, "Why was she so angry with you?"

She responded in an empty voice, "Her stillroom is not the place for household folk to go seeking her. When you have been here longer you will understand why, or Edmund Stonor will explain it, for one. But I thought that just this morning—this morning I forgot." In the radiant morning light the mottlings on her skin were smooth crimson, as if painted there. Her eyes told him what he had guessed, that they had known him from the moment of meeting his across the hall; he saw too that like nearly everyone else at White Ladies, she knew what he had been about the night before. Somebody was coming; of a sudden she shook off his hand as if he had been a mendicant, and so disdaining him went quickly away.

At supper that evening Simon found Charity sullen still, and old Mistress Flower sat grim between them. The servants whispered she had quarreled with her daughter-in-law, and Doretie, who waited in the upper chamber, reported the old woman had pulled the younger by the hair, calling her a wanton and a ribald that would lift up her skirt for any man. It appeared the first time she had taken notice of her daughter-in-law's lightness; perhaps, Simon thought, with a glance at Edmund Stonor, prim over his trencher, it was the first time she had been told. Afterward the old woman had moved herself into Charity's cupid-painted bower, announcing that thenceforward they would share a bed, until her son should be home again to play a husband's part.

When supper was over the lute stayed in its case, and Simon, rising, bade the company good night. As the old woman oversaw the servants clearing away, loudly directing and cupping an ear to catch reply, Charity drew nearer the young man, and, opening her hand, showed him his rings. She had had them by her half the day, she said softly; he might have had them earlier if he had cared to look for her in the stillroom. Simon remembered what Maud had told him, and maintained an uncomprehending countenance; he did not find Charity Flower remarkable enough to complicate for her sake the remainder of what he was silently resolving would be a very short stay. He slipped the jewels back on his hands, thanking her gracefully for taking so good care of them; they were of no extraordinary value to him, except for the signet ring carved with his seal. This, Charity said, she had found after some searching, lying apart from the rest; Doretie her maid, it might be, had been looking at it, but for a time she had almost supposed it to have been lost.

IX

In the parish church at Tickthorn, masons were making
the elder Mistress Flower's tomb. The old lady herself
took a lively interest in the monument's progress, and
came often to harry the workmen on; she wanted to see
it finished and impressing the countryside before she
should be dead. The alabaster effigy being already com-
pleted waited only for the painter from London, and the
sides of the sarcophagus were carved with mourning
figures under arches of flowers.

Simon liked to watch too. Often when the stonecutters
had gone and only the master mason remained, cramped
over the oolite block as he chipped out one by one the
hooded figures, the young man would sit curled on the
base of the font, listening to the tap and chink of the
hammer on the chisel head, and Gilbert's slowly expelling
breaths. He was a craftsman from London, not loved by
the village workers, because he was critical and apt to
push an underling aside while seizing the tools from his
hand to show how such a thing should be done; perhaps

because of this, being lonely, he enjoyed Simon's company, although amused that a young foreign lord should be interested in how an English workman went at his trade. "I expect it will be putting you in mind of what you've seen done at home," he said once, blowing white dust from a trailing stone fold. "If you study on it long enough, sir, happen you'll remember where it might have been, and what you were called there; maybe there's a wife and childer waiting for you, or an old lord grieving who's to be next of his name, with his son gone."

He had disappeared behind the effigy, working stiffly on his knees in the narrow space; the sarcophagus was only a little drawn forward from the niche where it was to be placed. The arch above was low and plain in the Norman style, and the aperture so big there would be room enough left for a man to sit at the coffin's either end. Simon said after a moment, "You're taking as great trouble with that side as the three that will show. Why bother, since no one will see?"

The mason's head hardly lifted; his shoulders in their haltering leather apron bunched awkwardly, then moved again with the swift, accurate swing of the hammer. "I met a craftsman about a year ago, I guess, that had been hired to make a shrine, somewhere up north in a grand fine church; he was to have three assistants, and a reward at the end over his pay. The bishop and chapter knew just what they wanted; it was to be so tall that ten men must stand on each other's shoulders for the upmost one to see over, with statues round the base and the top like a steeple, with crockets and pinnacles and suchlike. The bottom that would be seen nearest was to be as handsome as he could make it, and the next high part to be well done too, only a little less fine; but the top, they told him, was to be no better than was needful, when looking up from below. He did it like he was asked, and they were well pleased; but last week, when Sir Peter Priest asked me to climb up there"—he pointed suddenly with a dust-floured finger toward the thick roof beams—"to look at a crack he thought might be coming under the tower, I saw all around carved like life—bunches of grapes, and flowers, and little wild beasts, foxes and badgers and hares, and in the darkest corner the face of the man that did it, near three hundred years ago. They were ignorant folk, maybe, as we call them nowadays, but they knew the reason for what they were building, then."

Standing a little later in the church porch, Simon looked down the village street and wondered how he would pass the afternoon. The clothes he had been supplied with were thin for walking long out of doors, a device of Charity Flower's to keep him by the heels which he had early recognized, and privately despised: in one fashion or another, he would find boots and a horse to get him from Tickthorn when he chose. Daily, almost, he wondered why he lingered, not knowing whether Charity's little hinting glances and references to her stillroom distasted him less, or more, than Edmund Stonor's open hatred, or old Mistress Flower's frequent audible reckoning of what their nameless prize might eventually be worth. There was an emptiness and an aimlessness within him: even when Edmund, baiting him, recounted again how the Duke of York had been proved and confessed himself only a Tournai burgher's son, he could not muster emotion enough to do more than shrug in disbelief, and inquire what other nursery tales Master Stonor knew to tell.

At the other end of the street upon which White Ladies fronted with its carved breastsummer and gilded merchant's mark above the door, the land ran out to plowed fields and pasture, for the most part banked and ditched, and enclosed in hawthorn or sloe or crab apple with its bright-cheeked fruit. Simon was picking his way along a footpath by one such hedge on whose other side were the fat motionless backs of grazing sheep, when he saw someone run out of the warren which bordered on the foot of the path, and stand looking as if in urgency. As he got nearer he realized it was a woman, and when he was nearer still, he saw she was Maud Lovell.

He was too close now to turn back, although he would have liked to. Since their first meeting in the garden porch, he never passed her without being conscious of the foolishness of his situation; he saw from her eyes that she despised him, and was injured that he should have been so quickly judged. Then he saw a smear of red on her skirt, and blood dripping from her hand where she clutched the folds. She seemed to feel nothing from it, and addressed him as if they had not spoken before, like a stranger unknown to her who has happened by, and will suffice a need. "Can you lift a log? There's a dog caught, I tried to free her but she's hurt, and too frightened to be touched—"

"You've got bitten already, trying," Simon said, and felt for his handkerchief. She caught back her hand, wiping it again on her dress. "There's no time for that: I'll show you the way." She went before him, hurrying over tussocks of yellowed grass and through brambles that dragged and tore at her skirts as they passed. It had rained in the night, and the ground being low-lying, a good deal of the time they were both over their shoes in water; she made no comment, and appeared to expect he would care as little for it as she.

The dog was in a spinney of birches, a little half-grown mongrel bitch from the White Ladies stables, that Simon had noticed before with Maud when she was setting out to walk. Her head lay flat on the ground, the eyes as he saw being half-filmed already; across her spine was the log of a deadfall trap, thicker than a man's thigh and laden with the autumn rains, that had been set for hares.

For form's sake he knelt to look; but he had seen enough beasts dispatched at the hunt to know when an animal was near its end. The bitch snarled weakly at his touch, although no longer able to get her head round to bite. At length sitting back on his heels, he said, "She is going to die. It would be kinder to kill her at once, than let her be all day about it."

He expected she would recoil, or cry, and did not understand why the thing should so work upon himself, who had seen as bad or worse in hunting or in war. But she said only, "Will you do it, then?" He had known he must, and was feeling for his knife when the bareness at his belt reminded him, and he dropped his hand. With a dim memory of a young lordling at Saint Aubin who had owned an etched and gilded hunting *trousse* of dagger, knives, and cleaver, he searched for a stone, and found one heavy enough. He had supposed Maud would go away, but when he looked at her, she answered as if he had spoken, "She was ill-used in the stables, and is afraid of strangers. I will stay by her until you are done." He had not the heart to tell her the beast was past knowing now. As he had thought, it needed only one blow to crush the skull; afterward he rolled away the log, and kicked and scraped a pit in the soft ground to lift the dead animal in. There was a collar round her neck that had been sewn from a woman's girdle; he remembered his sister Margriet at Clairmont, and how he used to laugh at her for making ribbons for her pet dogs to wear. His heart was sore with pity which he could not bruise her pride in showing, but when, as he trod down the earth, she said quietly, "I am obliged to you, Master Lewis," he replied with a glance, "You will please me to put that nonsense by, my kinswoman. At our first speaking here, you knew as well as I that we had met before."

She made no response; he saw her swallow, and fell back to walk a pace behind her as they left the spot, realizing she wanted no company then; yet he felt her warmed that he had trusted her, and had told her so. One or two farm laborers met them, returning, who stopped and gazed curiously when they had gone by: as it seemed to Simon, more particularly at Maud. This made him think, and later that day, finding Charity alone, he asked if there were no servant that could attend Mistress Lovell when she walked beyond the village. The woman's fair brows lifted; she was sitting at the oak table in the parlor, making nosegays of herbs to strew in the privy rooms and bedchambers. Presently smiling, she tucked a posy of lavender between the embroidered border of her chemise and her breasts. "Since there are no blind men nor any lacking entirely their wit in Tickthorn, she is safe enough. This is a pleasant fragrance, crushed on the skin: have you ever smelt it so?"

He stood staring at her, while she continued to play with the sprays of lavender, folding and pleating the edge of her garment in such a fashion that, if he wished, he might see down inside. It was in his mind that he had never so much disliked a woman in his life as this one; his palm longed to inform her of it in the only manner, he thought, that she would understand. She read it in his eyes; of a sudden her cheeks went scarlet, and she pulled up the neck of her dress so sharply that the aromatic stalks tumbled in a litter of crushed gray-green and gray-mauve at her feet. Without speaking, he turned his back on her and walked out of the room.

From that time he made it his affair to know when Maud left the house, and in some fashion to join her, either at the door, or with apparent casualness in the village street. She made no comment when he gave as excuse that the house was close and he wanted fresh air, this being an attitude which he had found the English, in whatever temperatures, always able to understand; but one day, when the wind had worried their faces all the length of the climb up Tickthorn hill, and a misty rain blowing its dampness through jerkin and shirt to the shivering skin had three times made him sneeze, she looked round to catch his gaze, and her eyes encountering his began to gleam with laughter. Pulling her cloak higher about her neck, she remarked, "There is no need you should drown yourself to bear me company, kinsman. I have walked abroad alone since I was old enough to know the way."

Simon said calmly, "Have you? Well, you should not,

and I wonder at your brother." He saw the smile vanish like a quenched light in the indentation of her cheek, and was conscious of the wrath that had moved him against Charity Flower, familiar once more in his breast. He remembered Will Lovell's voice on the Coldstream road, peremptorily recalling her from the pleasure of a moment's talk with one person who did not know what was concealed by dusk and the shadow of her hood: if she had any need to be taught further the meaning of her affliction, that tone of warning would have made it clear. Yet it was not impossible a man might enjoy listening to such a voice as hers; she had a quick mind, and a good wit when remembrance had so far slipped from her that it could appear; and once when he heard her laugh Simon was astonished, for the sound was like spring waters, light-filled and as taintless as snow.

It was that afternoon that she spoke of her brother, from whom she seldom heard. A kinsman, Humphrey Talbot, had taken brother and sister together into his protection when the mother died, and was striving to advance the young man's fortunes, but the effect had been small. There was talk now of some association with Peter Flower, whose affairs were so prospering that he could use a gentlemanly spoken agent to travel for him to and from the Flanders marts; it might be this would prove the best Will Lovell could find to do. All his father's lands were gone, the better part of them—the two great Oxfordshire houses, some holdings in Wales, and the northern estates—having been given to King Henry's uncle, the Earl of Bedford. Since Bedford died, Humphrey Talbot had acted as the King's steward for the midland properties; Maud and her brother had even been present with him at Minster Lovell when Henry was received there, and lingered for a day of Wychwood's famous hunting, three years ago.

They were on the height above Tickthorn village, a broad smooth mound whose crest was thatched with trees. On the other side of the valley the Norman tower of the church shouldered above clustering roofs of tile or straw, and the wet green flanks of the hill sloped down between to merge with and become the village fields. "It is like Hainault here, a little," Simon said. "I suppose soon I shall go home."

The rain had stopped; a weak sunlight threaded the clouds, and the wind, taking gentleness, blew softly. It was late afternoon when they walked down the high street again to White Ladies, and found the doorstep deep in milling servants, village children, all palms and eyes, and the heaped gear from half a dozen horses and carts. Master Flower, seven voices shouted all together, was at home again.

Within the hall, the evidence of his arrival was strewn like sea litter left by the tide. More servants hurried to and fro, carrying cups of welcome and dishes of candied caraway or coriander seeds; benches and chairs were dragged awry; great iron-bound chests stood with lifted lids where they had been borne in from the carts while maids knelt to bring out what was inside—lengths of silk and cambric and fustian, chests of Canary sugar, white Castile soap and oranges of the season from Spain, and a pot of the syrupy green ginger that old Mistress Flower loved. She was poking in the jar with a little silver fork, kept especially for the purpose, when Simon and Maud entered, and found half the company hearing London news. It appeared that Master Flower had brought a guest, a captain of the English garrison at Guisnes Castle by Calais, with whom Peter Flower had long had dealings; gentlefolk of England, it was well known, were not shy of associating themselves for a profit with well-to-do merchants, offering in exchange the influence of their connections of family or at court, and although noticing no more of the visitor than the cartwheel glitter of his spurs, Simon could guess a good deal from Edmund Stonor's reverent hovering. He walked slowly past the apprentice toward the principal chair on the dais, where sat the grossest figure he had ever seen. The seat was large, but nearly hidden by the mound of flesh enthroned upon it: huge arms and legs, their monstrous girth bulging against the loose concealment of the merchant's gown; a belly that overhung its girdle, and neck hidden by the many folds of the shaven chin; surmounting this, a small head with close-clipped, fawn-colored hair. Beheld far off, the man would have been supposed some dropsical ancient, of no capacity or will but in laboring yet to live, but Peter Flower was not old. His skin was fresh and unlined, his mouth pink as a child's: it was a spectacle for laughter, except the eyes were not the eyes of a man one jested with.

At present however he spoke courteously, in a thin, flat voice, rising with the aid of a stick from his chair. He was sorry, he said, to have been so long in welcoming a guest to his house, and regretted to hear of Monsieur's misfortune; it might be that he could assist in discovering Monsieur's name. Simon suggested diffidently that there would be associates of the sometime Duke of York still in prison in London, who would undoubtedly know him, but he was not anxious to draw himself to the attention of the King's Council by searching for them; Master Flower smiled indulgently, and said that his Majesty with his customary clemency was no longer concerned about the lesser followers of the pretender, now he had the chief ones in his hand.

By this time the merchant had seated himself again, a chair for Simon having been brought forward at a signal to face his host's. Of Charity there was no sign, although muffled wails descended the stair from the upper chamber; Peter Flower had been no more than an hour at home, but his first act, as every occupant of the household was aware, had been to withdraw into the solar with his wife, there to beat her to resistlessness with the white-thorn walking staff which lay now—carved, gilded, and bound with brass—across his knees. All the while he was talking his smooth fat hand lay upon it, his light eyes, small-pupiled as a cat's between their puffs of lids, moving slowly over the younger man from heels to head. "It is astonishing, in fact, how easily the Tournai villain's friends were gathered in. At Southampton, for example, a parcel of Irishmen were taken looking for a ship, and the Cornish were scattered like rabbits from Romsey to Hengistbury Head: it is fortunate for yourself that you were found by Mistress Flower only three paces, I am told, from the ford where she passed by, returning from pilgrimage to make offerings that we should be blessed with a son. At that time, the loyalty of the people and the zeal of the King's good servants"—he bowed slightly toward the bronze and iron spurs, immobile on the rush matting of the dais—"ensured that few offenders escaped Lord Daubeney's net, but the country is quiet now: the

King is inclined to disregard what remaining small fish may have gone free, Heaven having granted him the larger ones to trouble him no more."

"All but one." It was the guest from London who had spoken, in a heavy voice that had a grate to it even pitched low, and Simon, who had been the last several moments thinking with pain of Jackie Atwater and his father, was recalled to himself with a shock. Instantaneous as lightning, remembrance flashed upon him where he had heard that voice before. His hand on the chair arm began to go taut, and relaxed just in time under the merchant's steady stare; like a distant echo he heard himself replying as Peter Flower interrupted, gently apologizing, to present the Captain of Guisnes Castle, Sir James Tyrell. It was borne upon Simon that neither the merchant nor his friend and patron was here by accident; maybe Tyrell, who had so nearly taken Simon de Brezy at Beaulieu, had done simple arithmetic when he heard of a fugitive discovered near the abbey, or perhaps there was a description abroad. Pleasantly smiling and turning the wine cup between his hands, he sat silently laying to his own procrastinating folly every revilement that three languages could devise, and was unsurprised to hear Tyrell say, "There's one of Warbeck's captains that was not brought in with the rest, a Burgoner called de Brezy. I nearly had him myself at Beaulieu, only he broke sanctuary to go over the wall: a young lord, French-speaking like his master"—a cold smile lit the cavern-deep eyes—"and the Tournai mountebank's dear companion, as they say, in cup and bed. I know the family he comes of, his stepfather is the traitor Philip Lovell who fled beyond seas after Bosworth fight—a fit nest for our bird to have hatched in. I had the story from Warbeck's closest councilors; it was when they began to understand what was between those two, they said, that they knew such a man could not be the prince he claimed to be."

Decorously serving more wine, Edmund Stonor murmured, "They say, the vice of all the French is lechery." He looked with meaning at Simon, smugly delighted at the foreigner's discomfiture. Simon returned softly, "And that of the English, treachery. Your late King Richard could have testified to that, when he fell betrayed at Bosworth." He had forgotten, until he spoke, that James Tyrell was the only one of King Richard's personal officers who had continued to his profit in the service of Henry Tudor. The little space of silence, spreading like cold, would have been its own reminder, had he possessed concern to spare for it; he felt like a man in one of those pairs of stocks on the village green, locked hand and foot with arms stretched wide, so that whatever comes, he cannot save his face from it. The hall below the dais might have been a church, all starings and rustlings; to hide his color he lifted the cup to drink again, and saw across it Maud Lovell's eyes.

In the tall leaded windows, paned with wrinkled, sea-colored glass, daylight was fading; a savory smell drifted from the kitchen, of meat and spices and pastry drawn hot out of the ovens; a servant came stepping discreetly at the master's sign to let down a wooden chandelier carved with stags' heads, and light its ring of candles. Simon had his hands on his chair arms, ready to rise, when he realized there was all of supper to be got through yet; then he wondered where Tyrell's men were hidden that he must have brought, and how soon they would be summoned to take him prisoner back to London. But the host led the way presently to supper in the parlor, for which Sir James had supplied a buck, furnished on a warrant that had been delivered to a New Forest keeper the day before; there were compliments and thanks and graceful hesitations, while the first slices cooled on the broad serving blade. As for Simon, he did not expect ever again to taste the flesh of red deer without a turning of his belly. When the meal was over and the last ewers and towels carried away, he pushed back his chair, thinking, If it is coming, it will be now. But neither Peter Flower nor the burly Guisnes captain made any move to detain him when he excused himself; in the outer hall there were only the underservants, sitting down in their superiors' places, and the door into the garden was unlocked. He went into the porch, which had stone seats on either side, and stood between them staring over the darkened garden, until Maud's voice behind him said, "Edmund Stonor sent a drawing of your seal to London, he boasted of it at supper. It was to find out whose it might be, he said, that Master Flower showed it to Sir James." She was sitting in the shadow, her hands idle in her lap. When Simon made no reply, she asked quietly, "Do they know who you are?"

He answered without turning, "Very well indeed. What they would like to find out now, I should think, is whether I do myself." He had wanted nothing in the world so much as peace to himself; out of any in that household who might have come, he hated her the most for intruding upon him, and for having understood, alone among them, that the guest they had called Master Lewis was that Simon de Brezy whose name Tyrell had linked shamefully with the burgher's son, the discredited Prince of York. But she remarked pensively, "I always wondered why you said that you could not remember your name. For a while I thought it was so you might stay and be near—her." That brought him round, incredulous as if she had flung a pitcher at his head. Her eyes, more accustomed than his to the gloom, made out with clarity the haggard wretchedness of his face; when he saw her staring his hands curled as if to strike something, and without averting her gaze she said, "What he told of you and the man Warbeck, was it true?"

He threw back violently, "Ask Mistress Flower!" with an angry jeer, and then stopped, ashamed. A pale half-moon rising beyond the garden wall showed her motionless still, inscrutable as Justice with the scales; she had wrapped a cape around her head and shoulders, which, loosening, had fallen partly away, and the marks on her face looked like gray plated metal in the light. After a moment he spoke with his palms against the frame of the little window above the seat. "I should not have said that, it was a lout's brag. No, the story is not true, though that will never prevent someone telling it again. It would be far too good to waste, for example, in Brussels or Malines."

She was quiet, regarding her hands; he had never met a woman so self-contained, and yet he could sense her thinking, and her concern for him. In a little while, when he had taken his knee from the bench and sat down beside her, she asked, "What will you do now?"

"Get away tonight, if I can. Tyrell may have men about the house by now, unless he and my host have not yet made up their minds whether they will send me to London, or take a double ransom. I was a fool to stay here so long."

She was untying the strings of the cloak, a capacious garment which fell to her shoes. "Your clothes are thin, you had better have this. England is cold in November." He had been reflecting on the same thing himself, and wondering where he might come by something to wrap round himself on such a night. As he took the cloak he saw her looking at the neck of his shirt, which had been embroidered intricately in variegated silks; her lip curling, she said, "The woman is too foolish to live. Those flosses were got for her in Antwerp by her husband's man, the best that could be had. If he had heard nothing but what was to her praise, the work on that shirt would have told him as much as Edmund Stonor."

Uncomfortable, Simon said, "I heard her crying. Will he have injured her?"

"No more than will keep her abed late tomorrow, and her bodice worn modestly for a week. Do you not trouble yourself." The moon had slipped behind a tree, and the light was like speckled silver, antique and dim. He was silent, searching for words, and she added, "You are supposing it is envy speaks, and you are right. Though she is as common as a cart track and any man may have to do with her all the ways he could wish, it is a thing no man has wished to practice with me, nor ever will."

Her hair, which was silky black, grew from her forehead in a little peak; on the slender column of her neck the skin was fine and fair. He remembered what he had been told, that her kinsmen were sending her to a convent, and imagined her muffled to the chin in the habit of a religious, with wimple drawn down to her brows. He had heard that nuns when they made their vows had their hair close-cropped; he did not know if it was true.

All at once the illumined lattice of the porch window, lit from without by the light streaming over the garden from the hall, died into blackness; within, servants were quenching the candles and making the house ready for night. The moon having climbed beyond the roof of the porch, they sat together in the darkness, hearing each other's breath; and Simon knew as if he had been told it that her hand lay with opened palm on the seat between them, and if he should put his own upon it, would not draw away.

As to the reason, he could not flatter himself. She was her parents' child, ripe for life and sick to see it passing before she had tasted it; soon the cloister would open, and, if her kindred chose with judgment, it would be such a place where the chance would not arise again; moreover, he had given her no cause to suppose himself particular. It was that last knowledge which drove him to his feet, a heat like summer in his face, saying, "They will be bolting the doors soon, we must go inside." It was too early yet for him to get a horse past the gate unheard, but to give her, as he told himself, a moment alone to be quiet in, he ran down to the foot of the garden, which was flanked on one side by the stables, and on the two others by a high wall. Vines grew over it, their tough stalks supplying good foothold; he hoisted himself up and peered over the edge, but saw nothing. If Tyrell had men with him, they were keeping no watch tonight, it seemed. Coming back, he found her standing by the door; she had left the cloak for him, folded on the seat where he could find it when he came down to the stable later on. For an instant they stood looking at each other, or trying to in the obscurity through which their eyes had begun imperfectly to see; he would have liked to kiss her cheek, but, he thought, that was not what she wanted of him. So he put his hand on the latch, and pushing open the door went after her into the house.

Beyond the screens the hall was empty, its candles extinguished; the room was like a cave, made mysterious by the dying glow of the fire, and red wavering shadows moving on the walls. In the pantry on the other side of the passage, plates chinked and clattered still, the sounds coming muted, hushed by distance and the broad spaces of desertion between. Approaching the stair to the upper rooms, Simon saw the door to the parlor where he had dined with Tyrell and Peter Flower was ajar; that room also was in darkness, but a track of light came from the merchant's closet which opened from it, and the voices of men talking together. Simon paused briefly, listening; then, having motioned to Maud that she was to go on upstairs, he pushed the parlor door wider, and went softly in. As he stood in the gloom, making sure of tables and footstools before stepping among them, he heard Flower say, "Make yourself easy, sir. If it is true he lacks knowledge of himself, he has no cause to flee; if not, he will think he is safer here even so than anywhere in England, since he believes that we do not know him. He has neither money nor clothes; a horse, which he would need, must come from my stables, and until he has gone to bed and young Stonor knocks on the porter's door to tell him so, there is a watch above the gate. Isn't the money worth a risk? A thousand marks at the least he is worth: no one will care if we get it from him before he is sent to London, and if he supposes it is to buy his way back to Flanders, so much the worse for him. I shall hope to see his face when they clap on the chains."

They had made themselves comfortable in the tiny room, with hippocras and pastries between them on the table, and wax candles in a latten stand. In one corner, an earthenware wine jar sat to its neck in water within a wooden cask, and the curve-legged brazier held a fire of shimmering coals. Slouched in a spindle-backed chair, his hard horseman's buttocks accommodating themselves without visible discomfort to the uncushioned triangle of its seat, Tyrell said, "I had rather see his stepfather's."

His dark face showed a flush of red beneath its brown; his hand on the goblet moved slowly up and down the stem, then, reaching for the flagon, refilled the cup to its brim. While Peter Flower stared contemptuously he downed the contents to the dregs, spat, and looked pointedly over his shoulder at the untouched jar in its cooling cask. Simon was moving soundlessly nearer across the shadowed parlor when a hand out of the darkness closing on his wrist made him swing about, heart and breath together impacted in his throat; but it was only Maud, pointing in silence at the silk-plumed tail of the kitchen cat, stretched delicately where he had been about to set his foot. The reaction to laughter was so strong an impulse that he had to clench his jaw against it; since there was no use now in trying to send the girl back, he laid his finger to his lips, and, stepping carefully over the drowsy animal, edged to the jamb of the candlelit doorway, and stood flat to the wall beside it. The cat, unfolding like a wraith, slipped after him.

"Philip Lovell," the merchant was saying, "a knight and gentleman, bravely noble and nobly just: King Richard's beloved friend and sharer of his bosom's most secret counsels. I remember hearing once that you two were not friends, although you served together in that same King's household." He had gone to get the other bottle, which, unstoppering, he decanted into the emptied flagon, adding maliciously, "You were not in London, maybe, when the harlot Jane Shore was put to penance, walking barefoot in procession with a taper in her hand, for her evil living that had been throughout the King's brother's time; Sir Philip having been unable, as it was said, to dissuade the King from this punishing of the whore, went himself beside her all the way, to the displeasure of the bishop and the great marveling of the people. Another man would have seen the inside of Fleet Prison for it. King Richard's good spirit, a worshiping citizenry had called him even before then; it must," said Peter Flower, "have been a spirit absent upon its private affairs, when King Richard set about to murder his brother Edward's two sons in the Tower, because they had been named before him once as King Edward's heirs."

"They were bastards both," Tyrell said thickly. "They could not in law be crowned." His hand, which had been uncertain before, was unsteady as a drunkard's as he fumbled with the cup; yet, watching slantwise from his hiding place, Simon could see the hippocras which the captain had poured himself lapping still untasted about the brim.

"So King Richard claimed, but was not, apparently,

enough convinced by his own argument to let them continue nonetheless to live. And yet"—the thin, high voice was pleasant and meditative—"it has always been a strange thing to me, that after our present King (whom God protect) killed King Richard and took the crown, he was able, as it would seem, to find out nothing at all from the Tower guards about what in truth had happened to those two boys. He has said King Richard murdered them, but he has not shown how, or when; some assert the tale is slander merely, put about to defame the dead King, and it would be certainly to our King's advantage to prove it once for all. It would rid him, for example, of the nuisance of young men like Warbeck, who while doubt remains will not have been the last to rise up naming himself King Edward's heir."

Rattling on the table boards, the cup was set down from Tyrell's hand, drained of contents except for the sloppings that had trickled down the sides. He sat staring at it; and then Peter Flower's pale plump fingers slid across the table and filled the goblet once more to its lip. "How amusing it would be," he said, "if in fact the young man Warbeck were what he has pretended to be: King Richard's nephew, King Edward's inconveniently unslaughtered son."

Tyrell shook his head, moving it doggedly from side to side like an unfamiliar object newly discovered between his shoulders. "Nay, he is not, they are buried these fourteen years—" His speech had dropped back into the uncouthness of the countryman which, under half-achieved court accents, he had always been; he muttered again, "Fourteen years," and lifted the cup to his mouth, using both hands to steady it. Master Flower put up his brows; he seemed bored, and played with the furred facing of his gown. "You are positive. The Bishop of Lincoln did not know, or said he did not, and he was King Richard's Chancellor. How is it you are wiser, that were, if I remember, his horsekeeper?"

Having swallowed, Tyrell peered at the other man across the goblet's brim. His eyes were narrowed and cunning, with a light far back at which even from his distance Simon shivered; he looked like a person who has long enjoyed an abominable joke exclusive to himself, and is deciding now to part with it for the stir to be made. "I know," he said, "because it was my two men that held the pillows to the bastards' faces, the night Buckingham sent for the Lieutenant of the Tower, and so I might have time enough, made sure Master Lieutenant should lie at Westminster until morning."

Whatever Peter Flower had expected, it had not been this. His big body became utterly still; in the rigidity of his face was the apprehension of a secret delivered in wine which, when the owner has sobered, may be recalled in blood. He waited, fear and curiosity contending together; then he said softly, "Buckingham? Would you be meaning the Duke?"

"Who else should I mean? He was Lord Constable, and King Richard's kinsman; after his master was crowned and went on progress into the West, there was no one in London that had power to deny him."

"But you were the King's servant, not Buckingham's. He had a thousand hands to do his bidding: why choose you?"

Their voices had fallen, whispering like reeds when the wind moves through; resting his elbows on the table,

Tyrell gazed in silence above his clasped hands, and the candle flames, moveless as spears in the heavy air, burned unregarded in his eyes.

"He sent for me one night, when the court lay at Greenwich—" The rough voice when it came was so blurred and low that Simon had to creep nearer the door to hear. "He told me the King had grave business that needed a true man who loved him and would do him service. He said it was the King's wish his nephews should be dead. Most secret it must be: on a night the Lieutenant of the Tower would be gone, and a man that had made himself business within the walls could go into the place where the children slept, and come out again with never a glimpse of him but by those he had chosen to be of his company—he said the man that achieved this would lie in the King's heart to his life's end, there would be no one in England he would more dearly love. I told him, and it was so, that I had no wish for rich rewards if I might serve the King my dear lord, and he took me by the shoulders and smiling into my eyes said, It is by such faithfulness that a prince in truth may know his friends."

A candle died; the shadows of the two men changed with its passing; to see them now, murmuring together, was to see another lamplight flickering that had been quenched fourteen years ago. Buckingham, Simon thought —why had no one thought of Buckingham? Golden-tongued, irresistible of wit, the brief gaudy Ahitophel of King Richard's star-crossed reign: all that and more he had conceived himself, until he learned there were some things in which Richard Plantagenet meant to be king alone. It was then, Philip Lovell had always believed, that the Duke of Buckingham began seriously to remember that he was a Plantagenet too. His design in London accomplished, the Duke fled back to his Welsh fastness, the last credible heir of the Plantagenets, to spread banners against the infanticide Richard, and found too late he had raised up instead the friends of Henry Tudor across the seas. Buckingham died by the axe for his mistaking; Henry Tudor sailed back to Britanny to await another day, and King Richard returned to London, to learn from his lieutenant Sir Robert Brackenbury that the boys were gone.

"Before King Henry had slept one night in London," Tyrell said, "his care was to prove the children were dead, and that King Richard was to blame for it; but he found he could not do both. The Tower officers knew Brackenbury had been sent for to dine with Buckingham, he was not so clever at hiding his track there as he had thought; and since the Duke had declared for Henry Tudor so soon after, our new King was in the same fix as the old one: he could not make the deed open without raising suspicion that he had been himself accomplice to it . . . Brackenbury, I have heard it told, supposed the King had wished the boys removed to some surer place in the North or West, and thought no more until Buckingham was dead and the King came back to London: but that was only what was said after, long after—'Gentle Brackenbury,' folk called him, he died at Bosworth and lost all his goods—" The whispering voice, which had been as steady as the tread of soldiers' feet, wandered and grew indistinct; the light sank lower, and the red glow of the brazier sprang up against the darkened wall. "I thought—in the beginning I still wished to think I had done the King that service he had desired. All winter I waited for just one word, a sign to assure me of his thanks and love; but he never spoke, and once being not in his proper mind from another matter, he struck at me so there was blood. Then I understood. If he had known, he could never have treated his best servant so . . . He gave me lands, somewhat, and offices a little; but that was not why I had done for him what I had done."

The last candles were failing; the fire smoldered low, stifling in the airless heat of the tiny room; impatient, Peter Flower leaned from his chair to thrust open a shutter with his stick. Cold air swirled in, and the whistle of a gathering wind that brushed Simon's cheek and, seizing the hall door behind him, slammed it shut. Startled, he and Maud recoiled together; in the gloom a stool tipped over, and suddenly the bright crack of the inner door leaped into a broad oblong, with a man's shadow black before it. Instinctive as beasts, they made together for the door into the hall, Simon snatching the girl's hand to drag her along; there was a sound of stumbling and a gasp, and as he groped for the catch he heard Maud scream, "Simon, run!" Then Tyrell's voice spoke, very near: "I should not, if you value her life. Take your hand from that door, and come back inside."

The latch was beneath his fingers, smooth iron, chiseled and pierced and gilded, with a surround of raised lilies and leaves. After a moment he lifted his hand, and turning walked back through the parlor into the inner room.

As he crossed the threshold, going before Tyrell and Maud, a sword point stabbed over his kidney; he stiffened and began to swing about, furious at the pain and the wantonness of it, and halted as if struck at Maud's smothered cry. Tyrell said, "You lack wit, my young master. If you take one step without I tell you, she pays." He had moved back a pace, the long sword dropped a trifle, bracing the girl before him by a brutally crooked arm. His deep-set eyes, swept shadowless by the light streaming from the closet, showed a man not sobered, but steadied dangerously by a mortal fear; momentarily Simon hesitated, then obeying the curt nod went on into the little room and, standing to one side of the door, let the two behind him enter and go round the disordered table to its farther end. The candles, revivified by the new air and Peter Flower's attentive hand, fled up like torches to shed a light of noonday over all.

It was a cramped, low-ceilinged place, which containing four persons seemed crowded to its linenfold walls. Holding Maud hard against him, Tyrell said, "Monsieur de Brezy, you have recovered memory of your name. What a fortunate chance."

Simon spoke quickly: "The girl knows nothing. Send her upstairs, this is of no concern to her." It was useless, as he had known it would be; Tyrell only displayed his teeth in a grin. "Folk that put their ears to door holes happen on things they've no business to know. Is her understanding less than yours?"

For the first time Simon risked a glance at Flower, and in that fleshy, immovable countenance saw what he had hoped. "If you mean to get rid of everyone that heard you confess to murdering your late King's nephews, you'll need be more handy with a shovel, even, than the last time. Besides, corpses make questions, above ground or under, and Master Flower wouldn't like it in his fine house. Ask him."

Flower said in his colorless voice, "He's right there. You cannot kill them: the girl has kin."

"You fat bag of guts, keep your two busy thumbs outwith my affairs," Tyrell said quietly; he had not bothered to turn his head. Simon observed pleasantly, "He's thinking of his beautiful thousand marks. So were you, up to three cups ago."

There was a little silence; and then Flower spoke again, more softly. "Strip them and put them abed together to be found with witnesses tomorrow morning: there is the stuff that will keep them very douce until light." He pointed at the jar of hippocras. "They can say all they want then, nobody would believe one word."

"So you tell me, since it is never your skin anyway," Tyrell responded shortly, but his eyes, briefly resting on Maud, had become thoughtful. Presently he laughed to himself, and remarked to Simon, "Jesu, I could wish you a sweeter couchfellow. Do you keep dwarfs also, friend Flower?" Using the tip of his sword, he pushed the silver flagon straight across to the edge of the table. Within its embossed bellying sides, ample as an alderman's, the sweet thick wine lapped darkly, hardly below the level of the brim; there was a smell of ginger and cinnamon. Staring over it at the younger man, Tyrell said, "Pick it up, and drink. When it is empty Master Flower will bring more. I shouldn't throw anything, if I were you: remember your mistress, whose beauties you are soon to behold."

In the tiny room, Simon had only to reach out his hands to lift the jug, heavy with its burden. The fumes were pungent and sickening. To Maud, he said as if they had been alone on the windy top of Tickthorn hill, "I am sorry," and then, lightly raising the vessel toward her, "This to my lady." Though her lips were white, unbelievably, she smiled.

Spiced like a pomander, glutinously sweet, the hippocras slid over his tongue. He swallowed, trying to avoid tasting it, but his throat and the back of his mouth became viscid from the stuff with the first draft. As awareness of it flowed downward, curling and penetrating through a stomach that had taken little at supper, Simon began to wish he had not so despised Tyrell's venison: it was possible a second flagon might not be required. He lowered it for a space to breathe, and the tail of his eye saw a shadow move. It was the cat, nosing silently and daintily from the parlor, drawn by the crumbs which had fallen from the table. The private feast had been a generous one, the pasties well stuffed with meat; its leavings had fallen wide. She threaded the legs of the table, paused to sniff, and padded on, noiseless, to investigate something between the back of Tyrell's legs and the brazier. Simon took another drink and said to Peter Flower, "Have you tried Irish whiskey? It would be a great saving for your cellars, if you do this often to your guests."

Between the brazier and the pleated paneling of the wall, there was scarcely a tall man's single stride; between Tyrell and the brazier there was even less. The cat having discovered refreshment to her taste settled for a pleasurable repast. Simon drank again, as meagerly as he dared, put the jug on the table, and rubbed his forehead; and Tyrell said smiling, "So soon? It wasn't for your head

that Warbeck kept you, it seems." He added to Peter
Flower, "Isn't it sad to see dissipation in the young?
Times aren't what they were in our day. Even his
stepfather, that I have no cause to love: I don't think in
fifteen years I knew him drunken with wine. It's a shame
what we are coming to."

The shutter had blown to again, and the atmosphere
of the room was like mud, hardly to be breathed. Simon
groped uncertainly, feeling for Tyrell's vacant chair; having located this, he took a step round the table, and while
trying to lean on the arm managed with his elbow to
upset the flagon. A clumsy lunge in its pursuit brought
him a step closer to Tyrell: whereupon several things
simultaneously occurred. Unsuspecting, Tyrell began to
retreat the half pace necessary to maintain the distance
between them; his arm across Maud's breast slackening,
she bent her head and sank her teeth through lawn wrist-
band and protesting flesh to the agonized bone; and
Tyrell's foot with all his weight behind it descended upon
something silken and sinuous that yowled, twisted, and
fled hissing from the abruptly clamorous interior of Peter
Flower's closet. Impelled by a kick, the Captain of Guisnes
went backward with the sword flying from his hand,
and landed backside to brazier, his head loudly meeting
the wall. An indescribable bellow rose, mingled with wild
thrashing and the stench of singed wool, and as Flower
started lumberingly from his chair Simon flung round to
sink successively his right fist and left knee low under the
yielding featherbed of the merchant's belly. After that,
Tyrell had company in his distress, and there was an instant to look for the sword. He discovered it in Maud's

hand, being proffered across the congealing dregs from the flagon.

A residual question remained as to Tyrell, who had ceased clawing at his lower garments to roll muzzily to his knees. Picking up the half-emptied wine jar, Simon leaned over the captain, and, with a pleasure he had not known he possessed will to relish, smashed the earthen bottle across his head.

Scattered coals from the brazier smoked on the woven matting, and Maud was methodically crushing them out with the wooden sole of her patten, removed for the purpose. A hand's reach beyond her James Tyrell lay unmoving; the only sound in the room was Peter Flower's shrill sobs. Simon walked to the door, and with his back against it said to the squirming, doubled mass, "You are not dead. Be glad for that, since I can think of no reason why I shouldn't skewer your arse."

He was breathing hard, his body trembling with strain and a leashed, primitive fury which even in the violence of the last moments had not wholly spent itself. The liquor in his stomach lingered, squalidly reminding; having bolted the door, he threw open the shutter once more and leaned briefly out in the gusty air. The wind, he observed with thankfulness, had cleared away the clouds, and a waxing moon hung white above Tickthorn hill. At length withdrawing his head from the window, he stepped round the table and stretching down his hand helped Maud to her feet. "If I should go on crusade against the Turk, I would rather have you with me than twenty lances. After all this, can you ride?"

They used Tyrell's shirt, torn into strips, to bind the slack-limbed owner and Flower both, and stuffed their mouths with wads of cloth, carefully bandaged and knotted against ejection. When this was finished Simon stood looking at Peter Flower, of whose face little remained visible except the fleshy triangle of his nose, and two eyes above, glaring like an animal's out of its hole. "We are now going to steal a pair of your best horses, and the maiden returns to her kinsmen. It was unwise of you to forget them in your dealings with her, these months: Lord Talbot may pursue the matter. *Enchanté que j'aie fait vôtre connaissance, Monsieur Flower.*"

In the hall beyond the parlor the fire was gray and rosy now, and threw only a faint glow. Here or there in the shadows a servant snored; even with the thickness of two oak doors to muffle sound, it was lucky, Simon reflected grimly, that they were so driven at White Ladies as to care for nothing, once they had reached their pallets, but sleep. The garden entry was a few steps away, but when Maud would have gone toward it he caught her back silently, laying a finger to his lips. Then, with infinite care slipping off his shoes, he signed her to await him, and disappeared up the unlighted stair. The gate porter's door was at the top; underneath was a gleam still. Simon knocked softly, twice; a yawning voice answered, acknowledging, and a minute later the light went out.

Next the porter's door was that of the apprentices' chamber, with his own beyond. For a moment Simon hesitated, thinking of young Stonor on the other side, but the youth would not be alone, and the night was early; there was nothing for it but to trust in Edmund's continued patience waiting for the Frenchman to come to bed, and hope that before exhausting it he would fall asleep. He crept back downstairs, and found Maud with his shoes beneath her arm, having just slipped the bolt of the garden door.

Twenty minutes later they led the horses quietly through the courtyard passage into the street, the unbolted gate and lookout window behind them blind under the moon. There was not a stir in all the village; a prankish wind sported among the dripping hedgerows and bare, pale birches from which Peter Flower's great house had been named, and it was cold enough to set the marrow in Simon's southern bones.

They traveled north, because Lord Talbot as Maud believed was now at his home in Gloucestershire, but beyond that she had hardly more notion of the road than Simon; when the path forked and he stopped to choose a direction she waited wordlessly, muffled in the cloak which he had retrieved hastily from the porch and returned, with a briskness which demolished argument, to its first owner. They passed no one, nor heard any hoofs behind; night was no time for honest wayfarers to be abroad, and the other sort Simon was happy not to meet. Spectral in the moonlight, the track wound over sparse uplands and through patches of woods that grew black to the edge of the narrow road; sometimes a fox slipped past, peering with eyes like beryls, or the striped vertical mask of a badger thrust from the undergrowth, startled by the soft pat and hurry of the horses' feet.

Daybreak was cloudless, with a dew like rain; they sat among some trees in unobtrusive view of a distant town until the watch bell rang, and the gates having opened a thickening stream of carts and travelers began to flow through. Simon noted with pleasure that it was market day, and with Maud beside him entered inconspicuously behind a miller's wagon bulging with sacks, and in front of another, powerfully reeking, of uncured hides. His first care was to get money, for they had none; but he sold his seal ring to a goldsmith, and having left Maud in the loft room of a nearby hostelry went in search of a tailor's shop, where he bought ready-made a cloak for himself and, more hesitantly, some boys' clothes, which he took back to the inn rolled under his arm. "If we are followed, it will be a man and woman they are asking for," he explained as he shook the garments out, and was relieved when she appeared undisturbed. "Am I to be your servant, or your brother? Whichever it is, you had better be taking me from the tooth-drawer's." She picked up her cloak, demonstrating with the hood so he saw only her eyes. Her voice spoke no more than a schooled, dry amusement, but his color rose and he said abruptly, "Is there nothing else of you to consider, that you think day and night of one hand's breadth of skin? You dwell too much upon it." She looked at him half smiling, the prints of sleeplessness, of barely assuaged hunger and the un-obliterated memory of crude pain like thumb smears under her lids. "I have not dwelt upon it since we left White Ladies. Don't you realize these are the best hours I have known in my life?"

Tierce-sext was in every bell mouth as they rode under the gate arch once more; the sky had been now twelve hours clear, and it was November. About noon clouds began to gather, and a short time later opened firmly for the rain to descend; it was still coming in huge, wind-driven torrents when, unsubstantial as silverpoint in the dusk of late afternoon, the spires of Oxford lifted, delicately slender, beyond the dim low line of the city walls.

The room Simon found therein for the night differed improvingly from the morning's in a single respect: one mounted to it not up a ladder, but by means of a stair. That particular apart, it was much the same: small and not over clean, the lesser of two chambers which faced door to door across a tiny landing, the other being the landlord's common offering to travelers who had not the money to pay for private sleep. Simon considered the frail door, unevenly hanging, of the little room, and laid within inches of his hand the sword he had taken above Tyrell's unconscious form; they had entered the city gates within an hour of their closing for night, but to the Captain of Guisnes Castle, clinking with gold, the difficulty would not be insuperable. The apartment was three parts filled by a single bed canopied with cheap painted cloth; beside it was a chest with a tallow candle, vilely smoking, and on the opposite side of the room a three-legged table, where, shunning the common room below, they supped on peascods and small roast birds bought at a cookshop, and ale from the innkeeper's cask. There was no fire, and they were sodden to their skins; Simon heard the girl's teeth chatter and said, "Get out of those clothes and into bed: you will be warmer then." He pulled the hangings together at the foot for a screen, and was throwing to the floor his crumpled outer garments to make a sleeping place for himself when footsteps crashed on the stair, and the door shook under repeated blows.

The sword was on the chest. He made two strides to reach it, and swung round to face the noise, to which voices had been added. For a minute longer the uproar continued, varied and indecipherable; then someone bawled out from below, and the pounding ceased. Dragging and creaking, the footsteps withdrew to loud complainings, and Simon released together the sword and his breath. "Drunk, only," he said. "And looking for somebody that he thought insulted him downstairs; he got the wrong door. Well."

He had meant only to reassure her; from the first thundering of the drunkard's fist she had made not one sound. But the silence went on, and it was as impossible to keep from turning as to forbid blood and life from his warm, living heart.

The last of the boys' dress lay on the floor; she had been snatching for the sheet when her hand stopped, and had not moved again. He stood looking, the pulses like hammers in his wrists and throat, for the fate that had spoiled and branded her to human sight had compounded irony with its evil: from the silken-skinned hollows of her neck to her slender feet, she was flawless and fair. She lay moveless under his gaze, her hand unstirring on the sheet; above the bare, unregarded breasts her eyes meeting his were unfathomable of all but what urgency could read. Then, his foot taking him toward her, they turned away.

She had put up her arm that he might see nothing, in the moment of his hands' possession, beyond the curtain of her hair. He took her wrist and slipped his palm behind her head, forcing around her face so his kisses fell impartial as dew over the planes whole or marred of cheek and brow, and traveled, sensually exploring, to her acceptant mouth. "No, no, my own sweetheart," he whispered. "I love you."

X

Late that night, in one of the troughs between love and love when they had told each other everything, Simon said, "I am your father's cousin's bastard: it is the kind of thing that, if it were known, would need more than a bishop to dispense us from." She answered softly, "How could you make it known, and name your mother? We shall do very well." They had already sworn to marry, kneeling face to face with their hands on the cruciform hilt of the stolen sword; since they had lain together the contract was binding, although Simon had no wish to invoke that argument to get Lord Talbot's consent. As for the other, he was still thinking about it when they dismounted next evening in the cobbled Gloucestershire courtyard, and realized he could not in honor conceal the truth of his parentage in asking Humphrey Talbot for his kinswoman to wife. Just to imagine himself confessing it made him feel sick, but the experience proved less abrading than he had feared: Humphrey Talbot only stared at him for a space, and remarked, "Well, all things are got in Rome. If it troubles you, make a visit there one day and buy your bull, although I should be careful who you tell your secret to. Priests are knaves, and Roman ones the worst. You say it's not known in Burgundy?"

"I have been told it is not. Madame la Grande, the dowager Duchess of Burgundy—she knows, and I have told Maud; apart from these, only madame my mother, and"—he had never said it before; the word was like a fish bone in his throat—"my father."

Talbot turned the wine cup in his hand. He was a lean, sinewy man with hair that had been ten years before the color of a fox's brush, and the detached air common in one who has possessed neither wife nor children, and come to prefer it so. His eyes were like a fox's too, pale and quick, except their color was clear green-blue. After a little silence he said in a neutral voice, "Well, I met Philip Lovell once, though he has probably forgotten: you need have no fear of me. What you do with the thing is your affair, but I should think five persons in two kingdoms could keep it safe for you."

Simon said quietly, "And the gentlewoman's brother." He thought of Will Lovell, who was at present he knew not where; clearest of everything about him, he remembered that dark, disdainful eye. Reflectively considering, Humphrey Talbot said, "In my opinion, there is no reason that he should know. It is possible besides that it would be as useless a pain for him as for yourself, the comparison between your situations being what it is, and he has cause already for bitterness."

"He would have even greater reason for it if I were dishonest with him in this," Simon rejoined briefly. Perhaps because, at bottom, he cared as little for Will Lovell as did the young man for him, he could not yield him the advantage of being less than scrupulously dealt with; but he was unwillingly sorry for him too, remembering that draggle of borrowed men, and added, "I have heard he has been unfortunate, and one cannot wonder if he is angry. Are memories so long, that he must pay still for what his father did?"

"To a degree, certainly: there would have been difficulties for anyone in his position," Talbot responded dryly. "But he cannot learn the world owes him no special compensation for the misfortune of having been born his father's son. Also, nothing will satisfy him but that he gets back all of what he is pleased to call his lands, and he might as reasonably wish for the jewels from Saint Thomas' tomb. I told him so, last time he was here, which is the reason I suppose that I've heard nothing from him these three months past."

They talked then of other matters: the repeating tomorrow of the precontract before Lord Talbot's priest, the crying of banns, the question of settlement and dower. At some time too, it would be advisable for form's sake to secure dispensation from affinity, Philip Lovell being as the world supposed stepfather to Margaret de Brezy's son; but the marriage ceremony need not wait on that. Simon was amused that his host showed more interest in the extent of his fortune than in his relations with the English government, which in some fashion he presumed were to be mended. It would be unthinkable for Humphrey Talbot, a rising Tudor man, to bestow even his most obscure kinswoman upon King Henry's unreconciled enemy, and when the subject arrived Simon discovered he could bear with comfort the idea of begging pardon of Henry Tudor, who from what he now knew appeared to have as much right to the throne he sat on as any other person left alive. Once or twice, early on the ride from Wiltshire, Simon had found his mind on the man who had styled himself Richard Plantagenet and fooled half Europe into acknowledging him King Edward's son, but it was no more than a recollection strayed: the greater part of his thoughts had been of two children in a shadowed room, thrashing hopelessly against the pillows which were crushed to their mouths and nostrils while the block shape of James Tyrell watched unmoving from the door. He had wit enough to guess beforehand what Humphrey Talbot would say to that part of the story, and indeed Talbot left him in no doubt where both safety and advantage lay. "It may have happened as he told it, or the man is perhaps even more mad than he would need to be for such a tale to be true: either way, you'll get no thanks and bring great danger on yourself by repeating it now. Never fear, he'll keep as far from you as he is able, having Flower to be afraid of too; the best for you will be to forget the thing. Anyway"— smiling again, he clapped the younger man's shoulder— "you'll have better business to be concerned with, from tomorrow." He was, Simon reminded himself again, a good Tudor man; but very probably also it was as he said. So they put their minds to inventing an excuse to account for his departure with Maud from Wiltshire— Talbot remarked chuckling that at White Ladies Peter Flower and James Tyrell, with more difficulty, would be doing the same—and spoke of the matter no more.

The marriage was performed just over a week later,

that being the shortest period in which as Lord Talbot insisted the necessary forms could be fulfilled without indecent haste. Simon suspected that the time required to get a letter to London and receive an answer back might have as much to do with it, but he could not blame Talbot for his prudence, who had had one costly experience in his youth of what it meant to offend a king. The great torment was being kept apart from Maud, whom he could not openly be with now except under her kinsman's or some grave servant's eye; they used to appoint times whispering at morning Mass, and slip out separately afterward to meet about the demesne: swift, thwarting encounters from which they both returned baffled and unsatisfied, counting the days. Sometimes Simon imagined how it must be if Talbot's letter brought back no fair reply, but a troop of men in harness sent to fetch a troublesome foreigner captive to London; what might befall him afterward he never envisioned, since he could think of nothing worse to happen than that he should be taken away, and not see Maud again. But it seemed Talbot knew what he was doing, for the messenger came back alone, and when Simon met his host at supper the red-haired man told him cheerfully that all was well. "Your memory having returned, and being now entirely persuaded of the man Warbeck's villainy, you are to be forgiven misdoing upon payment of a benevolence—since you're no subject, we can't call it a fine—and the kissing of the King's hand. He keeps court at Sheen, this Christmas; we'll wait on him together when you've enjoyed being a husband awhile."

There was a manor which Humphrey Talbot owned, in the Cotswold borderland between the Severn valley and the chalk Oxfordshire plain. It lay in a fold of three hills, with woods on each height of conifers and beech and hornbeam, so from this was called Three Shaws: the house was on the east slope, an easy, rambling place within a low wall, built of that natural gray stone of the district which the late-lying sun turned honey-gold. Simon saw it first on his way back, a pardoned man, from the audience at the Christmas court, when Talbot sent carts and servants ahead to make the house ready for them to lie in that night; because the place was inconveniently distant from the rest of his holdings he came there seldom, and let fall that he was thinking of renting it, if the proper tenant could be found. They were at supper in the parlor, a small oak-paneled room with solar above; the tall oriel window faced west, and was filled now with the sunset light. Simon said, "Would you rent it to me?"

He had taken the notion only as he spoke, but he knew Maud would want it too. He had seen her face when he spoke, as occasionally he felt constrained to, of the day when he should take her to Hainault; he understood the reason, although in a dozen weeks as he believed he had brought her to the point where, with himself, with the known folk of Talbot's household, she no longer had always in mind what her mirror told her. In Hainault, swarming with strangers, there would be the old shrinking all to unlearn again.

By Candlemas they were settled at Three Shaws, concluded tenants for ten pounds yearly, and Maud was pregnant with their first child. It gave Simon a reason, when next he wrote to Clairmont, for his further staying in England; his wife, he said, was too sick each morning for long travel now. The house was small enough so they could do with no more servants than they wished, but he hired a decent widow from the nearest village, who had borne three children living, to sleep in the chamber beyond the solar, and be the especial attendant of Madame. This caused their first quarrel, for Maud stormed she would have no woman to take off her petticoats, and, when he insisted, wept from rage and fled into the buttery, promising that if the creature stared she should find herself in the stewpond with the bream. They went the day through without being friends, and she would have made him pay in bed that night if he had known no better than to allow it. She was not a girl to enjoy mastering her husband, though she would try. Afterward, they were so loving together that no difference could be imagined between them, and the woman Lucy proving sensible and quiet, the subject arose no more. But from that time, or soon after, Simon began to notice a change; whether because of the life within, or from having two persons near who neither whispered nor signed themselves in corners as she passed, she was more free of manner about the other servants, or when a chance neighbor came to the door. The morning illness had passed; the thinly covered bones of cheek and jaw fleshed softly with her deepening bosom; she no longer turned her face into the shadow, when his hand strayed about her body of an evening in the lamplit lower room.

It was a small demesne of fields and pastures, with wheat and barley growing on the lower slopes, and sheep grazing above; there were cows and poultry too, and pigs that foraged in the beech mast of the upper woods until brought down by the hogherd to winter in the sties.

Simon had never farmed before, having had stewards in Hainault, but he meant to make it pay, and was up by first light, spring and summer, to be out with his men. Often in the busy seasons he ate a crust in the fields, and was not home again until dusk. Returning on one such evening with blistered palms and the dust and chaff of new-scythed hay pervasive as fog in clothes and nostrils and throat, he found the women of the household like bees on the solar stair, and in the room above his daughter was half an hour old.

She was perfect from head to heels, milky-skinned and chestnut-browed—Maud's mother, Simon recalled her saying, had had auburn hair—and continued in life with as tranquil ease as she had entered it. She was christened Françoise, because Maud had wished to commemorate her father, and Simon preferred her to be named as he would call her in his first tongue; in a short time, as the mother had not enough at breast, Lucy found a wet nurse in the village, a comely, damp-bodiced wife whose own boy was barely half a year old, amply able to nourish two, and strapping enough to assure the milk would not dry up in another twelvemonth. They brought her to live at Three Shaws, and found work for her husband too, since Simon and Maud exclaimed together when advised they might as conveniently send the child to nurse in the village until she should be weaned. This, they knew, would not properly be for two years or better; and already to imagine the nursery without its carved oak cradle and polished teething coral hung with bells beneath the hood was to feel the shock of limb torn away.

Sometimes that year, as he rode out to oversee the plashing of the lower pasture against straying cattle, or stood in a meadow of newly dropped lambs, discussing with the shepherd the likelihood of murrain that season, Simon wondered what his Saint Aubin steward would have said to see him now. Then his mind turned beyond seas; he remembered there were estates in Hainault and Holland which were more deserving of his labor, being his own, beside which Three Shaws was a little farm; and he told himself that when Françoise was only somewhat older and the fair season for travel arrived, perhaps they would go. But one morning Maud was sick as they sat at breakfast, and when he stooped fearfully above her, Lucy came hurrying to snatch the napkin from his hand, remarking tartly that his part in the business was finished, and it was ever for women to conclude what a man had begun. He was too greatly taken aback to reply—it was hardly six months since Françoise had been born—but when they had gone out, with Lucy alternately murmuring and shouting over her shoulder for hot bricks and a fire in Madam's chamber, he sat down to write to Lord Talbot and sent it by the man whose small rent he paid in exchange for his service on such errands, saying that he would renew the lease of the manor for another year.

Later, he began to wonder if she might be angry with him for giving her another child so soon: Lucy, he knew, thought hardly of him for it. He went up to the solar almost with shyness to see her among the pillows; but she, when he spoke clumsily of this, answered, "I used to be envious of madam your mother, because everyone told me how beautiful she was: even here in England people heard. But in all the years she has been married to your lord father, she has borne him only one child alive: it is my turn to be sorry for her now." He kissed her softly: they said no more.

It was Michaelmas Eve, a crisp autumn day with sun on the hills, when coming through the orchard above the house Simon made out horsemen in Talbot colors dismounting at the gate, and his brother-in-law Will Lovell among them. Even from a distance there was no mistaking the set of chin and shoulders, the impression, definite as intaglio, of an attention that is willing to be claimed if reason worthy of it can be found.

They had not spoken together since the time of the wedding, when Simon had felt compelled to describe exactly the nature of his relationship to William Lovell and his sister; this Lovell took in expected style, commenting sardonically that it was just unlucky for himself that his father too had not played the farmer beyond seas in a rich man's field, instead of sowing his seed at home. Later, when the priest was done, he had come awkwardly to wish the bride and her husband well, which since they were now brothers Simon accepted for the rough apology it was intended to be; but the acquaintance had not warmed, and as he walked down to greet Lord Talbot and his unlooked-for companion he was schooling his face to what hospitality the occasion seemed about to require. It appeared however that they were claiming no more than beds overnight, being on the way to London, where Talbot had affairs, and Will Lovell intended to continue toward Dover and Calais. Behind them Maud was descending the steps, moving slowly out of her heaviness, but smiling too; as she and Talbot saluted each other Simon saw her brother turn and look up the slope, through the orchard where apples hung bloomed with dusky red, to the fields that stood harvest ready, thatched with rippling gold; and it trembled on his tongue to say, "This place was here before I knew of it, and to you Lord Talbot would have let it cheap. Even now, there are other farms, and worse ways to live than in tilling one of them." But the words died; whatever medicine could be laid to Will Lovell's bitterness, it was not this. So in a moment he led the way inside.

Supper, though, was cheerful. The little Françoise, unsteadily walking since her birthday, was brought with pride to be presented, offering a smile of pink gums and teeth like buds, just through; later Maud played the lute and sang, an art to which Simon had introduced her, and then found himself surpassed. Often when they were together she would make music for him, but he took especial satisfaction in observing her do it now for others, and that as easily as if they had been by themselves alone. A year ago it would not have happened so. A great calmness of content washed over him; he was thinking once more of spring passages and the dawn-lit chases of Saint Aubin when she withdrew, excusing the weariness of her condition, and Humphrey Talbot said, "Will, our host's not too respectable yet for a gossip among friends: tell him of your visit to Wiltshire." Then to Simon, not waiting for Lovell to speak, "He was at Tickthorn a month ago, and near ravished of his virtue by Flower's widow. But she's more regularly furnished now, having taken the late Master Flower's prentice for her new husband—you'd remember him, Stonor's the name."

"Flower's dead, then?" Simon was attending to the wine cups, replacing the inch missing from his own at the same time as he served his brother-in-law. Lovell responded with a gleam, "Houseled, belled, and handsomely interred. It was his wife's doings that were cause of it, I heard; they say he put her in a chastity belt— he was an old-fashioned man—being obliged to absent himself in London awhile, but she struck up acquaintance with the locksmith of the village, which threw Master Flower into such frenzy when he learned of it that an apoplexy carried him off. But the tale's grown, most likely."

They lay back in their chairs, roaring with delight; then drank prosperity to Edmund Stonor in keeping the plow in the furrow, and so passed to those stories that are saved until men sit alone at table, with the wine halfway down the bottle. The soft September night had fallen; the lighted windows of the manor house blinked into darkness as the servants went one by one to bed; only in the parlor candles still burned while the talk went lazily on. Humphrey Talbot rose at length, telling his companions they were welcome to the heads they would nurse next morning, but he himself had done thirty miles on horseback that day, and was ready for sleep. Simon accompanied the older man to the door, bringing a taper to light him upstairs; as Talbot took it from him he glanced beyond Simon's shoulder at Will Lovell, leaning back in his chair with half-shut eyes while the drained cup dangled in his hand, and the red-haired man muttered, "He'll be no company to travel with tomorrow cocklight, but his horse knows every road from here to the Channel ports by now, I should think, and could swim to Calais too. Pest on the fool: I might have helped him to something in London if this is the life he wants, but no, he'll have none of my offers. I didn't tell you, he made acquaintance with your friend Tyrell not long ago, on business of Flower's in Calais, and there's no talking to him since. I know why he hangs after the man, being his jack of all errands for the crumbs to be got for it, but he'll be disappointed: Sir James has his own troubles nowadays, and if he ever was the person to help Francis Lovell's son to favor, the time is past. He could use someone now to do that kind of service for himself."

They stood together before the unshuttered lobby window, the night air gentle on their faces while the candle flame drifted and curtsied between. In the parlor, the silence was broken by a man's thick snore. Simon said softly, "Does he really think Tyrell could get back Minster Lovell for him, and the rest too?" Talbot rejoined with a shrug, "He hopes, lacking other means to it, so it serves for belief." Then he added, "And while we speak of Tyrell, bear in mind that these two years the chance of Peter Flower's witness was your shield from him: now Flower is dead, Tyrell is safe if pleasure or profit move him to try to injure you. As I said, he has other considerations just now to occupy him, but be careful just the same."

"Is Tyrell in trouble, then?" Simon asked idly. "Last I heard, he was one of the King's best-trusted servants."

"Not lately, I assure you. He had a visitor at Guisnes Castle this summer, the Duke of Suffolk: a well-watched gentleman whose brother was Francis Lovell's friend. Having fled abroad without leave, the Duke was persuaded to return to England, and Tyrell was sent for also to explain what he had talked about with such a guest. He cleared himself of intrigue, but no more than so; he has offices to lose; he steps softly these days, and would be glad of a way to restore himself in the King's eyes."

Will Lovell did not rouse as Simon came back into the parlor; only the cup slid from his relaxing fingers to clatter eloquently upon the floor tiles. The remaining light of the room dealt candidly with the contours of his face, smoothed of its guard, and with the long, expressive fingers—copies of Simon's own—that hung moveless at his side. It occurred to William Lovell's brother-in-law that, were he in those much-worn shoes, there would be many another shoulder more welcome under his arm than Simon de Brezy's to help him up to bed. He thought briefly of calling back Humphrey Talbot, believed he saw an eyelid flicker, and addressed himself to it amiably as he went about the room, checking bolts and trimming the candles. "'What is there between sot and Scot?' asked the Emperor of his friend John Scotus, both flown with wine. 'Sire,' replied the sage, 'the breadth of the table.' Stock and lock, fire and candle: all secure for a good night, and I'll give an arm to you, my brother, if you'll do the like for me—"

Abrupt on the window glass, something rattled. He turned to listen, and the noise came again: the dry patter of earth or gravel flung against the panes. For an instant Simon stood motionless, but there was no sound except the sleeping man's breath. Then picking up a light from the table, he walked to the outer door and, slipping the bar, went outside.

It was a little courtyard with plots of flowers and herbs; the orchard beyond grew down to the garden wall, which was low enough, Simon remembered, for any moderately active boy or man to climb. Holding the candle above his head, he called out quietly, "Does someone want me? Who is there?" A stir in the shubbery beside the house brought him round, his hand whipping to his thigh, and a voice said huskily, "Is it yourself, Simon?" It was Jackie Atwater.

He sat spread-legged under the withies, his back to the house and fingers flexed in the earth; his out-thrust feet were shoeless, his hose and jerkin like beggars' rags. When Simon exclaimed and knelt to raise him, the Irishman caught his hand away. "Wait a bit. There was someone with you at the window, a time back—" He was gaunt and unshaven, his black hair filthy about his shoulders; the one brawny arm where Simon grasped it might have been enclosed within thumb and forefinger, so emaciated it was, and clothes and body reeked. Atwater read his expression, and said with harsh humor, "It's the effects of prison, me butty, two fat years of the King of England's hospitality; and do your servants or neighbors get wind of who's visited you tonight, you'll enjoy the like of it yourself."

Simon was stripping off his jacket; the night was mild, but he had felt the shaking coldness of the ill-clad frame. "How did you find me, Jackie?"

"Oh, we get news now and again, do King Tudor's guests. It made a grand story for the guards to tell, about the fine lord from Burgundy that had got pardon from the King and was now a landed gentleman in sweet England's breast—They know of you from here to Oxford, and the place of your farm; I'd only to ask on the road. You should have changed your name, if you didn't want to be found."

Busy flinging cloth round the Irishman's bony shoulders, Simon said, "Is that what you supposed?—Stick out your feet, my stockings will go over them if the shoes won't, and there's gravel to walk across to the house." He eased them over the torn, raw soles.

"Man, you've got prosperous," Atwater explained wryly. "It's a sore disease for afflicting old friendships." He stretched stiff legs as Simon reached for the second sock. "It's a fair walk from London, I wore out the shoes of me three days back—I killed two men to get free, a Salt Tower guard and the old grandad bringing beer to the garrison, for his smock to get me by the Water Gate: I'd have taken my da with me, only there's nowhere his legs could carry him now, Mary be good to him, not though Master Lieutenant himself gave him his arm. You'd not know him, Simon, nor the Duke either, poor gentleman, after a year in that damned lightless hole."

It was like burial stones heaved up, the antic stirring of a corpse risen from a long undisturbed grave. Kneeling cold on the thymy ground, Simon said, "But I thought —I was told the King had dealt lightly with the Cornish and the others, that the Duke—the man Warbeck had been received into his household under easy guard—"

"Jesus." Coughing painfully, Atwater leaned his shaggy head on his knees. "Well, you might say that was true at first, if there's kindness in taking a man under your roof to make a living mock of him from daybreak to candlelight. I was in the Tower—Irish Yorkists don't get treated like other folk here, my lad: don't ever you think it—and I only heard a bit what was happening. He stood it as long as he was able, and then one night when the yeomen he slept between were sounder off than their custom, he got away. They caught him next day at Sheen, and fetched him back to sit all morning in a pair of stocks set up on barrels in Westminster hall, and another day until afternoon in Cheapside, with a paper held in front of him to read his confession from while the crowd threw bad eggs, or worse. It would have done his whoreson majesty's heart good to see him taken off at last, King Edward's son with dung in his hair—they say he cried like a maid, before the end. Did you hear nothing about it at all?"

Moonlight was bright above the housetop; Simon pinched out the candle beside him, drowned in the white enchantment, and hardly knew it as his fingers moved too slowly through the flame. "My wife was with child that summer, and near her time—I never thought nor heard."

"Afterward he was sent to the Tower, in a little underground room with straw for his bed and only the rats' eyes to see when the lantern had been taken away— and so he's been since more than a year, except once when the King sent for him to be shown to the Duke of Burgundy's ambassador. He could hardly bear a light to his face by then, winking and creeping with a beard to his chest, so Cleymound said."

"Cleymound?" Simon repeated the name mechanically, and added, "You heard a lot, Jackie, for a clapped-up Irishman with holes in his purse."

Atwater said slowly, "Aye." He wrapped his arms about his knees, and appeared thinking. "Cleymound was one of the guards, new this summer, a wee friendly fellow with a smile to show every tooth he had. He brought food at first, out of honest Christian pity as it seemed for the pig's swill that was our fare, and in a while he began to tell us what was passing with the Duke, and made great compassionating remarks about his wretchedness, saying that he for one would never blame the poor young gentleman for any way he tried to get his freedom. I told my da—I told him Robin Cleymound had the stink of pure informer with every breath of his mouth, and he should send him to the devil with his old bread and sympathy, but he could never bring himself to believe there were such folk. Send that he may be right, but I'll keep to my opinion! The minute Master Robin started talking about what prisoner was kept over the Duke's cell, I knew." He turned his head, looking at Simon with wide, cold eyes. "He meant young Warwick, the Duke of Clarence's son, and after King Edward's heirs the Plantagenet next the throne: for the which reason good King Henry has kept him close prisoner since he was eight years old. There's not a soul within Tower walls that doesn't know about the Earl of Warwick, and what Tudor would give to be free of him surer than doors and bars. He's found a grand way to it, that will get rid of the Duke of York too and the last of his Irishmen, all as tidy as a goodwife's cottage with her man away, and lawful too. They'll kick on ropes' ends for whatever treason Cleymound puts it in their heads is needful to break free, every last one from Warwick and the Duke down to John Atwater of Cork, the old simpleton, the old silly, childish-trusting fool—" A tear scored the grimed, sunken cheek, and Simon put his arm around the other man's shoulder. "It's sleep you need, my lad: come on now. When you've had that, we can think what's best to do." The only safe bed, he knew, would be a pallet in the master's room; he hoped Maud wouldn't mind. Leaning hard on his arm, Atwater said thickly, "It's good of you, Simon: I'd no thought, truthfully, than to ask a bit of money to buy passage back to Ireland, and maybe some food—"

"All a good horse will bear, and clothes too: it's my French taste, Jackie, but I can't admire the lot you're wearing. You'll go back to Ireland, then?" They were on the path now beneath the moon-washed housefront: a gift to anyone inside who might pass a window, and pause to see. Simon had never considered the way long, before.

"Aye, to make remembrance for King Tudor of the Duke of York's name, and Mayor Atwater's of Cork too —" The warm rich voice Simon had known on the Cornish marches was white with hate and weakness. Haltingly, to spare as much as could be Atwater's scraped and suppurating feet, they got themselves along. The outer door opened directly opposite the solar stair; as Simon pushed it open he felt the limping steps falter, the weight grow heavier on his supporting shoulder, until all at once it was gone, slipping with hardly a sound to the lobby floor. He knelt down, groping in the dark until his hands closed on flesh, and as he began to raise the unconscious man became aware that the light from the parlor door was less than when he had stood here with Humphrey Talbot. He turned, and saw Will Lovell's shadow thrown broad before it as he leaned watching against the jamb.

Since he did not move, Simon rose and faced him. The garden door, he recalled, had been ajar when he brought Atwater in; and voices carried in a night stillness. He wished it had been anyone else under his roof: Lucy or his steward or the youngest kitchen scullion; he wished he had had twice the drink on the table at supper, and that he could see the other man's eyes. Then Lovell said, "One of your late friends of the West, I presume?" He did not point: only his foot indicated fractionally the slumped form. Simon answered curtly, "A starving one, and in need. He wants sleep and a bed: I am seeing to it he gets them."

"In your own chamber?" Lovell glanced at the solar stair. "I take it my sister does not mind." As Simon drew breath to reply, he added, "Nor Lord Talbot either: this is, after all, his house. You stand to lose it for him, and all the rest he owns besides." It was a point Simon had been thinking about for half an hour, no sweeter for being rendered back to him now. He stooped once more, searching with his fingers for a heartbeat inside the dirty shirt, and, finding it, got down on one knee preparatory to gathering the unconscious man bodily in his arms. He had wondered if he could manage the weight; but it was like lifting Maud. Anger made his head light as from wine, and he said, "Lord Talbot knows nothing of this, as if need be I will testify: by mischance only this man came to Three Shaws while my lord was here, and I am not going to tell him, come tomorrow, because of it. I promised your King I would live at peace in his land, not turn away those that were my friends to die a yard from my door." He had got Atwater's body across his shoulder; having stood with difficulty, he left his brother-in-law to make what he wished of it, and carried the Irishman slowly upstairs.

In the solar, Jackie opened his eyes while Simon was

making the bed round him, and muttered, "Faix. It's nothing, man—just if there was a bite of food somewhere—" Refreshment for all-night was untouched beside the bed, bread and fruit and wine. Maud woke as he was wolfing them; Simon heard her stir, and whispered with his head between the curtains. He had thought she might reproach him for endangering them by his charity; but she dressed hastily, and after telling him to go down for a pannikin of water, began to get salves and blankets and linen to tear for bandaging from the chests.

Three days later Simon rode to Cirencester alone, and bought a horse, which he led home at twilight and tethered in the woods beyond the garden wall. This he saddled and loaded with provisions himself after the servants were asleep; in all the house only he and his wife knew of the guest who had lain three days in a disused storeroom of the undercroft, and until the dusk of next day's dawn, when Atwater bade them good-by, only they two had carried light and bedding and food, and tended the brazier in the locked, apple-scented chamber.

Talbot and Lovell had already gone their ways, the older man promising jovially to pass by Three Shaws on his return journey from London, Will Lovell with an inscrutability which did less than Talbot's manner to tell Simon that the secret of his visitor was still kept. He ought, he supposed, to have given some indication of thanks for it, but the courtyard was noisy with leave-taking, and Françoise tumbling about the horses' feet was trodden by one of them and had to be carried screaming into the house; in the confusion Simon no more than touched his brother-in-law's shoulder, and never watched as his cap and feather dropped down beyond the hill.

Françoise continued irritable after her fall, and the doctor brought from town said a bone had broken in her arm. He bound it with splints and told the parents to keep her from using it until he came again, but she was restless and woke crying at night, and this concerned them so they had scarcely attention left to notice it when Atwater had gone.

All this while, the child to come was growing too. Almost daily Maud felt it leap, as if impatient to begin its life; Françoise had been calmer even before her birth. Gifts for the nursery came from Clairmont, and letters, the latest of many; for more than a year now it had fallen to Maud as much as Simon to acknowledge these, which were not always in his mother's hand. One night lying in bed, she said, "If it is a boy, might we not name him Philip?" The pause continued so long she was distressed, and rose on her arm to touch one bare, brown shoulder. "Simon?" A long breath answered, and by the night candle she saw he was already asleep.

Simon was in Cirencester upon necessary business some days later, when a trader disappointed of a promised sale spoke to him in Low Country French, offering a young goshawk from the Valkenswaard market: a soft-breasted, iron-taloned bird in tooled leather hood, which when raised unblinded a glowing golden eye. It was long since Simon had taken time for sport; he carried her home, planning a day's pleasure, and was glad when next morning Maud said that Françoise being asleep, she would spend some hours at work upon the hangings of the chamber for her lying-in. The stuffs had come from Antwerp weeks before, all as ordered: cloths of velvet for a groaning chair and to warm the fresh-whitened plaster walls, satin for curtains and cushions, and a coverlet of miniver skins.

As the best streams were a distance from the demesne, Simon went on horseback, and was just passing the lodge when Will Lovell alone came riding toward it. He had not gone to Calais after all, he said, but offered no more than that; from taciturn he had grown to monosyllabic, but since courtesy meant either turning back with the visitor or inviting his company, Simon showed the hungry, impatient bird, and suggested that a fresh horse be saddled in exchange for his brother-in-law's tired one. It was a mild October morning, clear and sunny with a quick-drying dew; before nine o'clock the hawk had made her first kill, and was spreading wings once more. By noon the game bags were full, the bets lost and won; they walked back to their tethered mounts. Riding through the woods Simon led the way with Lovell somewhat behind, but this was less dampening than would have been his company, which had become more constrained with the hours; several times, glancing at him, Simon had wondered if he could be sick.

They were coming through the trees above the demesne when Simon saw riders approaching the gatehouse below, about half a dozen men. Then the brush thickened again, masking the view; he was down the hill and almost to the gate before he recognized the pennons, and the broadly built figure at the head. Instinctively he drew rein, his heart bounding in his breast, and when the gelding backed and sidled, was arrested by the feel of someone behind him on the narrow track. He swung about, his hand at his belt, while the hawk having been thrown from his wrist flew up with an angry beating of wings, and above the fringed and rosette-clasped headstall of the horse that blocked his path, he met William Lovell's eyes.

For an instant he was motionless, his mind incredulous of what it must believe; and his brother-in-law's voice said evenly, "You will not be harmed, if you have sense and do what you are bidden. If not—" Then with a drumming in the ground like thunder, the horsemen arrived.

He fought them at first from the saddle, slashing and cutting at their faces with the short riding whip which, apart from his hunting knife, was the only weapon he had; then, when they had unhorsed him, with the knife itself among the plunging, terrified hooves, and that being prised away, with teeth and feet and nails. Presently the weight of men grew more on his legs and arms, so he no longer moved; pinned flat to the earth, he heard as distant noises the repeated dull impact of boot and fist, and his own gasps like echoes upon the shocks. They ceased; the ring of faces, anonymous as eggs against the sky's pale blue, dissolved to let one replace them, and he was looking at James Tyrell.

He appeared smiling and at leisure. Fear, Simon noted academically, would have killed an enemy from behind; hatred required something better, and Peter Flower being dead, could afford it now very well. Was that all, the only reason for this? Sudden as lightning, a voice of certainty said inside his head—"Suffolk,"

218

and then, "Atwater." Just what was needed to re-prove a loyalty that had been lately questioned. The sight of Will Lovell at ease among Tyrell's men was more enraging than the stones which bruised his back, and he said, "It's bullies by daylight now, master captain, you're improving. You waited until night last time, to murder children asleep."

He spoke clearly, to underline by how many they could be heard; but Tyrell said merely, "I understood you were putting about some lie or other to slander me. We shall see, if it comes to it, which of us will be believed." He was quite untroubled. Sparks of light glowed deep in his eyes, which moved slowly over the younger man's body like softly exploring hands; coming at last to his face, they lingered there. Then with a laugh he stood aside. "Well, well. Bring him along."

Simon had expected to walk no farther than to the horses, which he supposed would be used to start at once for London. When he was pushed past them toward the gatehouse, he halted in spite of himself; but the men, although no more than carelessly rough, moved him quickly on. They had bound his hands with thongs cut from his horse's reins, and guards walked behind him either side, with knife blades pricking him along.

They met no one in the courtyard; within the hall, which was empty also, Tyrell addressed a question to William Lovell in an undertone, and at his reply passed on through. Climbing the stair to the solar, Simon found himself thrust in advance of the rest; he could hear voices above, Maud's and Lucy's, and then Françoise laughing. Tyrell heard too, and as the father stood motionless on the threshold, leaned past his shoulder to open the door. "Now," he said gently. "We will all go in."

The room was spread with velvet, and drifted over with snippets and ends of silk. On the other side of a table which was covered with work, Maud looked up; she was holding some flosses mixed ready for the needle, crimson and carnation and applebloom, which as she checked staring slipped from her hand. Françoise seeing her father wriggled from Lucy's arm to run to him; she waited clasping his knees, puzzled he did not as always stoop and lift her, while the men behind crowded in, and Tyrell briskly disposed them in their places. Will Lovell entering behind the others went quietly to his sister's side, and said, "There is no call to be frightened. Your husband is not so badly hurt as you think, and need never have been so at all. He is in trouble by his own great foolishness, but Sir James is not unfriendly here."

The wine-purple ugliness of her cheek had grown more vivid, sprung into relief against the whitening of her face; her fingers were stiff in the ungainly bulk of her skirt. "What foolishness," she said, "that brings men like thieves breaking in?" Tyrell answered genially, "A considerable one, madam, if treachery and treason may be called by so slight a word. This man your husband was excused misdoing once by our good King; he has repaid that mercy by taking felons into his house, feeding and furnishing them with necessaries, and putting them on their way in full knowledge of treason to come. If these are not offenses for gallows judgment, I never heard any, and the evidence is your brother's oath.

I came here today a private gentleman, but I need only carry this information to the proper place to bring the King's men with me next time, not my own. You should thank me for it."

He straddled a bench before the fire with his hands on the hilt of his sword. She said, her voice changing on every word, "My brother? My brother took this report to you?" Her hand groped, blindly seeking, and swung up clenched on the big cloth-cutting shears which had been lying on the table: the first object in reach that was hard enough to hurt. Lovell recoiled, tripping and stumbling while he tried to guard himself without striking her; one of Tyrell's men drawled, "Jesu, what a termagant," as he moved lazily to interfere, and Simon shouted furiously, *"Maud!"* He had been in terror she was too beside herself to heed, but she turned at his voice, the implement slipping from her hand. Scared by the noise, Françoise began first to whimper and then to cry aloud, straining her body against her father's knees, and the mother came quickly to lift her. As she straightened, holding the child, her eyes met her husband's; they looked at each other above Françoise's head, and Simon said, "You must go to Flanders; you know where to write, and my mother will come to meet you at Calais. You will love her, and she you." Her face was like a mask that has been set with living eyes; he had not seen her look so since he killed the dog below Tickthorn hill.

She turned away, carrying Françoise awkwardly, for she was not two months from her time, and he watched her go. He had hoped she would be sent out now with Lucy and the child, but guards kept both doors, and neither moved. He could feel two more close at his elbows, and the curl-armed paneled chair that had been pushed up behind him; at a signal now they thrust him into it, and tied his ankles with cords to the thick claw feet. Tyrell looked on with a smile. "I told you," he said, "that I came here on my own affairs; you have not asked what these might be. If I had wanted to see you fetched to London, I need never have been at the trouble to leave it. My business is not with you, but with your father." That there might be no misunderstanding, he made grinning a sign with his two fingers above his brows.

It was the blow of a cudgel, where one has expected the sword; and Simon saw that every man in the room had been ready for it except himself. In Scotland, in Cornwall, he had dreamed of this moment, and slept no more until dawn. Now the sawing of the tough leather bindings on his wrists told him that this time it was real. He looked at William Lovell, a long regard whereat the other's color warmed; and to that flushed, unquiet countenance he said at length, "I owe you more than I knew, it seems." The taut lips barely parted to let the answer through: "You slept soft from the hour of your birth, in spite of it. You will not die now for a name or two."

Tyrell was speaking again, his eyes beneath their deeply overhanging brows never leaving Simon's face; he had the look of a man that is nourishing himself on a tasty food. "Philip Lovell's bastard," he said pleasurably, relishing it; his voice invited everybody to share the jest. "Yes, I remember he was in Flanders in 'seventy-five, as it was presumed to fight King Louis, but he found better occupation, apparently. Who would have dreamed it of that upright gentleman." He added a joke that would not have ill-suited a stable yard, and rising walked slowly round the chair. Presently halting, he reached between the carved back and the ropes, feeling for one of Simon's hands; he was trying to pull off his seal, a new ring made to replace that which had been sold on the ride to Gloucestershire. It had the Brezy antelope on it, like the earlier one, but done facing the other way. Simon doubled his finger into his palm, not caring for that instant if it were to be broken as a result; but Tyrell drew back, and coming round fast to the front of the chair, brought down the iron hilt of his sword twice, hard, across the young man's face. The room disintegrated and split apart, flowering into a white blaze of light; salt warmth poured down his lip and chin and the back of his mouth; its taste was the last thing he knew until, after unknown spaces, water splashed his face. Out of his sight a woman sobbed, harshly and tearlessly, like a man, and his right hand was bare. In front of him, Tyrell stood tossing the ring in his palm.

"We need this," he remarked as if there had been no pause, "to send with the letter you are going to write your father, telling him you stand ready to be charged with treason. A man of position makes enemies, and I have mine; they have been busy with my reputation; I must show they lie. For this reason, I will forbear to deliver you to your deserts in exchange for Sir Philip's presence, which the law has been too long denied, once more in England. I've a place chosen in London you may direct him to; you can say"—his teeth showed briefly, wide-spaced and broken like an old worn battlement—"that I want to talk to him."

Braced in the chair, Simon stared at him. They had passed another rope beneath his armpits to hold him up; his head was one swollen, unbelievable pain, and there was a queasiness in his belly from swallowed blood. He spoke carefully, because his jaw was stiffening, and he wanted to be clear. "The lord of Clairmont has been under sentence of attainder in England since he fled arrest after Bosworth fight, fourteen years ago. If you've business with him, you must go to Burgundy; he is not so great a fool as to come here to you."

"True indeed, unless you ask him. I've the intention to return King Henry his great traitor as a service of faithfulness, and that, of course, is the reason for this visit today. Lucky for you it may be put an end to by the scratching of a pen, but as I said, I've no care about you at all." Simon might have believed it, if he had not seen his eyes in the moment before the sword came down. Had no other grounds nor need existed, in some fashion he did not yet understand, it would have been enough only that he was Philip Lovell's son. The familiar knife twisted, four years embedded in his pride; then, like an uneasy horse compelled back step by step toward what it has fled from, he set his mind deliberately to conjuring his father's presence. He saw a man's head, as featureless as if thrown upon light; he heard a voice speaking out of that shadow; but no more.

Hot sweat coursed his ribs, precursor of a welling sickness; he swallowed, to clean the foretaste from his tongue, and said, "No."

They had everything ready: a pen and Maud's pewter inkstand brought from the table where she reckoned the household accounts; tablets, sealing thread and wax, and a caster of sand. Tyrell stroked the thinning plume of the pen, his heavy brows inexpressive; after a moment he said, "That's foolish. I have the ring: suppose I write myself?"

"If you know him, you know he's not stupid. Rings have been stolen before." Françoise and Lucy, he was glad to see, had been taken out; he wished they would send Maud too. One of Tyrell's men moved forward; he was barrel-chested and scarred on the cheeks from pox, and had a sheep's tooth mounted in the gap where his own had gone; this gave him a hanging, lop-ended smile. He said, "I can make him write." Tyrell looked from Simon to the fire, which was low and red, and back again. "You hear? He can, too."

His deep-set eyes were on the hazel ones, which gave back a remembered stare. More than five and twenty years ago, before Simon de Brezy was ever born, James Tyrell had first seen those eyes. His own never changing their direction, he laid the pen with care upon the bench and motioned with his head; the man with the sheep's tooth left his companions, in workmanlike fashion turning back his sleeves, and Will Lovell sprang forward, exclaiming hoarsely, "No! You promised—you told me you only wanted—" As if a gnat had buzzed, Tyrell shook him off, and the wife's voice falling like a stone said, "I will write the letter."

She crossed the room with her heavy, burdened tread, turning as she passed the chair to face her husband. He spoke once, or tried to, before the guard's hand clapped his mouth; for an instant only she sought his eyes, her face quivering as if all the muscles had stretched and slackened to string; then taking up pen and paper she walked to the table and sat down before it. Tyrell followed quickly after. She said, thickly whispering, "The lord of Clairmont knows my hand. You want him here in England to his hurt: that much will be plain, however it is set down. If I ask him nonetheless to come, you will be satisfied and persuade my husband no more: is that so?" He agreed, smoothly.

Someone brought the box of sand; another as she wrote waited with wax and taper. It was Tyrell himself who presently took the sheet, and having sprinkled, folded, and sealed it, bestowed the packet with careful fingers in his doublet. Then jerking his head at Simon he said curtly, "We are ready. Bring him along." One of the men who stood over the chair remarked, "We'll need tie him to his saddle. Jesus, who's to be the packhorse to get him to it," and Tyrell responded with a flickering glance, "He can walk, or come on his belly at a rope's end. It's a good stair to do it."

For greater entertainment, they cut the ropes on his hands with the rest. In a little expectant silence Simon braced himself on his knuckles; Maud, twisting in her seat, struggled to come to him and was forced down by Tyrell's hand. The room swam, and steadied; and he got fumbling to his feet. The head of the stair was six paces off. He accomplished the distance slowly, feeling like a boat at sea; then as his fingers brushed the door curtain the floor tilted and rose up before him. The last thing he remembered as the new bonds dragged at his wrists was Will Lovell's face shouldered from the huddle, and his voice, as if beseeching: "He said—he promised he could get me back my lands." It was, Simon thought dizzily, as if he meant by that to explain it all.

PART 3: Sir Philip Lovell
Late autumn 1499

XI

"You should visit Italy, Philip," said Claude Bouton, who had just returned. "Nobody has lived that has not seen what is happening there. In Rome I saw a Pietà to make Herod weep, that a young sculptor called Buonarroti did; they say he can paint too, though not much caring for it. Man has been too long humble; he can do anything, one understands that only by looking at what some have done."

"Except elect an honest Pope," Philip said dryly. He sat balancing on one finger the gilt souvenir medal which Bouton had brought back with him, studying the while the fleshy papal profile, as virile and masterful as the possessor's own emblematic bull, and jaunty, curl-rimmed tonsure. Among other gossip, Bouton had recounted with laughter the tale of how Pope Alexander had had his chief mistress painted robed as the Virgin, and hung the portrait above the entry to his bedchamber. An earlier connection had given the Borgia his famous children; Cesare, the syphilitic favorite, as all Europe knew had murdered his elder brother for being made a duke before him.

The thin sun of November in Hainault came slanting through the window, making the medal's cheap gold flash and the brows of the older man to contract sharply at the brightness; to Bouton's eye, unobtrusively questing in the curiosity of a two years' absence, the fair-brown hair at his temples had startlingly lightened, its thickness stranded with new gray, and the lines about his mouth were of an obscure but settled pain. Not for the first time that day, the younger man's lips parted on a question, and closed once more as Philip added, "If I go anywhere, I should think it would be to England. Simon is a father there, and expecting to be so again: my wife tells me she would like to see her grandchildren."

"So I would suppose, but it is hardly possible, surely, for you?" As the Duke of Burgundy's Master of the Household, Bouton knew something of English affairs; he knew also, from Simon's mother, that although her son had lingered unconscionably with his family beyond seas, he did not expect to be much longer absent from his Low Country estates.

"It might be made possible. Bosworth is a long while past, and I used to be acquainted with some of the men that govern England now—Daubeney, for example, is the King's Lord Chamberlain. I knew him once, though later we chose different masters; he has had experience himself of exile for politics' sake."

Bouton drew down his brows, his mobile face a mirror to his thoughts; but it was left for another voice to say, "Monseigneur, before you put your old friends to that test, you must escape your new ones. I guarantee, you will stay this side of England while we have hands to keep you." It was Hélie de Grandmont who had entered, blond and smiling. Bouton, greeting him, noticed that in two years he had grown again, but supposed that being now nineteen he must surely have stopped at last; as it was, his head was only a finger's breadth beneath the lintel, and his wide shoulders filled the door. He brought wine when Philip pointed at the flagon, serving it as in his squire's days on one knee; their affection for each other was plain.

They were at Saint Aubin for Hélie's marriage to Margriet, whom Claude Bouton remembered before he went to Italy chasing doves about the courtyard with a dust patch on her cheek. In a bare season all that was ended; one afternoon three months ago while crossing the ladies' garden at Clairmont, Philip discovered her and Hélie de Grandmont kissing on the grass. They had seemed fixed as stones, that can change only with fusing into one; the amazement at intrusion showed in their dazed lifted faces, for the first moment blinded to what was in his, and in their voices which spoke then almost together, Hélie blurting, "Monseigneur, it was my fault," and Margriet, "Hélie is not to blame. He did not even want to, until I kissed him first." Two New Years' feasts ago for gifts she had asked for a French-dressed doll, and a bird in a cage; now within the tight-dragged cloth of skirt and bodice Philip saw the subtle roundings of puberty. It was time and more to bestow her; his extreme resistance to acknowledging it had been, he knew, a consequence of being her father; his wife, however, persuaded him, and it was true as she said that when he looked about him he saw no one of his acquaintance or knowledge he would rather have for her husband than Hélie, who from the time Simon sailed for England had been to him as a dear other son.

The wedding was to be splendid: the family of Grandmont, although old, was not rich, and Hélie was a younger son, for which reasons Philip, recalling in what circumstances he himself had married the lady of Clairmont, was resolved to make a show that would advertise his contentment in his son-in-law. They held it at Simon's great chateau at Saint Aubin, the costs to the estate being carefully noted for reimbursement, since even Clairmont was too small to accommodate the guests; less than a week before the first of the company was to arrive, Philip and Margaret made the slow journey with carts and sumpters, leaving behind no more than a few servants to keep household and direct any strangers at the gate. Because of that, and the deep wooded country ways baffling to strangers, it was another thirty hours before Lord Talbot's messenger, hastening back on his tracks from Clairmont, was able to deliver his packet.

There had been two days of journeying, and three of feasts; the wedding was a night and two days past, and some of the visitors were already gone. In the gallery above the hall musicians were playing a jigging tune, while the little bride in pearls and cloth of silver led the dance. Philip was in conversation with Claude Bouton when the steward came and whispered, offering a letter which the master accepted with lifted brows; the man who had brought it, said the steward, was being refreshed and would come when Monsiegneur desired.

There was a small room off the hall, hung round its four walls with tapestries and stuffed with the collected treasures of former Brezy lords; Bouton, invited by a gesture, followed the host in and stood gazing at a bronze cup two hundred years old, with a bird mounted on a pedestal in its center which, when the bowl was filled, made a sound of gurgling as the beak dipped so it seemed to drink.

By the light of a five-armed silver candlestick, Philip glanced once more at Humphrey Talbot's seal, which he had not seen since they exchanged formal correspondence in respect of Simon's and Maud's marriage, and with a knife cut the thread. The vellum sheet, inscribed at length in Talbot's compact hand, had been folded round a second letter, which in turn was bulky with an enclosure. When he broke the wax of the inner packet, something small fell bouncing and tinkling over the floor tiles to Bouton's feet. He stooped to pick it up, and as he returned it to Philip they saw together whose ring it was. Thereafter the younger man stood motionless, watching and waiting as Philip laid aside Talbot's communication, and rapidly spreading his daughter-in-law's letter, began to read.

This one it could be observed was short, but the perusal continued long enough for memorizing of each word. The players' distant piping brocaded the stillness with inconsequential brightness; the candles stirred, shadowing movement where no movement was in the Burgundian knight's collar with its hanging Fleece, and bridal-fine velvet sleeve. As the silence went on and he saw the hazel eyes had long ceased to travel the sheet, Bouton would have asked, "What is it?" But he realized

233

that for many minutes his presence had been entirely forgotten. At last slipping the letter within his doublet, Philip bent over Talbot's longer one; this he read with swiftness, and going then to the door said to the first servant he found, "Send the man who brought this to me."

He was a West Countryman, a trusted retainer of Humphrey Talbot's with the accent of Gloucestershire, who had been charged with explaining all his master had omitted to write. He had been with Lord Talbot, he said, when they reached Three Shaws and discovered the young man being taken away; there had been some horseplay in the house, seemingly, but he did not appear dangerously hurt, only much cut and bruised in his face. It was Lord Talbot who had insisted he must travel in a litter, and by strong representations to Tyrell got his consent; my lord did not believe he would come to more harm at present, although to ensure this the brother-in-law, young Lovell, had gone with the party to London. As for wife and child, Lord Talbot had taken them into his care, considering it unfit they should be left now in that house alone.

He ceased, and was dismissed with thanks to the steward, who would assign a bed; and Bouton, who had possessed himself of Talbot's letter while the messenger told his story, put it down again, remarking calmly, "He makes plain his opinion that you will endanger yourself to go." Three candles failed, almost together; the silence was as inscrutable as the sudden half-dark, but he knew the answer as if it had been spoken. Thun, thun, went the drums, tambours and tambourins marking the beat, and a lutist sang, "Oh sweet on the thyme, softer than vair, I got me a boy with golden hair—" His tongue was heavy with what in twelve years he had never breathed to words; but Talbot's precisely laid account had been discretion's self, and even now, in the frozen stillness of the man to whom each written syllable had been as sea-coldness upon the heart, Bouton knew that the person would not be thanked who violated it. He said at length, "A rare grudge, that is nourished near fifteen years. What was between you and Tyrell, to bring it to this?"

"Hardly anything, I would have thought once: a great deal, apparently, for him. He loved King Richard and wished to serve him, and believed I suppose that others should make room; for the rest, I was some years Richard of Gloucester's officer, and there were—issues." The vestigial light glimmered on the rich paraphernalia of the little cabinet, kissing smooth shining cheeks of ivory and crystal and gold; in the thick tapestries Saint Martin forever cloaked a beggar, and Leda yielded languorously to her swan. All at once Bouton sensed the other's quick movement as he bent to trim the blackened wicks; in the next instant, the rings of the door curtain rattled, and the light of the hall streamed in. From the threshold Margaret said, "Philip? There was a messenger, I heard, come out of England: is he from Simon?"

The letter which a moment since had lain upon the table was being held already to the candle, a wriggling furl of flame. But they had loved too long for him to lie to her and entirely succeed in it, and indeed it had been no more than a reflex to postpone the pain. As if an old tale had quickened before him to agony of life, Bouton remembered then that the bait which fed the

235

trap to draw her husband back to England was her son. He was a man curious about people and their ways, who had faced and charged a phalanx of those barbed two-foot-bladed spears the Germans call horsekillers, and eaten a good dinner after, but this, he discovered, he did not care to see. In a moment, unnoticed, he slipped away.

The castle of Lenaertsdijk was in Zeeland, a gaunt keep circled by old weathered walls that rose stark from the sole, low eminence of the plain. From its parapet one saw to the estuary of the Scheldt, and the salt spume blew straight off the North Sea. Philip came there from his business in Antwerp because it was near Flushing harbor, where he had bought passage under a name not his own, on a crayer loading with herring and sturgeon for Winchelsea. Stitched in his cloak was enough English gold from the Antwerp money changers to buy the Earl of Warwick himself, if he had wanted him, out of London Tower, and he had visited a swordsmith too. The ship's master was a Sussex man, and glad to take a passenger's fee; he had all but loaded his cargo, he said, and from tomorrow's cocklight would wait for a last barrel of oysters from Tholen or a fair wind, whichever came first.

Lenaertsdijk with its huddle of fishermen's huts was only half an hour's ride away. Since the castle was more fortress than dwelling, Philip had visited it no oftener than was necessary for overseeing in the past, but Margaret's first husband had liked the place well, and much of Simon's childhood had been spent there. Scratched on the coping of the inner well were the letters he had with labor traced there, Simon de B., when he was learning to write his name. There was a tower room where Margaret had brought him to nurse while still a baby, sitting in a thick seat below the window that looked north and west over the sea; it had been, as she and Philip learned after from each other, the year he left England to go on pilgrimage to the Holy Land, never knowing she had borne his child. These things wove about their thoughts now like spiders' threads, as in silence together they climbed the worn crumbling stairs. Three days' rain had ceased pockmarking the flat calm of the sea; with fall of dusk the Clairmont pennon above the keep stirred, lifted, and flattened from its staff as the breeze set for England.

XII

The captain of the crayer was friendly. He invited his passenger to come up beside him, and found him easy-mannered, although inclined to silences; later as landmarks appeared the master began informatively to point them out, until he realized his companion recognized them as well as himself. It was clear, he said respectfully, that the gentleman had crossed these seas many times before. They coasted past the seamed chalk cliffs and their guardian keep at Dover: "the key of England" for three hundred years; later the shoreline became all white shingly beaches, or flat marshland where at night green lights flickered. As they put into Winchelsea a sound like silver drifted, borne airy on the wind, and the passenger's head lifted as he heard. "English bells," he said. "There are none like them." The bearded sailor nodded, his eyes curious on the other's face. "Aye. It's in the founding, so they say: when I hear that, I know I'm in England again, near enough."

238

They parted at the harbor-side, Philip having first made sure of where in the town he should go to buy horses. He purchased two, and saddlery for both, and when the stableman offered direction of a guide, thanked him and declined. Even here on the southern coasts, he remembered the land well enough to be able to pick out a road; as he traveled west, skirting London and making direct for Gloucestershire, he could have ridden blindfold. A mild wet breeze brushed his cheek; his eye marked each grass blade, faded now like the white-gray sky to winter gentleness, and the air was clean from late-fallen rain.

He had had good crossing weather, a circumstance that in November was more good fortune than the rule, which had put him a week or more ahead of when Tyrell would begin expecting him, and Humphrey Talbot, in tendering discreet offers of assistance, had made sure to indicate where he was to be found. The porter at the manor gate said that Lord Talbot had gone for the day into Gloucester, although his return was hourly looked for; Philip asked then for Madame de Brezy, feigning a messenger's errand, and was brought in to her: a drawn-cheeked, gross-bellied child about whom her father's beauty lay like some hideous spoiled treasure, out of whose disfigured face there yet looked at him his cousin Francis' eyes.

She for her part, when he put back his hood and spoke her name, stood rigid with an expression he could read. Her letter had brought him to England, maybe to his death; she had used his life to bargain for Simon's and would do the same again, and now she must face him with it. Yet all the while her eyes clung to his, as if they would draw some strength or power to heal that had bled from her own heart as from a wound. When he asked about Will Lovell, she told him baldly what even Talbot's detached explicitness had failed from setting down. The account came breached by pauses, bare of defense or plea; it was her brother and she could not excuse him; he understood then the core of her bitterness and shame.

On the white plaster wall above them, a painted Fortune stood beside her wheel: the wry conceit of the house's present owner, done when he returned out of exile in the train of the Tudor king. The goddess waited with hand outstretched, ready to spin again, and seemed to smile. Philip did not know how long he had been gazing at it when he said, "Poor lad. I never dreamed matters had gone so badly with him . . . I wrote Talbot more than once, asking what help I might give my cousin's children, but he told me, none. No doubt he spared my feelings: I should have guessed I was the last person the boy would have received it from." She stared at him, the breath catching in her throat; then stumbling from her seat she knelt with her head on his knees, and he stroked her hair.

He left next morning, having arranged with Lord Talbot what he had come for: the immediate escort of Simon's wife and child south to Winchelsea, where a ship had been paid to wait for them. More than that service, Philip did not ask, and sensed beneath the courtesies Humphrey Talbot's relief. He had done what honorable duty required of him, but he took hardly less risk in receiving Philip Lovell than if it had been a dozen years ago, and his wars were over: he wanted no more trouble now than he could deal with, and a peaceful life.

The journey from the west parts of England to London commonly took anything from four days to ten, as roads and weather allowed. Philip did it in three, alternately thanking good fortune for the sturdiness of the Winchelsea horse dealer's animals, and a main road which ran direct from Gloucester through Oxford to London. He knew it like his hand.

The house Tyrell had appointed for their meeting was outside London walls, in the great ward of Farringdon Without; this Philip considered a circumstance of probable advantage, and took unobtrusive lodgings for himself in the same sprawling reaches, well clear of the city gates. It was now almost noon; having satisified mendaciously the lodging keeper's curiosity about his business and person, he went lounging out, an inconspicuous figure in creased, rough clothes, and after unhurried walking came to a courtyard wall behind which a tall building blinkered with shutters rose. The reek of cattle, drifting from Smithfield market, lay over the street. He strolled on past the house without pausing, and took up a position some distance beyond where he could watch unseen. There appeared a good deal of coming and going about the place; he counted three men—all brawny, tough-looking fellows—who arrived separately in haste and were admitted as if watched for, and then a group of them emerged all together and set off nearly running in the direction of Aldersgate. At the side of the house, above the sloping roof of a penthouse, one of the shutters hung askew; Philip was studying this with narrowed eyes when a bakehouse's maid came bustling along the street carrying a basket of loaves, and with the air of one that has done it many times, rapped on the postern beside the tall barred gate. It opened, and she went inside.

A dawning suspicion had brought the first small relaxing in days to the watcher's mouth. When the maid reappeared with her empty basket he accosted her, remarking in broad countryman's accents, "That's a busy place you've come out of. Would you like a penny?" She gave him a sharp look from an eye like a bird's, and rejoined smartly, "Yes, if there's another to rub against it."

He passed over the coins, and drew her after him into a covered alley that hid them from the house. "There's a man I'd like to meet in there, only I'd liefer his friends didn't know: a proud young cock I've followed all the way from Oxfordshire, for my girl's sake that he had his way with and then left with what he gave her. Maybe you'd know how I could talk to him? Black hair he has, and a pretty ladyship face and fancy way to speak: you'll know the sort. Simon, his name is."

She shook her head, thoughtfully regarding him as she leaned against the wall. "I never saw anyone like that, but I'll tell you something, my master: I'd keep clear of that house, for it's a den if ever there was one. All the time I've been going there, they had a man prisoner upstairs without law or leave, and nobody to know; only he broke out this morning, so I heard in the kitchen —left the breakfast guard with a knob on his head and half his face like a bag pudding, while the bird went out the window with someone's shirt for rope. He was a foreigner from beyond seas, some rich young man they'd a grudge on, the turnspit says. The whole house is in a taking, you'll get no one to pay you attention today." She added kindly, "And good luck for you too. Now you mind what I've said, for you look an honest man, even if you've the farm straw still in your boots, and you're too old sure to learn the way of dealing with such folk. Go on back to your parts: there's no meat for you in that place but you'll break your teeth chewing it." He thanked her meekly—she was about fourteen years old—and watched her go briskly off. Relief had weakened his legs so he was put to it to stand, and the lifting of the past weeks' load of fear and anguish was like a weight of mountains rolled from the heart. When, a moment later, Saint Bartholomew and Charterhouse bells began their solemn peal for the midday office, he bent his knees into the swill and mud of the little stinking close, and as humbly as any poor peasant for rain in drought, he gave thanks for the deliverance of his son.

Afterward walking away from Smithfield, he set himself to considering what Simon would do now. No more than Philip had done, could he risk assuming Tyrell would not turn next to Maud and Françoise for hostages; but the boy had neither horse nor money, and in all likelihood did not know the western roads so well that he could avoid leaving a trail of betraying inquiries behind him. If he chose to hide himself in London, he might make for Saint Martin's, a famous sanctuary; Tyrell had thought of that himself, apparently, since his men had gone toward Aldersgate. The more he pondered it, the less Philip was disposed to believe Simon would take refuge with the brothers. His pressing concern would be to convey Maud and Françoise beyond Tyrell's grasp; judging from his performance as so far reported this morning—here the father's eyes glinted a little—it seemed probable that, in one fashion or another, he would contrive to get himself on the way to Gloucestershire.

It struck Philip, until now only half noticing, that there were a great many folk abroad, even for the height of the day. It was a little, winding street, and mixed with the hum and jostle of the crowd the common din of the city rose: cooks' boys yelling praise of their masters' goods; shrill beggars each exhibiting alms bowl and sores; a harlot, hoarsely importuning, in the striped hood of her trade. From the best pitch, two preachers touted chances in a lottery: first prize to be a year's indulgence, certified by a bishop. When he reached the high road which debouched from Newgate, the people were so thick he was obliged at first to push his way, and soon could get no farther at all. He began to glance about, to see what kept them standing and looking; then he heard coming nearer the echo of hooves on the cobbled street, the slow scrape of wooden sledges, bumping and dragging, over the voice of the priest; and he knew.

It was some distance yet to Tyburn: a longer way than they had been already drawn from the Tower. They lay on the hurdles with their feet to the horses' tails, so their heads declined downward: two men, each chained hand and foot, one old and whimpering, his wits seeming gone, the other, as Philip now saw, young, with a tall gaunt body and trailing, dust-streaked ruddy hair. The Londoners hooted, some throwing filth and stones, others bowing in mock obeisance as the procession lumbered by—"God save your Dukeship," and, "Here's King War-

beck, riding to be crowned. Largesse, largesse." He made
no answer; his gaze was blind and fixed, as if he were
confined already within the close ritual of his death. A
rough cross had been thrust between the fingers of one
long hand, which Philip had last seen four years ago in
the Duchess of Burgundy's presence chamber, being held
out for him to kiss.

They passed; the crowd which pursued them pressed
up behind, to be enlarged by those observers falling in
after who had heretofore lined the way; and Philip
could not have disentangled himself had he tried. The
dark leaning walls of houses on either hand, with white
ribbon of sky unrolling between, began to diminish and
fall away; there were green fields, and a hospital for
lepers, standing alone. The crowd became silent, walking quietly to the squeak and jingle of harness, the slither
of the hurdles and hard dull ring of the horses' hooves.
To an older man next to him with a butcher's thick
shoulders and spotted apron, Philip said under his breath,
"Upon what charge were they condemned?" He was
thinking that in two years, Henry had been his own
time deciding upon it. The man looked surprised at
encountering someone who did not know, and replied,
"Why, they made a plot with the Earl of Warwick, young
Warbeck and the Irish mayor here with him, they were
to blow up the Tower and seize the government. The
Earl is to lose his head for it too next week, on Tower
Hill." He pushed forward, using his elbows and muscle-
strapped forearms to burrow through the mob, for the
van of the procession had halted, and in front of them,
mounted on its straw-strewn platform and skirted with
seats expensively for hire, were the tall uprights and rope-

245

hung crossbeam of the Tyburn Tree. The stands were filled with well-dressed spectators; to one side of the scaffold, a small fire burned.

One of the executioner's men descended to unshackle the first of the prisoners, and pushed him up the steps to the platform. An officer proclaimed the sentence; the priest, the hangman and his assistants, stood away; the copper-gilt head waited alone under the sky. It was the final moment save one, the end of a life in which all things had run to their conclusions; his wide questioning eyes seemed to wonder what could have been the reason for it all. But he read out, in a strained faltering voice, what had been given him to read, begging forgiveness for his troublesomeness and deceits, and testifying that he was indeed a stranger born, according to his confession past made. Some that listened were disappointed, having hoped for last-minute sensations; on the other hand, it might be that he had been told he would die more quickly so. As to the matter of his birth, from what Philip believed he knew, it was probably true enough. Not many months ago he had seen Margaret of Burgundy again, and found her looking ill and old; soon after the pretender fell into Tudor's hands, she had sued for pardon of the King of England, promising no more factiousness. It was not hard to guess why.

Now all was still; and if he had cared to indulge his soul's cowardice Philip could well have gotten away, for the people who had milled so busily stood like stones. It was not the first time he had witnessed this vengeance of the law; fifteen years ago Colyngbourne had suffered in just such a fashion, condemned to it by a commission which included Francis Lovell among its judges, for treasonable practices with the French, and—so said King Richard's enemies—a rhyme. It had remained for Philip Lovell to implore with passion some mitigation of the brutal sentence; he had failed; and bare horror at the long-drawn torment, shame like a filthy unwashable skin at being one of the government which had willed it, gripped him and lived again in this obscene duplication of its rites. Very soon the mind sickened and sought blindness like a drug; he did not know how long the strangulated body hung twisting and thrashing on its rope until the knife slashed through to cut it down; he could not have sworn it was upon that afternoon long past, and not today, that the broken scream had rung out: "Lord Jesus, yet more trouble—!" before the stench of burnt flesh choked his nostrils, wafting upward like an ancient offering to some grim, unappeased, unappeasable God. At the pitch of agony a new nerve is discovered, and still the flesh lives on . . . In Paris a man has looked on his four arms and legs ripped from his trunk by horses, and recognized the sight; in the Grand'-Place of Bruges Maximilian's councilors were killed by breaking, limb by limb; and Islam flays or impales alive. *Oh Christ, where art thou?* But long before the executioners rose red-armed from their work and the dispensing axe sheared down, all movement had ended: surely, surely he had been dead.

It was over; the severed head was held up and flourished by its hair to the crowd; and like a man with difficulty wakened, Philip looked about him, thinking to see in the surrounding, uplifted faces some reflection, perhaps, of what was in his own. But among all those near him, although a few were sober, others troubled or pale, he saw only one whose gaze had not yet begun to shift from the scaffold to the hurdle with its waiting second victim: in whose eyes he could read mirrored the same anguish of pity, as personal and amazing as grief.

He was young and black-haired, wearing clothes that had been decent once, and a month's black beard upon his chin. On his visible temple a recent bruise had yellowed; above the mask of stubble, only the lines of nose and brow were clearly to be discerned, and the curious lightness, anomalous to such coloring, of his eyes. Of a sudden Philip's heart began to knock against his ribs; several moments passed while he stood transfixed, unbelieving and unable to stir. The people round him were craning and pushing to see the Irishman brought up onto the scaffold, however; presently in the confusion he was able to thrust his way through, and quietly, so as not to startle him into an exclamation, he laid his hand on the young man's arm. "Simon," he said.

XIII

On a green breast of hillside, with the ascending heights of Hampstead at their backs and distant, sharp gray curve of the river below and before, they rested together, the older man leaning on one elbow, the younger staring in front of him, clasping his knees. It was a little pasture, hedged with hawthorn, where in summer cattle grazed, but the field was empty now since the Martinmas slaughtering two weeks ago. With a new shudder Simon tightened the grip about his legs, and Philip said, "You should not have waited for the second one: God knows, once is sufficient for any man to witness quartering done. I promise you, he was dead when they took him from the rope, and before that he hardly knew enough to be afraid. He was an old man, and his mind was gone." He bought wine hastily as they passed through Tyburn village; feeling now behind him, he unstoppered the bottle with his teeth and put it without comment in reach of the other's hand. Simon looked at the leather flask for a space before he took it up, and said presently in a muffled voice, "He was good to me once, when I was ill on the march from Taunton. I remember he fed me on Irish whiskey to keep me on my horse. He wasn't old then."

"No. Well, consider it in this light: he had lived a fair length of years, and while he was free to do it, he chose his path. I daresay Warbeck envied him."

He was relieved to observe some unclenching of the beard-roughened face, the first real sign of a mind becoming able to listen and apprehend once more. His throat was dry from prolonged talking upon gentle, random topics which he had pursued as they occurred to him, and could not now even recall; conversation it had never been, since Simon throughout had answered barely a word, yet Philip had known he was grateful. Leaning his forehead on his linked hands, the younger man said slowly, "Werbecque. No, he wasn't the one to undertake that sort of enterprise for himself. I wonder how he stumbled into it."

Philip was carefully noncommittal. "You've changed your opinion? You thought once he was the prince." Simon said briefly, "That was before I met Sir James Tyrell."

He recounted then what he had overheard at White Ladies, standing in the darkness while Tyrell and Peter Flower hunched whispering beyond the parlor door. "Tyrell's story was that the Duke of Buckingham set him on to kill the princes, and Lord Talbot told me he could believe it, besides that from what he's heard of Buckingham it sounds just his style: after King Richard and the boys, he was the Plantagenet next the crown. But I suppose you knew him too?" They shared the rest of the wine, Simon first passing over the flask before accepting it for himself. "I heard Tyrell say to Werbecque once that he had good reason to know he was not the prince. The Duke—Werbecque only asked him if he was quite sure. Right to the end, he carried it off; someone had been to a lot of trouble schooling him, and he looked the part too. Old men in the West Country that had known King Edward swore he must be his son."

"Nephew, I fancy. It was King Edward's sister he got his face from, the Duchess of Burgundy: you might say it was fairly given, since she was his mother."

They had been talking so easily that Philip spoke before he thought. The next instant he could have bitten his tongue through for it: not because of what he had said, but because he had said it without concern, in such fashion as, male to male, he might have been taken to jest. The little silence which followed was like a chasm opened; and then Simon said, "He was the Duchess of Burgundy's bastard? It seems hardly possible."

He spoke mechanically, his eyes on the withered grass. The set of his lips, the line newly drawn from cheek to mouth and the intent, unreadable gaze, all belonged to a man in whom the lad of a few years since was hardly to be remembered; Philip responded feeling like one who has ventured onto a stretch of half-frozen ice, whose every step must take him farther from the shore. "I believe it is probably true. The Duke of Burgundy was no uxorious husband, he spent whole months on his campaigns, and even in times of peace was no man for women. She was left much alone, poor lady. De Berghes, that is now the Bishop of Cambrai, was said to be the father: Maximilian has assured the English government it is so. It seems that Warbeck was reared to call the Tournai wife his mother, and at what time the Duchess of Burgundy told him differently is her secret now; for the rest, de Berghes was in London on embassy a year ago, and while there begged leave to see King Henry's most notorious prisoner, with whom, he said, he had been somewhat acquainted in days gone by. So Warbeck was brought, and in the presence of the bishop and certain others the King inquired of him why he had deceived the Duke of Burgundy and so many more besides with his false tales. Warbeck replied, it is said, that Madame la Grande the dowager Duchess of Burgundy knew as well as himself that he was not King Edward's son: to which assertion the bishop returned no answer. Warbeck was ill then from the conditions of his confinement, and by that time he must have known his death was sure; but I should have preferred his place to Henri de Berghes' then."

In the undergrowth of the hedgerow a bird cheeped softly; the air was so still they heard the rustle of her feet. Rolling over on his stomach, Simon said quietly, "I saw the bishop when he was in Scotland, he brought letters from Madame la Grande to Werbecque and the King of Scots. He and Werbecque did not much seek each other out after the first day, which they spent shut up long together. If Werbecque ever learned what the bishop was to him, I daresay that was the time when he discovered it."

He remembered his own pain under that scrutinizing episcopal eye, the sweating humiliation and terror of discovery: and all before the priestly father of a bastard adventurer as lawlessly gotten as himself. He would have been furious once, but that time seemed long ago. He had known better things, since then, to be angry about. He looked over the valley at the river, where a gilded barge with striped awning and pennons tremulous in the wind floated like a distant toy downstream toward London; and he said, "Monseigneur, I am sorry you were brought to England on my affairs. I never intended you to be, I should have been—embarrassed for you to trouble yourself on my account." He was aware of a movement beside him, like a sudden flinching at some intolerable pain. Philip answered, "If it was like that to you—if you were in any doubt I would come, setting aside with willingness every other claim of circumstance or person —then I have made more wretched work with you even than I dreamed."

Their two hands, motionlessly lying, were separated by no more than a finger's span of grass: the younger man's darker and drier of skin from summer labor out of doors, the elder's—it was his left one—with an irregularity still about the greater knuckles, where the bones had been broken and mended badly: a reminder of his escape from England after Bosworth, years ago. Furtively glancing, Simon recalled what the old groom Gregory Traynor had told him once about that injury, the circumstances of whose acquiring would have kept most men from returning where it was gotten for the rest of their lives. His mind emptied, passage space only for the comprehensions of his heart; he said, "No more wretched, Monseigneur, than I with you. I am sorry." He had wanted simply to be kind, whether from regret or pity he could not tell; but he found when he had spoken that it was quite true.

Later, as they made their way on foot back toward London, threading the farms and hamlets which bound the course of the river like tapestry along the valley flank, Philip said, "From the outset, there was hardly a thing I did not do wrong between us. I was afraid to show my love, for your mother's protection and yours; also I was ashamed before you, knowing what some day you must be told, and the worse matters grew the more it appeared a judgment which it would be impious in me to question. After Hélie came I could not put a hand right with you; I knew it, but could not guess why."

"You always seemed to have time for him: I used to hear you talking together, about everything and nothing . . . It was not the way you talked to me. I can't recall now what was the start of that last quarrel in your chamber. I came in, believing you back from Malines, and found him there—he told me eventually my place was not in your bedroom while you were absent from it, and that when you returned no doubt you would make time for me. I daresay I gave him good cause to say it. The next I remember is seeing you in the door."

Evening was drawing on. The late-day sun, declining westward, flared out between two bars of cloud, and vanished finally within the overcast; the light became gray once more, but the hills were dim green still which were embraced by the river's arm. They walked on, hardly noticing whether they spoke or kept silent, since each was happy in the other's company; and for this remembrance in the aftertime both were grateful, because it was the only evening, being at once the first and the last, which they passed so together in their lives.

Early next morning, dragging on his boots as he sat on the edge of Philip's bed, Simon watched him balance two swords across his palms—one, the useful and gentle-manly civilian weapon from Italy called cinquedea, for the five fingers' width of the base of its flat triangular blade; the other, as long but narrower with a plain steel grip, packed with its implements in a leather sheath which could be worn inconspicuously upon the outer thigh, concealed by a cloak. He remarked, "Holy Heaven, you're well armed. What's the dagger, or is it a sword?"

"A ballock knife," Philip rejoined gravely. "The vulgar Englishman likes it so well he is hardly dressed without it: your refinement will prefer this." He passed over the Italian sword, offering the hilt of inlaid ivory. Simon chuckled as he inspected the workmanship, which was excellent; he could have named the Antwerp dealer from whom the piece had come. "*Déa*, I'll be glad to see Hainault again. I've wished for Saint Aubin, many a time."

"It is your home, and a man is what he has been bred. You were reared a liege of Burgundy; I, though every interest flies against it, must remain also—what I must be." Philip leaned with crossed arms before the square of window, whose shutters had been latched back to admit the morning light. It was six o'clock, and the street was awake; above the cheerful, rowdy shouts and clatter of shop fronts being let down, the bells of all the parish churches of London, within and without the walls, were ringing in limpid multitude for early Mass and the beginning of the day. The several reeks, flamboyantly mingled, of poultry and pigs and horse droppings, swill-brimmed ditches and somewhere a tanner's works, made Simon's countryman's nostrils twitch and himself to long for the clean, uninhabited places; then he looked again

255

at his father, watching and listening, and held his tongue. He made himself busy instead with the packs which contained their possessions; presently joining him, Philip unrolled a cloak and threw it across the bed. "You will need this; it is not warm in England, this time of the year." Simon remembered Maud saying much the same to him, the night he left White Ladies; he wondered why it was he must do so much of his traveling in this country in November.

The horses Philip had bought in Winchelsea were waiting saddled in the courtyard; they had no need of a sumpter with their few things. The hostelry keeper came out to bid them good-by, and have a last inquisitive inspection; as they rode out the gate they saw him still peeping behind the door. Philip looked thoughtful, and remarked to Simon, "You might be advised to put up your hood. London is not Paris; one may walk end to end of it in less than half an hour, and I should be surprised if Tyrell has given up yet. If there is one thing I remember of him, it is that he could hold on." He himself wore a peak-brimmed hat with a long, old-fashioned liripipe attached, which was wound about the lower part of his face, as it might appear, against the wind. The day was overcast and cold; by the time they had crossed Fleet Bridge and entered within London walls by Ludgate, a light snow was falling.

It lay like lace, and then like wool, clothing their shoulders and forearms and the fronts of their thighs where they were bent to grip the horses' flanks; atop Ludgate Hill it swirled about the tall tower of Saint Paul's, and the gilded weathercock which topped the steeple was hidden from sight. The street became thick with it, and passers-by muffled in their cloaks of red or blue or russet looked like figures from a book of hours against the white. Rows of skinners' and leather sellers' warehouses, of drapers' and mercers' establishments, gave way to rows of taverns and butcher shops and fish-mongers' stalls; at length Philip turned south down a way of handsome houses and fine inns where rich men dined, at whose foot ran the life of London, the river Thames. One crossed over by the Bridge.

Entry was by a square-topped stone tower with port-cullis gate; beyond, borne on a score of whitewashed pillars, was a double line of shops and houses, with pas-sage between as wide as a street. Over the tower gate a few staves leaned drunkenly, so long they had supported their burdens of rotting heads, but two stood upright which had been planted there yesterday. Simon glanced up unsuspecting, and checked violently, his hood falling to his shoulders; for he recognized the faces of John Atwater and the man who had been called Richard of York, picked blind by crows, their heads cocked waggishly on the spear points seeming as if they had been of amused, unreverend ancients with their snow-whitened hair.

It was a busy place, with carts and horses, traders and travelers, all coming and going, for the southern port roads began on the other side of the river, and South-wark borough spread its bank, larger than many a town. As Philip reined back to draw nearer Simon, a party of Scots clattered under the portcullis without looking up-ward, and passed on. Scotsmen were a not unusual sight in London nowadays, coming as members of delegations public or private to further negotiations for the marriage of King Henry's eldest daughter to King James, but Philip still found it hard to accustom himself to it. To Simon, who sat with his gaze immovable upon the sentinel grotesques above the battlements, he said calmly, "This is nothing to them now. Come, or your wife will be before you at Winchelsea."

He spoke low, but a lounging, woolen-capped individual in the shelter of the archway who had been watching every man on foot or horseback that passed beneath the gate turned as he heard. His eye falling upon Simon, he withdrew as far as possible into the shelter of the pillar, and waited only until the two were safely past him before making off down Fish Street to one of its larger inns. Simon had noticed nothing; Philip, glancing casually as they rode under the tower, observed as well as the shadow allowed that he was pockmarked about the face, and a gap in his teeth had been made good by a substitute member which had once belonged, from the look of it, to a sheep.

Once over the Bridge and through Southwark, they lost the feel of the city and of men. The road to Winchelsea was lightly traveled, hardly more than a path, for the town's great days as a port were done; if they had been making for Sandwich or Dover they would have journeyed in company perforce, but this narrow, winding way curved solitarily over the backs of the Downs, blanched silent reaches against which the leafless branches of each clump of whin or scrub showed like pen strokes. The day had brightened with clearing weather as they crossed Blackheath, and the track of the horses' hooves followed in sharp, undisturbed intaglio, like a signature in the snow.

They rode as briskly as the way allowed, although realizing it would only mean they must wait the longer for Maud and Françoise at Winchelsea, for Simon was restless to press on. The land rose, and dipped, and rose again in gentle undulations; one saw no more, descending, than the white line of the next hill shouldering the white morning sky. It was from such a hollow that Simon, going before, disappeared at a canter over the height ahead; all at once the drum of hooves ceased, and soundlessness followed, empty as the air. An instant later, unbelievably far, Philip heard the wild scream of the horse.

Before ever he gained the crest, putting his beast at the steep ascent with shortened rein and iron-clamped sides, Philip knew. The horse jibbed and fought the bit, as if in like apprehension of what was beyond; Philip forced it sliding and sidling up the slope to the narrow ridge where the path bent sharply with the spine of the hill, and the gem-cut print of his son's trail altered, becoming blurred and scuffed in the crumbling, frost-weakened shelf which marched to the edge of the cliff and there halted, dropping half a hundred feet to the peaceful farmland below. In a wind-filled drift under the face of the cliff the horse thrashed, half rose, and sank again; its rider lay some distance off, immobile across the rocky outcrop which thrust like a blackened tooth from the snow.

There were hand- and footholds down the cliff, making a descent of sorts for a man; it was quicker than searching for a place where the horse could go. The brittle chalk tended to give under pressure and come away unexpectedly, but Philip hardly noticed the sudden consequent wrenching of his muscles, the tearing of his palms;

if he could have managed such a scramble better twenty years ago, or even ten, now was not the moment to repine at it. From time to time, between the endless spaces while he slipped and leaped and clung, he glanced swiftly over his shoulder, but in the meadow below only the beast yet moved and cried; the man was still. The last dozen feet Philip took at a single slithering jump, for he had seen as he got nearer the brightness of blood.

It was coming from his head, a great shallow gash across the scalp where the stone had ripped it, for he had struck on his shoulder, and rolled on downward until the outcrop broke his fall; the churned snow was all spotted with red. His body lay on its side, but strangely, as if the bones that supported it had softened to gristle. Automatically noting, Philip felt down chest and thighs, and flexed the legs: one smashed shoulder, very bad; ribs, so far as he could tell, all sound; the right ankle, perhaps not. He understood something of bonesetting, like any man who has survived a cavalry charge and gone in search of his friends after; as for the head, there was no knowing, and no remedy beyond binding of the wound to wait and see. He looked again at his son's face, as calm as sleep, and could not even pray; over and over, like the tumbling circle of a millwheel, accusation repeated that it was himself who had been familiar with this countryside, and yet he had let Simon ride ahead while he indulged his own preoccupation with looking upon what Humphrey Talbot's blunt honesty, demolishing illusion, had made plain to him he would not see again.

Across the breadth of the field, the dark chimney of a little, snow-mounded house—it was hardly better than a shepherd's hut—put up a thread of smoke: the only sign, in the dead marble waste, of sense and warmth and life. He knelt, and having with care and enormous difficulty stood once more—for the weight he carried must be no less than his own—he began to walk toward it with his son.

They were farmer folk, Kentish smallholders of the kind that for generations had supplied the London market stalls: the goodman thick and grizzled, his wife older-seeming, with a lined colorless face. Hearing Philip call as he shouldered open the gate, they met him together in the yard and with shocked exclaimings urged him in. The house was built of clay and wood and thatch, single-roomed below with a loft ladder to the only bed, but the earthen floor had been freshly spread with clean wheat straw at harvest time, and the fire made it warm after the cold outside. While the husband raked up a blaze, his wife made a bed in front of it, using a spare pallet unoccupied since the death of the only son from sweating sickness two years ago; an aproned young woman, the daughter-in-law, who entered from the rear with a young child at her skirts and the litter of the back garden sty on her shoes, ran, at sharp command, to mull eggs and honey in ale. Philip heeded her no more than the rest, but when her haste at the cupboard having overtipped the ale jug, the dame cuffed and cursed her resoundingly for it, the noise roused him from his crouched silent absorption before the hearth, and he looked round as she fumbled sniffing with the flagon to say quietly, "There is no haste for the drink: he will do better not to wake until I am done." Her eyes changed as they encountered his, her working fingers ceasing to move within her skirt; but he had returned already to his task: patiently, more delicately than a lover uncovering, exploring, disposing, with never precipitancy nor hesitation, no matter in what dumb destroying agony the mind kept its watch above. The blood was staunched, the worst savagery of the shoulder accomplished, and still the firelight alone made movement in the unstirring face. At midday the family offered timidly the first bowl from their pottage and meat; he shook his head, only afterward recollecting himself to thank them. The farmer had gone earlier with his cowherd and a flesh axe, to dispatch the injured horse, and bring down its fellow into the byre.

A little past noon Simon opened his eyes, to find them on an elderly man with gray-streaked hair and flaccid shoulders, who sat brow on fist beside him upon a straw-covered floor. The man's head lifted when the pallet whispered, and he was looking at his father.

For an instant they only stared at one another; and then each in silence put out a hand. The weakness of Simon's own clasp was, he found, no less than that of the shaken fingers which returned it; before that white, ill face, which in a few hours appeared to have put on twenty years, the young man was as embarrassed as if he had looked where he had no right to see; yet each, by what he had read in the other's eyes, was made too both glad and shy. The family rustled like mice in the corners, peeping sideways or with alert bright stares; and Philip said, "You will be happy to know you are less damaged than you might have supposed. Some bones will be their own time, I should judge, about mending, also a cut on the head; but you have two whole legs still, and no worse than a pulled ankle underneath one of them. My congratulations."

He spoke lightly, as constrained as Simon by what relief had shown, and by the household all pretending not to hear; watching as he bent to do unnecessary things with the surplus bandages, Simon said, "The last thing I remember is trying to get free of the stirrups—*Peste*, I must learn to move again." He was strapped in linen from neck to waist; there were more bandages about his head, and one shoulder was like a rock, except that rocks are not commonly imagined to feel: this one had a core of flame. Like a dream whose horror cannot be dispelled with waking, recollection returned of the instant his horse's feet had left the edge of the precipice, and he saw the valley floor waiting to receive him. He lay still, regarding the timber gridiron of the ceiling beams; the fire burned low, having been made up with turf while the dinner caldron hung above it, and a fair young woman in the inglenook put from her knees the child she had been clasping to bring a drink of something strong-flavored and warm. Simon took what his stomach could endure, because she seemed kindly and solicitous to serve; when, wordless yet, she had withdrawn once more, he added to Philip, "I am admiring your forbearance, Monseigneur. This would not have happened if I'd better looked what I was doing."

Philip rejoined briskly, "You're likely wrong: they've been quarrying below that cliff, our host says, and getting nearer the road each year." The thin horn panes of the single window were growing lucent from a westerly sun; he glanced toward it, as if in calculation, and rising, reached for his cloak. To Simon's expression of surprise, he said, "There's half the afternoon left, and a village I'm told only an hour down the hill. You're going to need another horse, and we won't find it on a steading like this one: oxen plow as well, and salt down better at Saint Martin's. They'll attend to your needs here—I've settled for our keep—and don't be concerned if I'm not back until tomorrow morning: if it comes on to snow again I'll wait for a fresh light." He stood smiling down. "We'll finish the journey in three stages instead of one, and still make Winchelsea before Maud. Excepting only the matter of your bones, there's no harm done."

Outside in the yard, he noticed a thaw was setting in; already his footsteps of the morning over the field and through the gate had sunk to black earthen ovals in the melting snow. The hills looked blandly far; tomorrow, if Simon were up to it, should be riding weather. In his hopefulness at this he whistled softly as he mounted, and gently chirruping to his disgruntled horse, turned its head toward the gate.

Next morning broke clear and mild; all night the slush had been running off, and last season's old dead grass reappeared, a degree more pale. To Philip, who had slept after all in the village below—the estimate of an hour's ride had proved a genial country guess, and he had spent the failing minutes of last evening's twilight knocking up the blacksmith to ask a bed by his hearth—the farmhouse lay unfamiliarly disclosed: a neat habitation of men, no longer half hidden, secret and alien in the snow's obliterating waste. The yard was all soft trampled mud. He dismounted in it, and having thrown blankets over the horse that he had ridden and the purchased beast, left them both for stabling by the farmer's man, and went inside.

The room was empty. At first he saw only the vacated pallet, its coverings gone; only gradually the sense came over him of a place lately violated of its order, and, still more lately, in part restored. The goodwife's spinning wheel had been pushed to the wall, its spindle snapped from the frame; the wooden bread safe gaped, broken and rifled, and the cupboard in which the ale was kept. There was other less explicable damage too—charred shells of carved beechen bowls, still in the mess of the hearth; the slashed pallet leaking straw—as gratuitous and spiteful as a misbehaving child's.

Silence was all around, and yet someone minutes ago had added new wood to the unkempt fire; the sticks had just started to burn. He shouted, not knowing if he expected a reply; only quiet answered, split by the crash of the farther door as he threw it open to peer into the byre. When he swung back, moving at a run toward the ladder-stair, he nearly tripped over the two figures of a woman and child, risen hand in hand from behind the dismantled trestles and table board. Philip grasped her shoulders so she flinched; he almost asked, "What has happened?" except that in sober truth, but for the one stark essential he did not care. So he said it plainly instead, endeavoring to still his heart's thunder in his breast, "Where is the young man that was here?"

She was trembling and trying to conceal it so as to reassure the child, whom of a sudden she thrust behind her back: afraid, he now perceived, of his anger falling freshly upon the disaster which had preceded it. Her hands wrung and twisted in her skirt, even as yesterday;

she said, "They took him—they came near as soon as you had gone, they made him ride just like he was. They'd been following him, they said, all the way from London."

His fingers unloosed her shoulders; he looked beyond her, as still as at some unguessed-for news. But there is a scent to calamity which wafts before it; surely he had been prepared for this since first he halted within the door? Yet his soul entreated: Make it not to be. Gaining courage now he had not struck her, the woman talked on, describing all that had occurred; in a little while his ear began to discern, like a bird's thin crying through the tidal roar of the sea, a kind of rough concern, even of pity, in her voice. For form's sake he asked if she knew whether one of the men had been called Tyrell. But although she shook her head, unable to recall, there was no need she should tell him. The marks, the signs of it were everywhere.

With creaks and whispers, to the rustle of skirts and boots descending the ladder out of the loft, the remaining household was daring show itself again. The herdboy passed with scared solemn face on tiptoe toward the byre; the old woman began turning and examining the broken spinning wheel, repeating a gesture of bewilderment she had reverted to, at intervals, since Tyrell and his men departed, loudly jesting, the afternoon before. Her husband moved in slow reinspection about the room, muttering and shaking his head. "Four good bowls that I carved myself; all the bread, and what ale they couldn't swill down their gullets thrown on the midden. Was it my fault they came on the fellow here? I never told him to crack his head in my pasture—" The child whimpered and dragged at its mother's skirts, asking for food.

Dover, Philip was thinking, for the woman had heard that named for their destination; they must be nearly there now. After that, Calais and Guisnes Castle, where, once inside, no one walked out again without Sir James Tyrell's leave: doubtless a letter of notification was on its way back to London already for the house at Smithfield, to be held for Sir Philip Lovell upon his inquiry there. Tyrell should have waited at the farm another day, and saved both their pains. Had he not once wondered whose was the second horse he pursued?

His mind had cleared of its confusion; his course being plain to him, he was cheerful and at peace. To the mother, who had gone to pour out milk taken an hour earlier from the cow, he said, "The child is hungry. Have you any food but that to give him?" She smoothed the boy's hair and answered, "Meal for porridge, enough to do him. I'll go without myself until we bake; they didn't touch the flour." She looked at him across the leather jug, her arm around her son. "You don't grudge anything you can do, not when it's for your own." Suddenly Philip remembered her staring at him yesterday as he worked on his knees, ripping his shirt into bindings in front of the fire.

He was making ready to leave, for he had far to travel before he could sleep. As he turned to the door he took money from his purse, and laid it on the splintered cupboard; the topmost piece, he noticed, was of King Henry's new coinage, having a representation of Tudor crowned, with orb and scepter in his hands. Philip stood looking at it for a space before he disposed it with the rest. "No," he said, and with an openness which conceded understanding between them, he returned her smile. "Not when it's for one's own."

XIV

From English-held Calais on the coast of France to the
Duke of Burgundy's harbor town of Gravelines was an
afternoon's easy ride; from Guisnes Castle, one of the
ring of forts within the English Pale which guarded the
landward side of Calais, the old walled seaport just inside
the Burgundian border was hardly more. The burly horseman who approached Gravelines' west gate in the last
light of the day had ridden with confidence thereto over
the King of England's well-kept highway; short visits to
his homeland apart, he had lived in the Pale for fifteen
years, and its geography was more familiar to him than
the East Anglian village of his birth. The authority of
his manner made up for lack of retinue; the wardens of
the gate passed him respectfully, with hardly a question.
One of them, at least, knew him.

It was getting on for night; the air was salt, and, nearer
the harbor, odorous with herring and cod. The solitary
traveler, now afoot, trod the narrow twilit streets with
assurance—like most of his countrymen from the Pale, he

knew the place well, having passed through it often on the way to the sights of Antwerp or Bruges—while leading his horse; at this time of the day there were few persons abroad. Presently he began to go more slowly, checking frequently to wait and listen; in such an interval a boot struck the cobbles within the mouth of an alley he had just passed, and he wheeled, his hand at his thigh, saying softly, "Who is there?" Notably, in this Flanders town, he spoke in English. A silence answered, though in the shadow something stirred; he felt himself inspected and remained as he was, permitting it. He said, "You sent to me at Guisnes. I have come alone, as you asked."

"Yes, it appears you did. As a matter of fact, you were observed as you arrived, and by one that could not be bribed, or bullied either, to give a false report. You see, Tyrell, I remember you." The shadows moved again; a man came out of them, and halted before the Captain of Guisnes. He was hatless with his cloak over his arm, and one hand rested on the steel pommel of the short sword which was belted to his side. By his voice already Tyrell had recognized him, and stood without yielding a step; he had no need, and he knew it, to fear that blade. After an instant Philip added evenly, "You will understand, I am sure, the precautions. I have no wish to be escorted back into the King of England's territories by a party of your men—waiting, perhaps, in a boat offshore."

Relaxing yet another degree, Tyrell put up his brows; he was almost jocular. "What necessity for that? I expect you there of your own accord, soon enough."

It was becoming too dark to see; yet both strained toward it, trying to identify each in the other that object of visceral enmity or detached dislike which had been the man of fifteen years ago. In his slow, thorough mind Tyrell gave himself the pleasure of imagining what Philip Lovell was enduring now; but in this the dusk kept its secrets well. As familiar to him as defeat or hate, he felt once more that impression of patient searching, of intent and thoughtful scrutiny trained upon him as if to explore the very cause and essence of his being; and felt it burn again like a point of light. But he reminded himself that of the two of them, it was not Philip Lovell who could afford patience this time. He was confirmed in the opinion within moments, for when the level voice resumed, it was to both as if a limit had been passed.

"You are holding at Guisnes Castle a liege of Burgundy, Simon de Brezy, the lord of Saint Aubin: he is my wife's son. I am here to tell you that if he is not set free without harm and conducted to this frontier by this hour tomorrow night, the matter will be referred to the Duke of Burgundy for discussion with the English government. You would be wise to allow it to be settled now between ourselves; you have no grounds for detaining the lord of Saint Aubin, and if you continue to do so, you are going to be in worse trouble than the Duke of Suffolk caused you last summer by his visit to Guisnes."

"No grounds, have I?" Tyrell retorted, undisturbed. "You're badly informed. The lord of Saint Aubin—shall we call him your bastard, and shorten the argument by half a length?—has been caught out in conspiracy and treason, while living in England under English law. They take out your tripes at Tyburn for what he can be charged with: how long is it since you saw that done? And by the way, there's a witness to prove every word of it."

Philip said quietly, "On the contrary, you have no witness to support such an accusation. I spoke with Will Lovell in London yesterday, Tyrell: you did less successfully with my cousin Francis' son than you believed. He sailed last night from Dover, and henceforward will live very far from England, making his life over with the help of friends that mean better toward him than you ever did. You have no case without his testimony, and you know it."

It was the last try: the final vain attempt—automatic in reflex, foredoomed in its futility—to penetrate a mind which was like a doorless room. Tyrell rejoined grinning, "Then you'd better ask the Duke of Burgundy to send off his letter. I guarantee to hand over Master Simon when I'm told to—that is, what may be left of him. It will be some while, I should think, before the order gets to Guisnes." He added carelessly, "He'd a bad shoulder when we took him in Kent, did you know?—I think it's broken. Someone that he met on the road, he said, had been at the trouble to wrap it up for him: I've left the bandages alone, so far."

There was a short silence. Then, as colorless as the dusk in which they stood, Philip said, "It appears to be a question of price. Very well." A link boy passed with kindled torch, guiding a patron on his way; by its brief gliding flame Tyrell eagerly scanned his adversary's face, but the light reached no farther than cheek and brow; his eyes were dark. The twin scuffling treads resounding from the cobbled paving dwindled into echoes which sharpened with distance; they died, and Philip said, "There are certain conditions. I have affairs that must be settled: three days will suffice. Also, I want a physician admitted to Guisnes Castle who will report by courier to me as to Monsieur de Brezy's condition; you may claim he has been summoned upon your orders if you wish, and it will be to your purpose as much as mine if you say nothing of this transaction to Monsieur de Brezy. When a time has been appointed for his exchange, the physician will administer a drug by means of food or wine; I should prefer him to be brought out asleep, and I daresay you will find it convenient also." He was cool and businesslike. To all this Tyrell assented without demur; only now it was within his grasp did he realize how much he had feared, and was afraid still, that at the last the fellow would change his mind. As briskly as if they had been two trading partners, they concluded arrangements for communication and notification in case of delay; Tyrell allowed these as the other was disposed to order them, saying at intervals only, "Yes," or, "That will do." Never one given to introspection, he was yet puzzled by the flatness of the moment, as if the bloom of his pleasure had gone. He had craved the savagery of a fortress demolished under cannonade; victory would have been in a face of hatred. Instead he felt himself set by, like a phenonemon of nature which accident has flung in the way, to be considered, perhaps, after understanding has arrived of the ultimate results.

Evening was merging into night; the house walls steeply ascendant on either hand dissolved and vanished within the greater dark. In such obscurity a man's voice must represent the man, and this, Tyrell now realized, changed less with time than his outward form. The wet sea wind, the smell of the harbor and of salt reminded him that this was the Duke of Burgundy's town of Gravelines on the edge of the English Pale; but he stood again in Middleham courtyard in the Yorkshire dales, while Richard of Gloucester, the King's Lieutenant in the North, kept hall beyond the castle door. The man beside him at this moment was the person whom, second only to wife and son, Richard of Gloucester had most dearly loved: so dearly and openly that if either had been less manifestly what he was, they could not have escaped calumny. It spoke for both, that nobody had ever thought of it. Tyrell saw again the two heads bent over a problem of fortifications and supply, of border raids or fishgarths or the sensitive politics of the city of York. In those days Philip Lovell had been steward of the Duke of Gloucester's household, but it was not for that reason that when they talked withdrawn together, no others broke in.

Alone in his private darkness, James Tyrell passed his tongue in careful silence over the surface of his lips. So long ago the ground had been prepared, to which Buckingham, the knowing husbandman, had come to plant his seed. Far off a watchman cried the hour, with horn and lantern trudging his round; each of the two that heard him became aware, by the interval of quiet which had fallen between them, that their business was done. And so they parted without farewells, and went their differing ways.

Several days later, in the middle of the morning among the soft marshes between Gravelines and Saint-Omer, two men stood dismounted beside their horses. The flat treeless ground made it possible to see strangers approaching from a great way off; the only landmark was the tall stone cylinder of a windmill, too distant for the slow creak of its sails to reach their ears, but useful in designating a place to meet. The sky was hazy blue, with a diffused winter sun; a few gulls swooped crying. The two men stared west without speaking, until one of them shaded his eyes and said, "Here they come."

An ancient wooden bridge lying directly in front of them spanned the thread of a nameless stream, whose casual course across this stretch of plain defined, by local consent, the boundary between the Burgundian province of Flanders and the English Pale. As he moved toward it his companion burst out, "Monseigneur—!" He bit off the rest, clenching hands and jaw, as the other turning looked at him and said, "Hélie, remember. For a little while from today everything, everyone, must depend on you: my wife, my daughter who is your wife, Françoise and Maud, and until he is at peace with himself once more, Simon most of all. I have trusted you." Under his gaze the young man's mouth steadied; again advancing to the bridge, Philip rested his hand on the rotting baluster head and stood waiting.

Even so far away, Tyrell recognized him. Involuntarily he expelled a long-pent breath, and his square hands lost their tension on the reins; a moment later, lifting his brows in elaborate simulation of surprise, he glanced at the soberly gowned individual whose companion rode a half length behind him and remarked, "He's on time. And got only one fellow with him; I'd have thought our gentleman would have wanted as many to look on as he could find, to admire his nobility." He wet his lips with his tongue—it was a mannerism which, in the past few days, had become almost habitual—and added conversationally,

"I've hated him for near thirty years. If I'd known once this time would come, some things would have been different, maybe."

The physician set his mouth, and made no reply. He had been informed, of necessity, about most of the circumstances surrounding his commission to Guisnes, disliked everything he knew, and was convinced that the one party to the agreement was as loftily misguided as the other was surely mad. But his business had been confined by stipulation to the person he was to attend; the rest, my lord of Clairmont had given him strongly to understand, was none of his affair. Five years ago he had saved him from smallpox, and for this.

The cart squeaked and rattled behind him; the pallet covers rustled briefly as Simon de Brezy, lying in drugged, unquiet sleep, tossed and muttered with the bumping of the springless planks. He was, the physician reflected after an anxious look, about due to being to rouse, one could not keep a healthy young man unconscious forever, no matter how others might think themselves qualified to instruct the doctor in his trade. The troop of Tyrell's men rode easily at the rear, relaxed against the moment when the captain should require them; one of them wore slung on his belt a singularly handsome sword of Italian work, the ivory hilt inlaid with what looked like gold.

As they drew up on the margin of the stream, Tyrell's eyes searched beyond it to see if the man awaiting him would meet his gaze. A tall, fair youth beside him stared indeed, eyes blazing in a face of grief; but Philip Lovell was watching the cart. At his sign the physician got down heavily from the saddle, and walked over the bridge. "He will wake soon, Monseigneur. You have lodgings arranged?"

"Yes, in Saint-Omer. His wife is there, and Madame de Clairmont his mother too. I have received your messages, Maître Jehan: I thank you for them." Philip turned his head. The torpid channel at his feet was almost narrow enough here for him to have bestridden it; on the opposite bank, the keen morning light defining each pit and line of its weathered skin, he saw for the first time with clearness his enemy's face. Momentarily he was still, all movement seeming reduced to the single rapid pulse-beat at his temple, the breeze's mothlike stirring in a strand of his hair. Then he said, "Tyrell. Send the cart across, under guard if you prefer. When I have satisfied myself as to Monsieur de Brezy's condition, I will come over to you." When Tyrell made no immediate response, he added with sudden crispness, "In that mill you will see, which is not an impossible distance, there are men equipped with horses and crossbows. While we keep to our commitments, they remain there."

He had always assumed like measures on Tyrell's part, and was unsurprised when, broadly smiling, the other returned, "Two can think of that." He glanced over his shoulder, whereupon three of his men came forward. They were armed with arbalests, and each carried a steel-tipped bolt which without further instructions he proceeded to fit to his bow. The back of the cart, Philip now perceived, was open. Tyrell waited while his archers raised delicately the taut charged weapons and trained them, stocks to their cheeks; to the father then he said calmly, "At this range, they could not miss. If you do anything I don't care for, they are not going to." He nodded to the carter, who shook the reins. The horse roused itself; the iron-shod wheels, dislodged with a noise of sucking from the mud, revolved jerkily and resounded on the bridge.

It was true as Jehan had said, that the boy was waking. The bandages were as they had been tied: apparently the setting of the bones had been sufficiently approved by the physician for them to be left now to heal. Philip reached down his hand, making to restore the disordered clothes; although the heavy lids lifted, the eyes gazed cloudily with their shrunken pupils, betraying no knowledge, offering no sign. But, he remembered, this was as he had wished.

Hélie de Grandmont's big, capable hands lay by his own on the edge of the cart; his expression as he looked down at Simon revealed nothing. Philip said, "When he was taken in Kent, he told them it was a stranger who had ridden with him from London, that he had hired on promise of money to point out the road. So Tyrell didn't wait, and took Simon with him on to Guisnes." He sent his fingers on the young man's moveless ones. "Don't let him grieve. You had differences once, but they are reconciled already, I believe, for him."

With such ordinariness that the significance of the gesture was nearly lost, he took off the foreign Burgundian chain of knighthood from around his neck, and from his belt the steel-pommeled Antwerp sword. These articles, after an instant's pause, were given without comment to Hélie; then drawing the horse's reins through his arm, he walked across the bridge into the Pale.

XV

That afternoon the wind changed to blow straight off the sea. It held so, with never an hour when a ship could put out for England, through seventeen days.

The towers of Guisnes Castle had cells high in their turrets, and others to which, even from the ground, one took a downward stair. One of these last Tyrell identified, with heavy wit, as the salle de Clairmont, remarking as a guard unslipped the bars that the apartment would have been in better readiness if they had received more warning of the guest. It was a round lightless pit with a grill in the ceiling which could be lifted for descent by ladder from the chamber above; entry had been originally down a stairway from the low outside door, the place having been meant in the beginning for stores, but this usage had been discontinued when decaying masonry began to let in the damp, and the floor now was never dry.

For the first hours, the greatest evil was the dark. The room above being windowless too, afternoon passed indistinguishably into night; the only sound was the chink of the iron chains rattling between hands or feet when he moved, and the soft wet trickle of the invisible sweating walls. Being cold, he tried to walk, counting the paces from one side to the other, or fumbling for a recognizable notch in the stone from which he could reckon his constricted steps. By and by he became thirsty, and then hungry, but when some time next day food and drink were brought, his stomach revolted from what the flickering torch of the guard displayed; he took only the water, in which scum was floating, and that because he knew he must drink what they gave, or seek moisture like an animal with his tongue in the midden about his feet. It was two days more before he discovered what his body could be made to accept for food, because there was nothing else. Racking pains began, surges of nausea and a worsening bloody flux; for long intervals he would crouch with his face in his hands, stifling the groans while spasm after spasm ripped his intestines as with knives. In respites between, when exhaustion lay heavier than the reeking, miasmatic dark, pictures of his life drifted and flashed like cracks in blackness; as a dream he remembered Gerard David and his world of light. He was convinced that whatever Tyrell had once planned or hoped to gain with him, it was no longer his intention that he should leave this place alive.

For Tyrell came each day. Like a close brooding chamber which transmutes the materials of life, that fetid pit held the conditions to change a man, and he did not mean to deny his eyes a single stage of the progression. It was as if a fearful compulsion drove him to seek with taunts or blows some response upon which

279

an ancient hunger still might feed; this Philip recognized, but knew no words to answer it. All his will was bent now to preparing his soul for death.

One morning very early the crash of the grill above his head started him from a kind of sleep. One of the warders clambered yawning down the ladder; at his belt, instead of the usual bucket in which the day's food arrived, there were some implements that clinked together as he moved. Without explanation, with no more remark than whispered cursing at an intractable shackle bolt, he hammered the irons from the prisoner's wrists and ankles; as he finished, the outer door was thrown open, and Tyrell appeared with two more guards at the head of the stair.

He came down with his heavy tread, and halted at the foot. The chill air of dawn flowed after him, a clean current unmixed with the swamp of the cell; outside, a waking bird chirped softly. In the gray thief-light the sick man's wrists were raw and festering, his lips within the unshaven beard cracked from thirst; the only sound was the harsh pant of his breathing as he held himself on one elbow, his gaze never leaving Tyrell's face. In his eyes, near black in their wasted hollows, Tyrell saw like the writing upon a palimpsest, brutally and imperfectly scraped, what had looked at him these seventeen days at Guisnes, what he had first seen across the steward's chamber at Middleham almost thirty years ago. Of a sudden his thick mouth wrenched as if in ungovernable passion; his hands clenched on the cross-piece of the sword. Then stepping back, he jerked his head at the door.

The astonishment of light, the blinding impact of

dawn's pale breaking upon eyes long kept from sight of day, were to Philip as great a violence as the guards' mishandling on the stair. A sweet cool rain like gossamer brushed his forehead; across the courtyard there were horses saddled, toward one of which he was roughly thrust. The wind had changed, someone said, and at Calais harbor a ship was waiting to carry him to England.

So after all, roped wrist and boot to his horse, with clothes sodden upon his skin from the subtly fingering rain and the voice of James Tyrell nearing and fading at his ear, Philip Lovell rode once more over the Kentish Downs to London.

He had been condemned by attainder before he fled England years ago; he learned now that sentence was to be pronounced upon him by a whole commission of judges and peers. For this a week's preparation was required, and in that time his abused body began a slow progress toward recovery. His room in the Tower was dry, and had been fine once with its own hearth and privy, and a mural above the fireplace of saints and shields of arms, now mildewed with age; he had a straw bed and a table, and there was even a window from which he could look down on the moat of the outer ward, and see the swans. He had been granted, it seemed, a royal bounty for the period of his imprisonment, which though frugal in King Henry's accustomed style, was enough to buy food and washing water and a little fire, and to replace with cheap frieze the rags of his clothes. The Lieutenant of the Tower came to apprise him courteously of the place and time of his summons before the commission, and to say that leave had been given for him to attend Mass in the prisoners' chapel if he so wished. The guards who walked on either side of him to this service each morning were civil too, although with covert glances when they supposed him unnoticing, and several times as he stood at his prison window he saw people clustered on the causeway below, pointing and gazing upward. It was a while before he realized they were staring at himself.

At length in the cool of a December noon he stood again beneath the big outer gate, and the Lieutenant offered him the warmth of a cloak, for he was to go on foot across half London for sentencing. The citizens stood shoulder to shoulder along the route to watch him pass; some whose faces he even thought he could remember called out encouragement or sympathy, or like old friends simply shouted his name. Always he answered carefully, telling them the King meant nothing for him but justice, and justice, he said, he had no more cause to fear than they.

In spite of Tyrell, notwithstanding Humphrey Talbot's gloom, he had never persuaded himself that Tudor desired his death: too few had suffered so for having fought at Bosworth, and he had been besides among the least-hated of King Richard's servants. Today on the bench of judges under the carved Guildhall beams he saw one face he knew well: the Roman coin profile and self-possessed, bulbous eye of Tom Howard, Earl of Surrey, who with his father had commanded King Richard's van at Bosworth, which nearly cracked Tudor's line. Surrey had paid with years of attainder and imprisonment for it; others had been punished in like fashion, or by crippling fines—a system which for a liege of Burgundy,

Philip was aware, could have led to complications, had he not been sure that this time neither Philippe of Burgundy nor his father Maximilian would make the slightest difficulty in whatever Henry Tudor chose to do. (A dozen years since Maximilian of Austria and Philip of Clairmont stood face to face in the grocer's parlor at Bruges: not five, since Maximilian sent young Simon de Brezy upon adventure in the law's and Philip Lovell's despite. Had he not once looked back to wonder what might come of it? Most likely not: he had kings and queens to treat with, and crowns to think of, now.)

The afternoon was heavy with overcast; inside the hall the warm light of candles inlaid deep shadows among the high roof beams, and touched waveringly the shields and gilding and colored window glass, the splendid robes of the commissioners and steel-tipped halberds of the guards. The judgmatic Howard gaze dwelt briefly upon the man before the bar, wrapped in a remembered tranquillity and the folds of the Lieutenant's cloak, and lifted even more briefly to the unreadable face. Unmoving, they regarded each other; but Surrey's function, like that of all his fellows on the bench save one, was merely to support by his attendance the procedures of the King's justice: then or later, he did not speak. It was the presiding commissioner's voice, as impersonal and astonishing as winter cold, that Philip shortly heard pronouncing upon him sentence of death by beheading. Execution would take place in three days' time on Tower Hill; the King, he was told, of his special mercy had waived hanging and dismemberment.

Outside, people who had waited for the news pressed so close the guards were obliged with shoulders and weapons to clear a path. Those citizens who stood nearest passed the word to their neighbors, so the whisper traveled east along The Poultry and Cornhill with the warders' slow tread; a few, Philip perceived with remote surprise, wept as they heard. At the Lion Gate there was a check while the drawbridge was lowered, and his keepers, alert, clustered near; all at once a clatter of hooves sounded, and some horsemen came riding down from East Cheap led by a boy not ten years old: a big-boned, copper-haired lad with the pink and white skin of a dairymaid, and wide pale eyes—even so far, Philip saw his eyes. It was the King's second son, Prince Henry, like any mischievous schoolboy stolen from Westminster to catch sight of King Richard's famous friend. For an instant he sat with head flung back, the long athlete's bones of his legs clamping the restless horse, staring through the crossed spears of the guards; he was composed and bright-eyed, curious only to see a man whose name he knew, out of a time that had passed before he was born. The wind whipped his red hair under the feathered cap; he wore a green and white tunic with hose particolored the same, and on his breast a great medal with the device of England: God and my right. The bridge groaned down, ponderous in its counterweights; suddenly he said something across his shoulder, whereat his companions laughed. Then they all clapped spurs to their horses and galloped off down the street, their felt cloaks and dagged harness leathers flying scarlet under the iron sky.

In his high prison room Philip stood once more at the window overlooking the moat, and heard the Lieutenant, after changing feet for some moments in the door, go without speaking away. The key turned with a rattle;

the warders' voices dwindled, drifting wayward as smoke up the stair from the guardroom below; the afternoon, which had been but half gone, seemed to darken even as he watched, so rapidly the day fled from him to its close. But that, he supposed, must be the inevitable illusion of men in his state. A chill wind slipped around the window bars, slyly winnowing so the strawings rustled between the table legs, and piled in drifts against the splayed bench ends of the single seat; it was the time of year when at Clairmont they brought in huge logs for the hearth, or lit fires of sea coal that burned with a green and turquoise flame. His wife's face passed before his eyes, smiling and tender; he smelt her hair. Sharply breathing, he laid his head on his arms across the scratched and dented table, and so sat until night.

Daubeney came two days later, well on in the afternoon. Riding in front of his servants along Tower Street, he saw on his left, in a broad open space of rising ground just north of the Tower curtain, a weather-bleached platform spread thickly with fresh new straw; bare wooden rails enclosed it, that would be draped next morning in solemn black, and at the top of the steps, carelessly set, was a basket large enough for a woman to carry to market, into which a man working by himself was measuring clean sawdust. His mouth setting, Lord Daubeney went on; the Lieutenant was waiting at the gate, and bowed him in.

It was approaching the hour when a keeper would bring the late-day food; Philip hardly roused at the clashing of the lock. But there followed neither step nor chink of keys, and he turned at length from the window, frowning as his eyes left the sunset dazzle to seek out and arrest upon the man who stood alone just inside the door. As if in doubt, he said slowly, "Giles Daubeney?" He appeared nonplussed by surprise, or the reclaiming of his thoughts; in a minute visibly bestirring himself, he came toward the visitor with outstretched hand. "Giles, I'm sorry. It must be I was wandering, I hadn't expected anyone, and it's been many a year—Man, come in."

He thrust forward the stool. Daubeney said hastily, "No need of that, for me. You should sit yourself, Philip, I hear you've been ill—" He had looked, because he could not help it, at the black scabby rings like bracelets about the other man's wrists; Philip saw the glance, and as he walked back to the window drew down the cuffs of his shirt. "A remembrance," he said, "from half a month at Guisnes, which I daresay was no worse than what Warbeck experienced hereabouts for better than a year. I saw him die at Tyburn: it was like a beast, or a shell."

The sky behind him was cool blue, in which a vein of scarlet was growing. Thinned to ghostliness, his face against it expressed a tense and deadly passivity; his eyes in their darkened circles were bright as from fever, but very steady and clear. Lord Daubeney, committed to an embarrassing errand, found himself unable to meet those eyes. From the Tower's inner ward a bell began to sound the curfew upon which the gates were shut, its deep bourdon reverberating outward like rings in water; a horseman belatedly departing thundered beneath the gate arch out over the causeway; someone shouted, and the portcullis crashed down: common noises all, for the man who would be alive to hear them again tomorrow night. His lips tightly compressed, Daubeney paced the room; without looking up or checking in this movement, he said, "Philip, the King neither desires nor intends your death."

What reaction he expected he did not in fact know, being unaware how much his voice had already betrayed. But a long silence answered; ending it, Philip said with a mildness that had an edge, "Excuse me, then, for misunderstanding him. He is late to tell me so."

Doggedly persisting, Daubeney rejoined, "He is telling you now. He knows you, by repute, and that is in your favor; also he takes no pleasure in needless spilling of blood. He has never wished you to die for an offense committed so long ago: an offense moreover which has been forgiven many others—I have his leave to say so much—of less worth."

"Giles—" Philip spoke softly, his hand gripping the window ledge he sat on so the fingers' cartilage cracked. "Giles, I have had merchant dealings before today. What is it I have to sell, that your King would buy?"

They had known each other more than twenty years. Immobile against the room's farthest wall, his thin, slope-profiled countenance reddened by distaste of his commission, by the comprehension of that intent, exploring scrutiny and the sunset's furnace glare, Daubeney said, "He desires your testimony, before witnesses, that the two children King Edward's sons were put to death in the Tower in the time of their uncle King Richard's reign, and that those murders were performed by King Richard's clear and absolute command."

"Ah!" Philip leaned back slowly. He fell quiet, revolving it in his mind. "Well, I see his need: Warbeck was only the latest illustration of it. And it's true enough that young Perkin was an imposter; by chance quite latey I had confirmed to me what I had long believed, that soon after their uncle's crowning, the true princes died. Now I realize how useful the proof of this would be to King Henry, and he may hear all I know with my good will, except I cannot credit that I have one fragment more of information than the King himself has had this very great while. None but a man as insanely gullible as the murderer—need I name him to you, Giles? —could imagine the crime was traceable only so far as Buckingham, a gentleman never famous for holding of his tongue, and yet no farther, to himself." As Daubeney stood rigid, the gentle humanity of his face transformed to stone, the meditative, equable voice went on, "Morton, who was Bishop of Ely then, had the Duke of Buckingham's confidence to the end, and stands now at King Henry's right hand. Am I to presume the good bishop never told his new master what Buckingham told him? Acquit me, please, of being an entire fool."

He ceased. Morton: Buckingham: Tyrell—the last name hung unspoken in the silence of the little shabby room. There was scant need, even as Philip had said, for him to utter it. Giles Daubeney, Chamberlain to King Henry and a man of integrity and compassion, knew his duty and proceeded with it, saying brusquely, "We are far from my business here, Philip. The concern is this, that if you bear witness as set down for you, your sentence of tomorrow morning will be remitted."

"I am unlikely to have forgotten it. But you know as well as I that King Richard did not command his nephews' deaths."

288

"Your opinion in this is not required."

"I know that too. Can you tell me then, since we have the sow finally by her proper ear, why Tudor, having waited so many years for this, has devised it now for me?"

Upon that, at last, Daubeney faltered. He started to walk about again, paused, and shifted feet so as to avoid the pitiless gaze. Presently he muttered something about "known probity," and "unimpeachable testimony, coming from the late King's dearest friend." He was honest enough to look ashamed, seeing irony in the other man's eye, and after a moment Philip said dryly, "I see."

He rose and took a turn about the room, halting briefly by the table where Daubeney now saw, beside a pen and stand of ink, a folded paper tied with a thread; then, going back to the window, he stood looking out. Evening was near; the vein of scarlet had become a vast streaming fissure, and the sky was as if charged with blood. He said, "And if I swear, what then? Am I to have my life, and freedom too?" Daubeney responded with briskness, the worst being done, "I am empowered to guarantee it: not immediately, but very soon. You are not yet so old as to set no value on your further days—"

He was unaware by what sound or gesture he was interrupted, so that the words which would have followed quenched on his lips: only in some fashion it was made plain he had said all that was essential to his meaning, and that it was enough. Nor could he tell, despite his straining to read what was visible of Philip Lovell's face, whether it had had any effect upon him, or if so, of what sort. Time passed; at length turning, Philip went to the table and picked up the thread-secured paper, holding it in both his hands. "Giles, I've been wondering how this could be sent, and if there were a way I might feel assured it would reach—the person for whom it is meant. Will you be responsible that it is dispatched beyond seas? It is a letter," he glanced down at it briefly, "for my wife."

He held it out. Speechless, Daubeney allowed himself to accept the sheet; it was the confirmation of its texture crumpling in his grasp which impelled him finally to say, "I cannot believe I understand you." His fists were clenched as though they gripped a weapon; Philip apprehended his anger, and looking him in the face replied gently, "My old friend, among all those still living in England that I know, I had presumed you the one that could."

"But—!" Daubeney shook his head; he seemed dizzy, and took one hand from the letter to drag his fingers through his hair. "Philip, you have no choice. I understand your reluctance, indeed I honor it, but no one could possibly blame you. . . ." He felt resourceless, like a fish in air. "Come, be sensible. You have no choice."

"With respect, Giles: being a free man I do, and I have King Henry to thank for teaching me the value of my estate. I doubt he ever meant to supply so clear a demonstration of it." His patience was like a rock; Daubeney discovered rage mounting to be so borne with, and spoke quietly, having mastered it.

"Philip, reflect a little. This kind of scruple might do well enough for some, but we both know, you and I, the way great decisions are taken, and the alternatives to—intelligent policy. See now: the more that simple folk are taught King Richard was an evil king, the more content will they be with him they have now in King Richard's room, and from this contentment will derive our English peace. You have often shown yourself a man concerned for the land's—the people's—good. You should put aside considerations of friendship and your personal honor, and have regard for larger things."

"*Raison d'état,*" Philip remarked; for an instant Daubeney even thought he heard amusement in his voice. "Well, I've met the proposition in King Edward's time, although in those days we were still inclined to look across our shoulders while we argued it, out of respect for what God might be thinking too. Nowadays we have got more bold, one encounters the doctrine everywhere . . . Men being as they are, it will be a good while probably, maybe even a few hundreds of years, before they stop and look around again, and see where *raison d'état* has brought them." He was silent for a time, the only sound the swift, light whisper of his breath. "What is it? Am I to love my life so greatly, in your view, that there must be nothing I will not do to preserve it? That indeed were to become the slave of every man. And a slavery suffered all in vain, seeing that at best your King and you can offer me no more than this: that I die not tomorrow, but another day."

Twilight had fallen, assuming within itself those shadows where the flesh of his cheeks and jaw had sunk beneath the firm spare planes of the facial bones; his eyes were like mouths of caves, a profounder dark. Yet Daubeney saw with astonishment that all was said, and nothing remained which could cancel it. Momentarily he stood unmoving, his long serious face bent in trouble above the letter in his hand, feeling over words as if they had been so many keys, one of which he was still persuaded must open for him. But they had become strangers with no common tongue, who must speak their innermost thoughts in translations whereby half the sense is lost. He remembered their first meeting, in Calais Castle the summer of King Edward's war; he had been only young Master Daubeney of Somersetshire then, whom someone more influential led along the tables after supper to present to Sir Philip Lovell, the Duke of Gloucester's friend.

He pushed the letter in his belt, and turned to beat on the door to bring the guard. As the lock grated and the invading torches streamed in, he said, "They will know below where I lie tonight. If at any time before morning you should reconsider—"

Philip shook his head. He asked after an instant, "Shall I have a priest?"

"The Lieutenant's chaplain—" Helpless, Daubeney added, "It's a poor creature," and was surprised by a flickering smile. "Are we not all of us, before God?"

Their eyes met. Almost Giles Daubeney found himself refusing the offered hand; but it would be improper, as well he knew, to maintain anger with a man so near the heavenly judgment, whose soul moreover required now not the censure of the faithful, but their prayers. So after all he clasped it, and without speaking again followed the guard downstairs.

Night came. The Tower swans slumbered among their reeds; downriver at Greenwich, King Henry received an equerry of Lord Daubeney in his bedchamber as he was undressed, and having bade his gentlemen good night retired behind the drawn curtains of the bed to lie awhile, staring with fixed impenetrable eyes before he slept; elsewhere in the palace Daubeney himself searched out work unregarded for days or weeks, and labored feverishly over it until the candles guttered; kindled new ones, and sat at length with hands idle on the parchments, watching the shrinking flame. In the east of Europe daybreak glimmered; there were Turkish spears on the Acropolis, and from his Austrian hunting lodge Maximilian set forth with blowing horns to chase the chamois into the Tirol snows. London was dark yet upon its river, smoothly flowing toward the sea. It was a long way now from its beginnings, being so near the end; far upstream in the amber stone villages and gentle hills the springs rose: a clear face silently welling among the white-stemmed grasses of the water meadow; a tiny trickle coursing from stone to stone, pebble dislodging pebble, stream emptying irreversibly into stream, until fresh currents met with salt and a ship could ride upon them to the sea.

In the prison room above the moat, the guard at his departing had left a lantern, whose failing radiance shone yellow on the dim painted figures of the chimney breast, on the man's body stretched moveless on the pallet, and his wide watching eyes. He could not guess how long it was since compline had rung, nor how many hours remained to him until dawn; the candle when it died left only the black window cleft to read, pricked with unknowable stars.

Last night he had dreamed he was with Meg again. If he had not gone to Bruges, if someone else had been the burghers' messenger, if on a summer night he had not lain down with his beloved, Erard de Brezy's wife, to beget his son . . .

She had been his life's great passion, for love of whom he had committed his life's most grievous sin; and even now he could not wish the thing to have never been, though his soul should be redeemed thereby from its offense. *They say that Paradise and Calvary, Christ's Cross and Adam's Tree, stood in one place* . . . His eyes strained through the blackness as if in question. About lauds, he slept.

the maneuver required charting; meantime Empson, who had never taught himself to accept a snub, went unregarding on. "I had expected you to be present, my lord; it was my impression a few years ago that Sir James was not your especial friend. Well, he has had his deserts. One might have supposed that to be involved once with Suffolk, and emerge scatheless, would provide adventure enough, but the man seems to have lacked the simplest will, afterward, to seek safety in disassociation from the Duke. Almost to the end, it's said, he believed himself to be charmed against the King's anger, being persuaded he had been so good a servant, in some particular, that not a doubt could touch him. A curious delusion for a man to harbor who had survived four reigns, but experience did not teach him, apparently, how to read his prince."

Stiff with discomfort, Daubeney was striving by sheer unresponsiveness of posture to force de Puebla aside; it was his companion, the Burgundian knight, who filled the silence, saying, "Clearly, it did not. A misfortune that the gentleman was so late in finding his error out." Something in his voice made de Puebla look sharply at him, but the courtyard was hushing so the gilded vanes that whirled above the towers were plainly to be heard, and seizing his chance, Daubeney took hold of the visitor's arm. "Monsieur," he said, "here is the King." Behind them, and to the farther gate, stretched a billow of bending necks and shoulders; advancing through the wave was a slender man with bony haggard face and lean chest which seemed almost hollowed by the weight upon it of an ornately jeweled collar. His eyes finding Lord Daubeney, he turned slightly toward him, and the Chamberlain said kneeling, "Your Majesty, the lord of Saint Aubin, Simon de Brezy, emissary from the Most High Prince Philippe of Burgundy, with letters for your hand."

It was Simon's impression, as he waited on his knees for the King's greeting, that Henry was being an uncommon length of time about giving it. Well, he had not asked, himself, to be sent on this errand, and his reasons for accepting it had nothing to do with his liege's duty to the Duke; King Henry, if he found himself discomposed by the sight of Simon de Brezy at his court, was welcome to tell Philippe of Burgundy so, and explain it how he wished. But the spare, cold hand with its delicate fingertips moved forward at last, emerging from the black hanging sleeve, and when he had kissed it, Simon said, "Your Majesty, I bring a letter from my lord the Duke of Burgundy, expressing his true sorrow at the death of the Prince of Wales your son. I was to say for him too, that as he is himself a father, he is as well able as any man living to comprehend the fullness of your grief."

He offered the roll, extended on his palms between the thrown-back folds of his black cloak sewn with pearls. Politeness, and his own inclination, made him now raise his head, his eyes meeting the sunken ones of the King; they were still, gazing at each other across the scroll. Then Henry said, "I am obliged to my good cousin, the Duke of Burgundy. Though it has pleased God to take from me in two years two of my three sons, yet I am consoled, tell him, by that son who is left me, the prince Henry, England's undoubted heir."

He took the letter—there were veins like conduits on the backs of his hands, and his nails, Simon saw, were blunted with gnawing—and turned it a little, back and

300

forth. It was remarked that of late the King had aged; some people believed this dated from the time nearly three years ago when he had signed the warrant for the young Earl of Warwick's death; however that might be, he was not the man whom Simon had once come to London to get a pardon from, and ask leave of to live awhile in England with his bride. If this was what it cost to keep a crown, then King Richard when he fell at Bosworth had been the luckier one. These reflections were perhaps too plainly to be read in the younger man's face; it was possible too that the unindulgent self-command of Henry Tudor's lifetime was affected yet by the disaster, so lately fallen, of his eldest son's death: not ten days had passed since "the rose of England," the hope of Henry's house, had been laid in his grave. For as he gestured finally for Lord Daubeney and Philippe of Burgundy's envoy to rise, he said in his suave, cool voice, "Monsieur de Brezy, it is long since we had the pleasure of receiving you at this court. You have been less time than that, however, out of remembrance, since not three years ago you wrote a letter to Lord Daubeney, concerning—if I recall correctly—certain processes of our justice here in England, with which you were not in accord. Two letters, now I think of it."

"One only, your Grace," Simon replied evenly. Of all the eventualities he had fancied might arise from this unwanted mission, here was the least believable and most gross. He stared up into the unblinking hooded eyes, and anger trembled in him like a coiled spring, straining toward release; he said, "The other was a blank page, signed with my name, for Lord Daubeney to write above it what terms you would accept, or what fine you would name, for discharge of a prisoner then in England. I was sorry that I was obliged to send a messenger: I would have come myself if I had been able."

"Ah yes, I have it now. But you must realize it was no matter for fines: we have our statutes, and the penalties for their violation are strictly set. It would have been improper to have pardoned for money or conditions a felon already sentenced under law." He brought this out with unimpaired composure, steadfastly regarding the other's face; Simon did not know why Lord Daubeney of a sudden flushed dark red, and looked at the marble paving stones. Faintly smiling, Henry added, "Well, it was a saving for your purse. You must be a rich man, monsieur: or else a very incautious one." Simon answered as if it were another person he heard, "As to that, sir, it seems I was not rich enough."

The pause this time was the King's. Simon saw Empson's mouth fall open, and knew he should be concerned by rights for the Duke of Burgundy's trade agreements. These, however, he reckoned to be safe; and for the rest, he judged it sufficient achievement that his hands had not reached forward of themselves to take the King of England by his skinny throat. He heard again his steward who had been his messenger to England, rain-drenched and stinking of his horse, stammering with tears the bare, deadly news; once more imagination pictured the winter sky white above Tower Hill, the bloody lifted blade. He said to himself, Some things are too dearly bought. I did not ask—I never wanted he should pay such a price. Who can tell what value may be in it, that which he saved? He was twice the worth of me.

Henry was speaking again, as contained as rock. He

said, "You have leave, sir." His expression as the younger man rose to his feet, bowing hat to knee, had become nonetheless first absent, and then reflective; he began to walk slowly on, and halted after a few paces, saying across his shoulder, "Master de Puebla—?" The little doctor bobbed and beamed, and limped forward delightedly at the King's sign; his salary from Spain was always late, and there was a free supper in Henry's eye. The King leaning lightly on his arm, they passed together beneath successive arches of raw new brick or gilded wood, while Henry spoke leisurely and indifferently of this or that, and the court trailed discreetly behind. On the threshold of the chamber of presence with its walls new-painted in white and blue, Henry asked, "And were you in London today, Doctor?" De Puebla shook his head, glancing sideways; the King, he knew, was well aware he had been at Richmond, having given him good-day only that morning as he came from Mass in the palace chapel. "I mean," Henry pursued, staring at the breadth of limewash and azure checkering handsomely embellished with portcullises and roses, "at Tower Hill? You will have known Sir James Tyrell was to suffer there."

"Indeed, sir, I had heard." The Spaniard cast down his eyes. He had been fifteen years in England, and affinity of temperaments had made of him and Henry Tudor as near cronies as their situations allowed; he knew an introductory note when it was sounded. Sighing, Henry said, "It was long before I could be convinced of his malice. He had served me well, or so I believed; when Nanfan at Calais swore that Sir James Tyrell was trafficking still with Suffolk, the greater traitor, it seemed to me the whole world must be false if Tyrell was. Yet I did not know then the half of his villainy." He turned and raised his voice, addressing the throng of attentive faces behind. "For only last night, seeing he must die and there was no remedy, he told Master Lieutenant at the Tower that he himself had been sent by King Richard in the same summer when that King was crowned, to dispatch to their deaths those blameless innocents King Edward's sons; and this, with only one servant to help him in it, he had done. Such a man, lords, was the man I had cherished and lifted up, all unknowing, for near twenty years."

A startled silence followed. De Puebla, whose mouth had flown open, was by reason of this unable to comment at once, but Empson in a moment rushed in. "And great reward he doubtless had of that foul prince, his late master Richard, for it. Why, your Grace, what need have you to mourn the loss of such a servant? Rather you should be glad the truth is known at last of the children's end. Here's a finish to those young men who would claim to be one of them, and so trouble your Grace's peace; copies of Sir James' confession, sent abroad to the princes of Europe, will ensure that no more like Warbeck arise . . ."

"Indeed," said de Puebla blandly, "my master the King of Aragon would be very interested to see a copy." A little smile had begun to flicker about his mouth; the King's eyes swerved to his face, then dropped again in contemplation of his nails. "Unhappily," he said, "in the confusion and distress of the time, Master Lieutenant neglected to have Sir James' words written down, or to secure a witness to them. Only this afternoon, when Sir James was already dead, was the report of his confession brought to me. A foolish mishandling of the event, but the gentleman cannot, unfortunately, be called back to life to testify once more. Doctor de Puebla, do you sleep here tonight, I shall have letters for you tomorrow for Spain . . ."

They strolled on, and the doors of the privy chamber closed after them. In the silence which attended their depature, Simon heard a whisper behind him, "So much for Tyrell, the useful man. It must be something to serve one's prince better after death than when one was alive . . . Doubtless we shall hear next that Master Lieutenant mistook where Sir James told him to dig for the bones." Someone replied softly, "Well, it's at least as reasonable as that story three years ago about the Earl of Warwick being executed for conspiring against the government, when everyone knew the poor wittol couldn't have told a church by daylight. Now there was murder for you, all under law." "He was King Edward's brother's son, and the King of Aragon refused to send his daughter to marry the Prince of Wales while there were any of *those* left around. He was probably wise in his estimate too. The good of the state, my dear fellow: one must have the balanced view." They moved off.

Simon said, "You are not well, Lord Daubeney?" He could not keep a dryness from his voice; and certainly the Chamberlain's face when he lifted it was both tired and sick. But he said after a moment, "My lord Saint Aubin, the King has commanded me to be your escort and attendant for the period that you are in England. Apartments have been made ready for you and your servants, and I am so charged that, should there be anything you require, you have but to ask."

He spoke calmly, a great officer doing his duty in his master's court; if he had had thoughts of his own an instant since, he had put them by; yet Simon was aware of something in his voice still, as indeed he had been aware of it ever since King Henry's Chamberlain, advancing to greet the Burgundian envoy outside Richmond gate, had been apprised of that envoy's name. The room recovering from its hush had begun to buzz with comment, wary or inquisitive or amused; far down the hall the King's servants were spreading the high table for supper, while courtiers passing the outer door peered hopefully in at their proceedings, and either lingered or went hastily on. They seemed to Simon distant figures, as small and quaint as if viewed through a far-held optic glass: Maud and Françoise waiting at Saint Aubin, and his little son Philip, now almost three years old, were more immediate and real than these busy, hurrying folk. Daubeney was talking on, mentioning some ceremony of formal welcome for the Duke of Burgundy's emissary tomorrow; he ended on a pause, having no more words with which it could be filled, and they looked at each other. Then Simon said, "Sir, these are courtesies enough. If you are surprised to see me here today, you cannot be more so than I should have been myself at it a month ago; and I am not here now for the Duke of Burgundy's sake, who in other circumstances I would have thanked to send someone else on his errand, instead of me. Three years ago, not quite, my mother the lady of Clairmont had a letter out of England, carried by your messenger and enclosed in another written by yourself . . . May we walk apart?"

He wondered for a minute if he had been properly

heard, for Daubeney only stood gazing down the room without reply; at length, however, turning from the crowded chamber, he remarked quietly, "It is pleasant this time of day beside the river. Come then, my lord."

Outside the sun was warm yet, the sky still blue; beyond the landing stage the grassy bank lay deserted down to the waterside. They paced slowly along it, leaving the boat stairs behind; somewhere a bell began to ring, a sweet solemn note, and Daubeney said, "That is Sheen Charterhouse, one of our holiest places. One may hear their vespers bell at evening all along this stretch of river, and a good way toward London: it is a peaceful sound."

They had come to a huge willow which lying out from the riverbank barred the natural path. Leaning his arms on the thickest bough, Simon said, "Lord Daubeney, I have been asked a question by my mother which I cannot answer from my own knowledge with certainty, and lately the case has become so with her"— his hand tightened briefly on the old rough bark beneath its fronds of new green—"that is, she has been told tales that both in England and other places the custom on occasion has been altered, or abridged, and she cannot content herself any more with what I of supposition alone can tell. So I must ask you, who will know . . . What are the circumstances of the prisoners' execution at Tower Hill?"

"They go out," Daubeney replied steadily, "usually in the morning, and are confessed and hear Mass. There is not long after that, as a rule, to wait. Do you want me to tell you about Sir Philip Lovell's death? I never saw a man more tranquil in himself . . . Very true it is we

307

must all come to die, but he it seemed had made such terms with it that he walked only as if to an appointed resting place. It was a clear bright day, although cold; climbing the slope outside the Lion Gate one can see the river, and the gulls flying over. He paused once and turned to look: I do not know his thoughts. There was the usual crowd around the scaffold, and the usual persons waiting on it. The warrant was read out, and the Lieutenant gave him leave if he wished to pray awhile, but he said he had done that already. The executioner then approaching, he forgave the man his duty and gave him a purse, and kneeling down, almost immediately made the sign for him to set on with his work. So it was done, and the axe cut through his neck with one blow."

The Carthusians' bell was still. Downriver a faint trumpet echoed, salute of some barge traveling from London; the sound repeated, nearer now, triumphal as a summons. Simon said, "You did not write of this."

"It did not appear to me at that time the wisest course. Later, I thought of it on many occasions, considering if I should set it down at least for you, so you might tell Madame if you saw fit . . . I met her once. It was, I think, before you were born, one summer in Calais: she was Madame de Brezy then. I trust—I hope she is well?"

"Reasonably well. She lives these days much retired, she does not care for Clairmont and has given it to my sister and her husband for their own. Sometimes she comes to Saint Aubin—she has promised to be with us at Michaelmas, for my wife's next lying-in—but she prefers to live mostly now in a house she has bought in

EPILOGUE: Richmond
May 6, 1502

name, for discharge of a prisoner then in England. I was sorry that I was obliged to send a messenger: I would have come myself if I had been able."

"Ah yes, I have it now. But you must realize it was no matter for fines: we have our statutes, and the penalties for their violation are strictly set. It would have been improper to have pardoned for money or conditions a felon already sentenced under law." He brought this out with unimpaired composure, steadfastly regarding the other's face; Simon did not know why Lord Daubeney of a sudden flushed dark red, and looked at the marble paving stones. Faintly smiling, Henry added, "Well, it was a saving for your purse. You must be a rich man, monsieur: or else a very incautious one." Simon answered as if it were another person he heard, "As to that, sir, it seems I was not rich enough."

The pause this time was the King's. Simon saw Empson's mouth fall open, and knew he should be concerned by rights for the Duke of Burgundy's trade agreements. These, however, he reckoned to be safe; and for the rest, he judged it sufficient achievement that his hands had not reached forward of themselves to take the King of England by his skinny throat. He heard again his steward who had been his messenger to England, rain-drenched and stinking of his horse, stammering with tears the bare, deadly news; once more imagination pictured the winter sky white above Tower Hill, the bloody lifted blade. He said to himself, Some things are too dearly bought. I did not ask—I never wanted he should pay such a price. Who can tell what value may be in it, that which he saved? He was twice the worth of me.

Henry was speaking again, as contained as rock. He

forth. It was remarked that of late the King had aged; some people believed this dated from the time nearly three years ago when he had signed the warrant for the young Earl of Warwick's death; however that might be, he was not the man whom Simon had once come to London to get a pardon from, and ask leave of to live awhile in England with his bride. If this was what it cost to keep a crown, then King Richard when he fell at Bosworth had been the luckier one. These reflections were perhaps too plainly to be read in the younger man's face; it was possible too that the unindulgent self-command of Henry Tudor's lifetime was affected yet by the disaster, so lately fallen, of his eldest son's death: not ten days had passed since "the rose of England," the hope of Henry's house, had been laid in his grave. For as he gestured finally for Lord Daubeney and Philippe of Burgundy's envoy to rise, he said in his suave, cool voice, "Monsieur de Brezy, it is long since we had the pleasure of receiving you at this court. You have been less time than that, however, out of remembrance, since not three years ago you wrote a letter to Lord Daubeney, concerning—if I recall correctly—certain processes of our justice here in England, with which you were not in accord. Two letters, now I think of it."

"One only, your Grace," Simon replied evenly. Of all the eventualities he had fancied might arise from this unwanted mission, here was the least believable and most gross. He stared up into the unblinking hooded eyes, and anger trembled in him like a coiled spring, straining toward release; he said, "The other was a blank page, signed with my name, for Lord Daubeney to write above it what terms you would accept, or what fine you would berlain said kneeling, "Your Majesty, the lord of Saint Aubin, Simon de Brezy, emissary from the Most High Prince Philippe of Burgundy, with letters for your hand."

It was Simon's impression, as he waited on his knees for the King's greeting, that Henry was being an uncommon length of time about giving it. Well, he had not asked, himself, to be sent on this errand, and his reasons for accepting it had nothing to do with his liege's duty to the Duke; King Henry, if he found himself discomposed by the sight of Simon de Brezy at his court, was welcome to tell Philippe of Burgundy so, and explain it how he wished. But the spare, cold hand with its delicate fingertips moved forward at last, emerging from the black hanging sleeve, and when he had kissed it, Simon said, "Your Majesty, I bring a letter from my lord the Duke of Burgundy, expressing his true sorrow at the death of the Prince of Wales your son. I was to say for him too, that as he is himself a father, he is as well able as any man living to comprehend the fullness of your grief."

He offered the roll, extended on his palms between the thrown-back folds of his black cloak sewn with pearls. Politeness, and his own inclination, made him now raise his head, his eyes meeting the sunken ones of the King; they were still, gazing at each other across the scroll. Then Henry said, "I am obliged to my good cousin, the Duke of Burgundy. Though it has pleased God to take from me in two years two of my three sons, yet I am consoled, tell him, by that son who is left me, the prince Henry, England's undoubted heir."

He took the letter—there were veins like conduits on the backs of his hands, and his nails, Simon saw, were blunted with gnawing—and turned it a little, back and the maneuver required charting; meantime Empson, who had never taught himself to accept a snub, went unregarding on. "I had expected you to be present, my lord; it was my impression a few years ago that Sir James was not your especial friend. Well, he has had his deserts. One might have supposed that to be involved once with Suffolk, and emerge scatheless, would provide adventure enough, but the man seems to have lacked the simplest will, afterward, to seek safety in disassociation from the Duke. Almost to the end, it's said, he believed himself to be charmed against the King's anger, being persuaded he had been so good a servant, in some particular, that not a doubt could touch him. A curious delusion for a man to harbor who had survived four reigns, but experience did not teach him, apparently, how to read his prince."

Stiff with discomfort, Daubeney was striving by sheer unresponsiveness of posture to force de Puebla aside; it was his companion, the Burgundian knight, who filled the silence, saying, "Clearly, it did not. A misfortune that the gentleman was so late in finding his error out." Something in his voice made de Puebla look sharply at him, but the courtyard was hushing so the gilded vanes that whirled above the towers were plainly to be heard, and seizing his chance, Daubeney took hold of the visitor's arm. "Monsieur," he said, "here is the King." Behind them, and to the farther gate, stretched a billow of bending necks and shoulders; advancing through the wave was a slender man with bony haggard face and lean chest which seemed almost hollowed by the weight upon it of an ornately jeweled collar. His eyes finding Lord Daubeney, he turned slightly toward him, and the Cham-

XVI

The new palace at Richmond was very fine. Fire had
wasted the old buildings called Sheen, and King Henry
had built on the site anew, naming it for his former
earldom. The great hall was vast, its roof carved and
gilded; there were galleries, open and covered, which led
to the gardens and tennis courts and archery butts; and
the marble and freestone paving of the second court supported a fountain devised of lions and dragons, and
branches of Tudor roses. Today, the afternoon being fair,
numbers of courtiers had chosen to stand about it, admiring the cunning of the artificer who had so wrought
that each jet of water sprang from the chalice of a
lapideous flower; in one of these, indeed, a dead beetle
was floating, victim of the under-cistern's abundance,
and Master Councilor Empson continued to regard it, a
part of his tidy mind considering if the corpse might be
reached and removed without wetting of his sleeve, even
as he pursued discourse with the Spanish ambassador de

Puebla—limping, impecunious, and ingratiatory—who stood at his side.

"A good end," the Englishman was saying, "yes, I own I was surprised, but he made a good end. I have seen men calm enough right to the hour, and then all in a moment the nerve goes . . . but he was steady, very steady, to the last: paid the headsman his fee and knelt down as if he had practiced it, with never a sign. No speeches, but then he was not a man for that."

"What, no words at all? Some thought he would blame the King."

Empson put up his brows. "Why so? He was judged and condemned by law, a traitor proved. As to how he was taken, necessity, my dear doctor, is the master of us all. He might have sat in Guisnes for a twelvemonth if promises had not tempted him out. If he believed in truth that he would get a pardon after, he was the bigger fool." He turned, including by a gesture and the direction of his bow the King's Chamberlain, just passing. "We were speaking of Sir James Tyrell, who had his head cut off this morning on Tower Hill. But I think you were not there, my lord?"

Barely checking, Lord Daubeney replied briefly, "No, I had no care to go. If you will excuse me, Master Empson, Master de Puebla—" He had another man with him, a gentleman, who was plainly the object of his courteous escort: dark-haired, sumptuously dressed, wearing on a chain about his neck the Burgundian order of the Golden Fleece; plainly too the Chamberlain was anxious to move on his charge with all speed, out of Empson's and the Spaniard's way. Since de Puebla, carried by the crowd, was now standing directly in their path,

Bruges, near a convent of sisters to which she has made endowments. It is quiet there." Simon was silent then, thinking of that once busy town. Almost as soon as Maximilian had been freed of his captivity there, he had invited all the foreign merchants to relocate their trading houses at Antwerp, new hated rival of the West Flanders towns, and this blow had finished what, long ago, the silting of the Zwijn had begun. Bruges was a dying city now.

On the other side of the willows oars dipped and splashed and rose, shivering the suntrack into drops of sparkling topaz and chrysoprase, and a royal pennon streamed out; it was the King's barge, carrying young Prince Henry to join his parents at Richmond. The trumpets brayed again, and tiny doll figures of people began to gather upriver on the water stairs. "For what satisfaction it may afford you," Daubeney was saying, "Sir James Tyrell when he went out this morning to Tower Hill passed through the same gate. I don't know if you heard the circumstances of his arrest? He was besieged in the end at Guisnes, there being no other way to dig him from his earth; finally a safe-conduct was offered under Privy Seal, inviting him to come on board ship in Calais harbor to discuss terms. Believing in the Seal, he went, and was forthwith seized and instructed that he would be thrown over the side to drown if he did not send word at once to his men to open the gates. Given his position, with what he must have known was waiting for him in England, one could not have marveled greatly if he had chosen the sea. But I daresay it is in the disposition of a man to guard his life while he has power to do it, no matter what the price."

"Yes," Simon said. "It is what most men do." The sun disappearing behind the trees threw long beams of fire-gold; shadows were cool, and in their deeps upon the water the first mist curled like smoke. He remembered the green Hampstead hillside where he had sat the day Warbeck died, his father's voice, and his hand stretched warmly living on the grass. He had never been, as Simon well knew, a man with much use for the idea of vengeance; since this was so, it could not beseem his son to take pleasure in it on his behalf; nevertheless time and events had avenged him, and two more of Tyrell's victims besides, even though Henry was trying now to shift over the blame for the princes' murder equally upon King Richard, too. Simon thought how Philip Lovell would have smiled at that, if he had known.

With all his heart he longed for Burgundy. There was work in Hainault for him to do, there were cares which, if that vain fool Philippe of Burgundy fulfilled his ambition of locking the Netherlands to Spain, would reach farther than Simon de Brezy's feudal boundary stones. What would be the effect for Burgundy when Philippe or his little son, the infant Charles of Ghent, should be both Duke and King: even, when Maximilian was no more alive, Roman Emperor too? Philip Lovell could have advised him perhaps; but he was dead. It was Simon de Brezy, and his sons after him, that must find the answer now.

"One makes choices all one's life," he heard Giles Daubeney once more. "The ruler for his people's good, the private person out of regard for his own advantage, or from love or hatred of another, or even as the conceit may persuade him for his prince's sake. Our lives are ourselves, and we can do no more at the last, each one, than make our offerings from that creation."

The river was gray and empty since the great blazon had passed. The silent air seemed fallen into a waiting; the Carthusians no doubt were at their prayers. Simon noticed again how drawn and weary Daubeney looked, his palm laid with the half-consciousness of a growing habit to the side of his breast. It was nothing, he said, only they had come farther than he had been used to go lately afoot, and if my lord Saint Aubin would excuse him, after they had taken their supper he would rest. They walked back together along the river path, the younger lending the elder his arm, while before them the King's barge swung smoothly toward its moorings for young Henry Tudor to spring ashore.

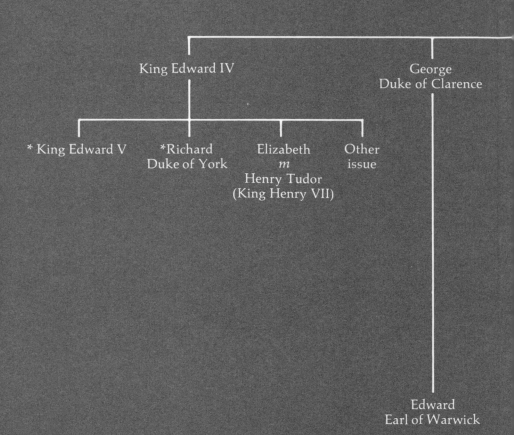

King Edward IV

George
Duke of Clarence

* King Edward V

*Richard
Duke of York

Elizabeth
m
Henry Tudor
(King Henry VII)

Other
issue

Edward
Earl of Warwick

*Presumed murdered in the Tower